PRAISE

"*Static* is a deep dive into the dark web of the American way of success and failure, and the unforgiving scream of the music of chance."
SALAR ABDOH, AUTHOR OF *A NEARBY COUNTRY CALLED LOVE*

"*Static* reverberates with the drumbeat of why we make art... funny, witty, and energetic... will hook you like a beautiful, catchy song that you'll be humming for days."
WILL MUSGROVE, AUTHOR OF *ASPHALT DREAMING*

"A heartfelt, moving debut about the downtown New York music scene, brimming with wasted talent, floundering ambition, broken hearts, and betrayals—and wonderfully redeemed by the possibility of second chances."
ELIZABETH GAFFNEY, AUTHOR OF *METROPOLIS*

"Music pops out of every page in multi-sensory detail—the warm crackle of a needle on vinyl, the sweat of a crowd, the vibration of strings, the digitized reanimation of a sample, and the cacophonous ambient symphony of New York City."
WILL HAGLE, AUTHOR OF *MADVILLAIN'S MADVILLAINY*

ABOUT THE AUTHOR

Originally from Charlottesville, Virginia, Brendan Gillen lives in Brooklyn and earned his MFA at the City College of New York. His short stories have been nominated for the Pushcart Prize and Best Small Fictions, and have appeared in *Wigleaf*, *X-R-A-Y*, *Necessary Fiction*, and many other journals. This is his first novel.

bgillen.com

BRENDAN GILLEN

STATIC

www.vineleavespress.com

Print Edition
ISBN: 978-3-98832-073-5
Published by Vine Leaves Press 2024

Cover design by Jessica Bell
Interior design by Amie McCracken

For Mom, Dad, and Shannon

"… and softly chant, They is, they is, they is."
Tobias Wolff, "Bullet in the Brain"

1.

PAUL STEPPED INTO THE BODEGA ON BLEECKER AND SULLIVAN. INSTINCT and routine guided him to the open-faced cooler along the wall. He eyed the shelf of pre-prepared wraps and sandwiches, which sat in a tidy row beneath a flotilla of colorful beverages. He pretended to browse, then selected two turkey bacon wraps. He made his way to the narrow middle aisle, inspected a bottle of shampoo, and waited for a young mother and her little daughter to leave the aisle. When they were gone, he discreetly slipped one wrap, then the other, through his open fly, keeping his back to the camera in the corner. He felt the cool cellophane slide down his leg until the sandwiches came to rest against the bottom of his pant leg, which he had tucked into his sock. This maneuver he had first observed in the movie *Kids*, the scene where Casper steals a forty—an impossibly brazen and bulky item—and saunters out of a bodega much like this one.

Paul went to the counter where the mother was paying for detergent and a bouquet of flowers. The mother shushed her daughter, who was tugging on her yoga pants and begging for a bag of fruit snacks. When they left, Paul asked the cashier if he had yesterday's *Times*. By the time the man had bent down, rustled through a box of old papers below the counter and re-emerged to tell Paul, "No *Times*," Paul had nabbed two

Snickers from the low-slung tray and slid them into the pocket of his parka.

"All good," Paul said, and for the first time in weeks, he meant it.

He went around the corner, put the sandwiches in his shoulder bag and descended a set of metal steps that led to a glass door long since caked over by a manic jumble of stickers. Beyond, was the oddly pleasing flat smell of dust. Low ceilings, narrow aisles, walls coated with faded ephemera. The impression was entropy and implosion. It was a throwback and a stalwart. And to Paul, it was everything a record store should be.

From behind the nicked and battered counter in the back of the shop, Dante tipped his chin. Paul nodded back, shuffled by the morning's sole digger, a rumpled kid in a brown hoodie flipping through the reggae rack. The early hours were like this: slow and languid, dotted by bored students, older jazz heads and eager tourists. But by afternoon, the shop would come to life, buzzing with a milling array of customers navigating the bins, sizing up the records others cradled in their arms with snap judgments of moral fiber.

Dante rested his elbows on the counter and scrolled through his phone. He wore a Delicious Vinyl tee—one of a series of vintage pieces he wore like a badge—and a black beanie meticulously cocked atop short dreads.

"What's this?" Paul asked. He gestured toward the speakers hung in the corners from which a floral voice trilled.

"Thai folk," Dante said without looking up.

"Mika?"

Dante nodded, his phone-thumb twitching in mini spasms.

Of course. Last week it was a collection of Gregorian chants, before that, Turkish psych. It was a custom of theirs to go around the horn picking the music that played aloud in the store. He could just see Mika flipping through the racks, pushing the huge frames of her glasses up the narrow bridge of her nose. Without fail, she opted for something leftfield as though to prove a point.

"I don't get it," Dante said, scanning his phone. "People are still obsessed with Radiohead. It's like, Thom Yorke farts and it's considered a profound artistic statement." He looked up and held his phone screen aloft for Paul to assess an Instagram post. Then he registered Paul's appearance and twisted his face in confusion. "The fuck happened to you?"

Paul cleared his throat, played dumb. "What do you mean?"

"What do I mean?" Dante studied him closely. "You win the lottery or something? Cause I know damn well you didn't get laid."

"Appreciate that."

"For real. What happened? You can't just roll in here looking like Mr. Rogers. You're scaring me."

Reflexively, Paul straightened his shoulders, sniffed. It was true: he had entered Dead Wax in a bubble of giddy lightness. Not because he'd gotten away with a free lunch; by now stealing was easy. And not because he felt most at home surrounded by stacks of records, though this was true. It was because he felt something he hadn't felt in quite some time: hope. He and Bunky, his bandmate, had just received a bit of fresh news. They'd been given a second chance.

"It's about—wait, what the fuck happened to *you*?" He touched his chin and winced.

"Ah," Dante said, "this?" He proudly displayed a raw half-dollar scrape that hadn't yet scabbed over. "Tried to kickflip the twelve-stair at the courthouse." He smacked his palms together and Paul winced. "Teeth survived though." He curled his lip back to prove it.

"Wish we could say the same about your brain."

They heard Mika's voice before she materialized from the stockroom with the deadpan gaze she wore like an accessory. Her Kool Aid-red bangs, the same color as the frames that encircled her pale blue eyes, fell in an angled line across her forehead. "You know we don't offer health insurance."

"Psh, do I look worried? I'm a quick healer, Mika. Been skating this city twelve years and only broken like, six bones. Seven if you count my ear."

"You can't break an ear," Mika said.

"Ear*drum.* Tried to nollie a low tree branch and—you know what? Forget it."

"But you almost broke your face," Paul said.

Dante raised a finger. "Almost. Takes more than a scuffed-up chin to stop me."

Mika expelled a puff of air, set about straightening records that slumped in their racks. She looked up at Paul and narrowed her eyes. "Why are you so chipper?"

"Rolled up in here looking like a bowl of sunshine," Dante said.

"I mean," Paul said, "if you really want to know, me and Bunky are headlining the Farm tonight."

Dante and Mika stole a glance.

"See?" Dante said. "Knew he didn't get laid."

Mika snickered.

Paul's shoulders sank. "Fuck both of you."

"You know I love you," Dante said, fighting laughter.

Paul glared back.

"I'll take the bait," Mika said. "How? Thought you guys were in a rut."

This was true: he and Bunky had been in a rut. It was one thing not to release any new music in two years, which nowadays may as well have been two decades. It was another thing entirely not to complete a single song for six months running. At this point, the rut was starting to feel more like a ravine, and Paul knew he was largely to blame. Bunky, despite his own issues, was still laying down some of the filthiest basslines Paul had ever heard in his life. He, on the other hand, had found it increasingly difficult to produce the lived-in, soulful beats that had first caught Bunky's attention, and propelled their brief ascent. By now it was no secret to either of them that his struggles started right around the time Sara decided to leave him to pursue her own music career and turn his heart into tartare. But tonight. Tonight they would set things straight, chart the course that was rightfully theirs. Paul said none of this to Dante and Mika; with these two, vulnerability was a foolish game. So, what he said instead, with surefooted nonchalance, was, "Greg still believes in us."

Which was partially true. Greg, the Farm's promoter, did still believe in them. He was, after all, the first to give Paul and Bunky a shot, and over the course of their development had become a friend and a trusted sounding board. But Greg's faith alone was not responsible for tonight's opportunity. No. In reality, he had called Paul that morning in a breathless panic looking for a last-minute fill-in. The British post-punk band that had been booked to headline had had to cancel because their drummer was arrested taking a leak off the Williamsburg Bridge. Still. A chance was a chance.

"That's huge," Dante said. He must have clocked the wariness in Paul's expression because he doubled down. "I mean it. Time to get that wave back." He held out his palm and Paul slapped it.

"You guys want to swing by?" Paul asked. "Always helps to see some familiar faces. Can put you on the list."

"Nah," Dante said, shaking his head, "no can do. Told myself I'd put in work tonight. Truth is, I'm riding some momentum myself right now. Almost finished writing a new joint."

"Get out of here," Mika said flatly, "you know how to write?"

"Hey. Miss Prolific. Talk to me when you finish a track."

"I make music when I feel I have something to say," Mika argued.

Dante guffawed. "In that case? You should have a discography like Scratch Perry."

Paul wasn't entirely sure what Mika was trying to say with her songs. To even call them songs was to imply at least a base level of user-friendliness. Under the moniker Drones, she recorded dense electronic sludge that sounded to him as if she had jammed a mic into the guts of a garbage disposal. Her tracks made Lou Reed's *Metal Machine Music* sound like Mendelssohn. He had once tried to codify her music. "Kind of an ambient, electronic thing," he had innocently said when he first heard one of her tracks curdle from the shop's speakers. It was a tactic she often deployed to drive customers from the store near closing time. "Genres are bullshit," she snapped in return, a comment that perfectly embodied her almost militant views on authenticity. "Categories are purely a manifestation of the consumerist impulse, Paul." He bit his tongue, and held back on addressing the irony of her managerial position in a record store whose interest it was to make money, and which adhered to the very categories she railed against.

"I may not be prolific, Dante," she replied, her back now turned as she went row to row, sorting and straightening records, "but at least I have the balls to follow through on my chosen mode of expression."

She had a point. Dante loved to talk about being a rapper while doing very little actual rapping. He liked to tell Paul all about his aesthetic, which drew more from the Southern, syrupy stylings of Houston or Memphis than it did his home borough of Queens. But whatever style he did possess was undermined by a fractal attention span—he rarely went more than a minute or two without slipping his phone from his pocket and refreshing for likes and updates—and a preference for kickflips over kicking rhymes.

"You can't rush greatness," Dante beamed.

"I've got an idea," Paul said. "Why don't you two just collaborate already and get it over with."

Dante smirked. "I'll collaborate whenever Mika's ready."

"Um," Mika said, shoving back a slumping row of records with an emphatic thud. "I wouldn't *collaborate* with you if the last three people on earth were you, me, and James Blunt."

Dante screwed up his face, and straightened the beanie on his head. "That's cold."

"I'm going out for a smoke," Mika said. "Allow that to sink in." Paul had to admire her: she embraced the role of villain with ruthless ease. There was a heart in there somewhere, you just had to dig for it.

They fell quiet, awash in the thrum of Northern Thailand. Dante went back to his phone and Paul set about opening a roll of new release posters for the window display. He finished pasting up one of the posters and was set to start in on another when he felt his phone buzz in his pocket. He hesitated, felt it buzz again. He relented and checked it. Sure enough: a pair of texts from his landlord. The first message was crammed with dollar signs, the second with question marks. He ignored them and went about his business, unrolled the next poster from its plastic sheath.

"Yo," he said at last, breaking the meditative air.

"Mm," Dante said.

"What do your parents think of you doing this?"

Dante looked up, tried to read Paul's face. "You mean like, working in a record store?"

"Well, yeah. And, you know, rapping. Making music."

Dante shrugged. "They don't really care what I do, to be honest. Long as I'm making a little bread and staying out of trouble."

"That's the way it should be."

"What about you?"

Paul demurred, directing his attention back to the box of posters.

"Don't do that," Dante said, folding his arms.

"Do what?"

"Bring up some shit and then pretend like you didn't do it for a reason. Like you don't have something to say."

"My folks think I gave up music after high school."

"For real?" Dante said. "What do they think you're doing up here?"

"Working in a cubicle."

"So what? You're a fucking adult, bro."

Paul shook his head. "It goes deeper than that though. It's like I constantly need to prove to them I'm not a complete fuck-up."

"Well, I guess that leaves you with one option then. Make it happen."

"No pressure."

"Aye, relax. You're the one who brought it up. What's up with Bunky anyway?"

"He's got his own problems, but talent like that doesn't come knocking too often."

"Facts," Dante shrugged. "Kid's nasty."

"We just gotta get that feeling back. I'm telling you; tonight is exactly what we need."

"Takes work to get it back though. Like, writing rhymes used to come so easy to me as a kid. Back when it was just fun." He scratched a spot on his scalp through his beanie. "I guess what I'm trying to say? You just can't take it all too seriously."

At that moment, the door jingled, and Mika entered the shop. Her eyes jumped from Dante to Paul. "Did I just walk in on therapy?"

"Nah," Paul said, "forget it."

"Big show tonight," Dante said. "Paul's ready to make some noise."

Mika crossed her arms, tipped her chin. Her ruby-red hair quivered. "Are you now?" She studied Paul for a moment, and he swore he saw her pale eyes soften a touch. But just as quickly, the flinty gleam returned. "Funny, because I could've sworn you were allergic to work. There's a stack of boxes in the back that need to be logged. Go make some noise where no one can hear you."

The stockroom was cramped and musty, a noticeably grimier climate than the one on the sales floor. Dust and mildew from battered boxes of used records created a dense pocket of claustrophobia. A boxy PC, yellowing with age, sat atop a cheap fiberboard desk. This was Paul's domain, his haven and workspace since Mika hired him as a staffer.

He sunk into a rolling chair, hunched over, and sliced the tape holding together a Uline moving box. The shop had just received several crates of used LPs, the fruits of an estate sale. It was his job, as always, to price the records, log them, then place them in the bins on the sales floor. He began to flip through.

Not a terrible haul: a ring-worn copy of *Superfly*, latter-day Roy Ayers, and a wholly unnecessary amount of Hall & Oates. Paul lifted out a selection of about a half-dozen records, and slid the albums into his shoulder bag. The cheap used records were far and away simpler to steal: easy to come by and easier to forget. And he was always careful not to take too many. He had begun stealing early on in his Dead Wax tenure and without giving it much thought. It was an impulse he'd nurtured since he was a teen when stealing albums was the only way he'd been able to get his hands on them; his mother and father had little in the way of discretionary cash, not that they'd have bought him records if they'd had the money. But at Dead Wax, he didn't even really consider it stealing. He was purely supplementing his hourly wage, feeding his bank of samples for beats, contributing to the universe of music. Besides, how many copies of *Private Eyes* did the shop really need?

He booted up the computer with a whir and a clunk and set to work, losing himself in the numbing repetition of his tasks. He punched digits into blank spreadsheet cells, tore open more boxes, slipped a battered copy of *Hot Buttered Soul* into his bag because to him, "Walk On By" sounded its best and most alive through the murky static. It was a record he already had, one he'd bought on a trip to Dead Wax when he was just a customer. Or, more accurately, a loiterer. After soul-destroying days as a gopher at Scrimshaw/Duff, he would burn whole evenings meandering the aisles, consuming liner notes, listening to stacks of wax on the turntable by the register. Eventually, he would begin to feel the heat of scrutiny from Mika and Dante—though he didn't yet know their names—and resort to carrying an armful of dog-eared psych, jazz, and funk records to the counter to take home. Dead Wax was, he felt, a spiritual refuge. And though he rarely spoke to anyone in the shop, he knew he was amongst a community of kindred souls—loners, nostalgists, fetishists—who, by merely spending time in the shop, were staging a protest against the codification of music into an ether of ones and zeroes.

Though it had been a Bleecker Street staple long before he arrived from Ohio, Paul had witnessed the many roles Dead Wax had played for the city's independent music community: hangout, venue, promoter, ticket vendor, crash pad, and for many bands—including him and Bunky—source of first record sale by way of the consignment crate at the foot of the counter.

They found a fan of *Clockwork* in Dante.

"Shit knocks," he said enthusiastically by phone after he'd given it a listen. "We'll take ten and let you know if we need a re-up."

They'd gone through eight boxes when Paul was hired a month later. As a part-time utility man, he swept the floors, scanned for stray stock, and absorbed a barrage of daily harassment. "Consider it a badge of honor," Dante said. "Your real payment," Mika would say, "is the boundless knowledge we selflessly bestow upon you."

When he was finally brought on full-time as a stockist to log inventory, he was thrilled. He felt he was finally settling into the life he was built for. That he was paid sixteen dollars an hour for it didn't much matter. He had joined the rarefied air of record store clerks, and the even more heightened tier of record store clerks who not only shilled obscure music but made it themselves.

He zipped his bag shut and thought about what he had said to Dante. The feeling. That's what it all came down to. Did he want the band to succeed? Of course. His bank account was

on life support. But what he really wanted, what was impera-
tive, was to recapture the thrill. The joy he had felt when he
and Gallo began making songs together, his first taste of band
life. The same warmth that descended upon him when he and
Sara—her violin and his drum machine—made what he still
considered to be some of the best songs he'd ever recorded. The
same blend of yearning and possibility that accompanied his
early partnership with Bunky back when it felt like something,
anything, might happen.

***

The hours slid by contentedly until two minor incidents gave
the afternoon a pulse. The first occurred shortly after lunch
when a bespectacled man with a horseshoe of greying hair
walked in to sell a stack of first-press Blue Note LPs. Paul was
filing an armful of new releases when the man approached
the counter. He watched as Dante slid the records from their
sleeves, whistling as he inspected their condition. Records like
this—Sonny Rollins, Hank Mobley, Kenny Dorham—didn't
just walk right into the shop very often, much less in pristine
shape. The man seemed to part with them reluctantly, looking
on wistfully as Dante tallied up his offering price.

"My kids won't appreciate them," he shrugged. "Hopefully
someone else will."

Paul empathized with the man, feeling a certain vicarious
sadness as he witnessed him sell off what were obviously
objects of deep personal meaning. He wished he had the money
to buy them himself, guarantee the man they were going to
a worthy—albeit shabby—home. Like any collectible, records
came with their own story, developed their own personality,
became as reliable as old friends. And he knew the records

would move quickly—Dante would post them on the shop's Instagram page—snapped up by a younger version of this very man with a taste for the finer things, or, more cynically, by an enterprising capitalist who would flip them for an even more outlandish price. In either case, the half-dozen records would help cover a sizable chunk of the shop's monthly rent.

The second incident unfolded just as the pale disc of November sun dipped behind the low buildings of Bleecker. By then Paul was finalizing the pricing of a box of budget classic rock when he heard an eruption of laughter on the other side of the door. He poked his head out to see Dante snapping a photo of Mika—straight-lipped, middle finger raised—standing next to a young man with a shaggy mop of hair. It took Paul a moment—until Dante began belting the chorus to "You're Beautiful" to be exact—to realize what was up: the young man was a dead ringer for James Blunt. As Dante later told it, in the aftermath of the uproar, he had thought the guy *was* James Blunt. He even worked up the nerve to ask if he was the mellow crooner himself, at which point the illusion was punctured by a gleeful combustion of laughter from both clerk and doppel-gänger alike. Paul gave Mika credit for being game and chalked it up to further evidence of her and Dante's awkward court-ship. And he couldn't help but see the episode as some sort of merry talisman.

On a normal day, as late afternoon bled into early evening, it would have been Paul's turn to close up the shop, punctuating the day by yanking down the thundering, graffiti-scrawled metal grate and fastening the chunky padlock. But tonight, he had more pressing business to attend to, so Dante agreed to assume the duty.

"You owe me," Dante said as Paul headed for the door.

"I don't have much to give at the moment," Paul said, "but I won't forget it if that means anything to you."

"It does," Dante said, "especially if you save me a guest verse when you and Bunky get a deal."

It was Dante's way of saying good luck. Mika looked up from a stack of receipts at the counter and nodded in his direction, her own way of wishing him well, or at least not ill will. He nodded back, shouldered through the door, and strode headlong into the New York City night.

2.

PAUL SCANNED THE BUOYANT FACES LOOKING UP AT HIM ON STAGE: open and expectant, chins tipped, awash in candied colors. Bunky stepped into the cone of light. He ran a hand—the knuckles of which were tattooed SINK in old-timey letters— through his stringy hair to clear it from his face. With the hand that was inked SWIM, he gripped the mic and introduced them with the same unassuming phrase he'd used from the beginning: *We're They Is. Get to know us.*

They launched into "One Step"—the first track they'd ever recorded together—just as they'd rehearsed. The foundation was a polyrhythmic drum break edged with the crackle of dust. Paul triggered it by tapping out the beat on his drum machine. It was emblematic of their sound, the pricklier cousin of the moody R&B served up by Portishead or Everything but the Girl. The lifeblood of the song was Bunky's bassline, warm and subcutaneous. Paul watched his bandmate find the groove on his toothpaste-blue bass, then lift a tattooed hand to the sky to instruct the sound engineer to give him more volume. Steadily, the low end enveloped the room until Paul's legs vibrated where he stood. To offset the purring menace of the rhythm section, Bunky introduced his viscous croon and sang about *Being man enough*, about *A father's love*, about *A thunder loud enough to touch.* He fed his vocals through reverb until a heady swirl embraced the room.

Paul again scanned the crowd.

Those who weren't outwardly dancing stood slack-jawed and searching, ready to succumb. He looked over at Bunky and his bandmate nodded back, cool and confident, a look Paul hadn't seen in months. Here again, it seemed, was the guy with the monster basslines, happy to just *play*; the guy Paul had been so excited to partner with in the first place. For the song's outro, Paul layered in a bubble of woozy record scratches, dragging a gutted Etta James record back and forth beneath the needle of his turntable. They interrupted the burst of claps and whistles by surging into their second track—kick drum tough as a manhole cover, snare cracking like whiplash—and Paul felt a thrill run up his neck. This was it. Where he and Bunky were supposed to be all along: casting a spell on an audience, what amounted to a cosmic sleight of hand.

He'd had no illusions that a headlining gig at a small club like the Farm alone was enough to relaunch their careers. But it was a confidence boost. And he knew all it took was one review, one IG post, one lucky break to shake them from their complacent stupor, to regain the momentum that had bloomed around their first record two years back. So here they were, grabbing an opportunity by the balls and would be damned if they let it go. The question was no longer *what had been holding them back*; it was now *what would stop them?* The answer, Paul felt, as his lips formed a sort of snarl, as his beat wound around the room, was *nothing*.

Nothing would stop them.

But then, like an uninvited dinner guest, another question—sharp-edged and dangerous—elbowed its way into his brain:

The fuck was Sara doing here?

Because she had, unmistakably, stepped into the room. Bunky was mid-chorus when Paul saw her pull open the door in the back, a sliver of warm light from the barroom beyond announcing her silhouette. He felt a cold spark in his chest. She hadn't been to one of his shows in ages, a few months before she'd picked up and left him for L.A. Now she was here, unannounced, to see him play. His heart sped in his ribcage, and it was only when his eyes drifted back to Bunky glaring at him that he realized he had missed his cue for the second verse. He improvised a bridge and found his footing before anyone in the crowd seemed to notice. Bunky stared at him through slit lids as he began to sing again. *Fuck.* He had to focus. He also felt a magnetic pull to find Sara again in the crowd. He scanned, spotting her once more, the way she swayed with the groove.

But it was right then, as her head tilted side-to-side, that a light beam swooped across the room and passed over her face where she stood by the sound booth: it wasn't Sara at all. The woman was the same height, had her dark hair swept up in the same way, moved her shoulders—a kind of off-kilter shimmy— the way Sara used to; she was even mouthing the words to the song. But the nose was too slender, the ears a little too prominent. And her blonde friend was someone he'd never seen before in his life. The reality mowed him down like a truck. In a matter of seconds, he had gone from thinking the woman he loved had, by some spell of magic, come back to catch his ascendance, to thinking about how he would salvage a song that he had sent off-balance by fucking up the tempo. Bunky was forced to draw the song to a close prematurely by dropping out the bass, letting Paul fade down the beat on his own.

He tried to regain his composure, tried to conjure the electricity, but the spell had been broken. He and Bunky were no longer a body in lockstep, but rather two separate entities who happened to be playing the same songs. There had been a rupture, like a pin to a balloon. It was a delicate thing, the exchange between crowd and performer, and once a fissure had disrupted the energy, it was damn near impossible to repair. Bunky didn't look at him for the rest of the performance.

Paul let the drum break of their last song fade and merge with the murmur of the room. Bunky mumbled "Thanks"—there was a bemused, polite applause—and they began to break down. Paul powered down his turntable, and his boxy MPC sampler, and placed them in their cushioned metal boxes. Bunky brooded over his velvet-lined case, laid to rest his bass, and didn't say a word. The heat of disappointment radiated from his area of the stage like a repellent magnetic force. Paul felt hollowed out and cold and couldn't bring himself to address his bandmate. They had headlined a show for the first time in months and hadn't bombed exactly, but they hadn't stood out; they had been *fine*, which in many ways was the worst thing you could be.

With the lights up, the room looked much smaller than it had in the airy darkness. A handful of kids milled about performing a casual march to keep shoes unglued from the cup-strewn floor. From his periphery, Paul saw a figure glide from the side-stage shadows. Greg greeted him with a dap and a grin. He wore a western shirt—the kind with snappy metal buttons—and, atop his round, red face, his trademark pageboy hat that Paul still hadn't worked up the nerve to tell him was much too small. He un-balled his clammy hand, pressed into Paul's palm a crumpled wad of bills: their cut of the door split. He could tell without looking it was modest—maybe five-hundred tops for him and Bunky to split—though for him, right now, anything would do.

Paul expected Greg to say *Tough luck* or *Get 'em next time* or any number of coach-like aphorisms. Instead, he said, "Solid set," and it was possible he believed it. Paul had to hand it to him: the guy was relentlessly positive. He continued: "Last one fresh?"

"Brand new," Paul lied and winced. Greg deserved better. The truth was that it was their oldest full song. And their most popular one, or at least the one that had jumpstarted their fleeting attention. They had simply sped it up and segued in and out of Sade's "Paradise" to fill out their set. The fact that Greg didn't recognize it—Greg, who by sheer proximity and exposure was perhaps the non-band member most familiar with their work—said everything.

"Right on," he said. "More where that came from?"

"Working on it," Paul said and glanced away. At least that part wasn't totally false. He and Bunky were always working on it. But there was a big difference between working on it and having the stuff you were working on *work*.

"That's what I'm talking about, brother." Greg raised his lumpy knuckles, which Paul tapped with his own. Then Greg's face rearranged itself into a sort of constipated smirk and Paul had a queasy hunch what was coming. "So," he said, nudging Paul with his elbow, "Sara around?"

He tried not to flinch at the sound of her name, to laugh at the cruel irony of it all. That he had already unspooled a thread of lies made this one easier. "She had to duck out," he said. "Rehearsal in the morning."

Greg tilted his head back and narrowed his eyes. "You gonna lock that up or what?"

It was Greg's playful way of saying, *She's out of your league.*
Paul did his best to hide the pain and said, "Soon."

Greg winked like a conspirator. Then his face fell serious and
he looked over his shoulder as though someone might have
been listening. He looked back and lowered his voice.

"Listen. Feathers need an opener, aright? Couple Fridays
from now. Warm up gig before they go on tour. If you guys
want to test more new stuff? All you."

Paul tried his best to look grateful. After all, Greg didn't owe
them shit, especially after tonight. He knew Greg's largesse
was due in large part to the fact that he simply *liked* Paul and
Bunky, considered them *good people*, a rarity in the music business. "Appreciate the look," he said, dipping his head in genuine
gratitude. "Let us talk it over." He stole a glance over at Bunky
to ensure he hadn't heard. Confirmed: he'd already hopped
down from the stage and was lugging his cases out of the room.

But, why? Why did it have to be Feathers? He pictured Dee Gallo
grinning beatifically through his new band's steady rise and
wanted to punch the air.

Greg shrugged. "Fine. But you gotta let me know by morning.
Their manager—some young shitkicker—keeps busting my
balls. Guy told me he'd snatch my soul. The hell does that even
mean?"

***

Around the corner, Paul found Bunky stuffing gear into his
rust-pocked Pathfinder. He slammed the hatch with a show
of force and the keys clipped to his belt loop jangled like a
warden's.

"What'd Greg want?" he snapped. His grey t-shirt, still dark
in patches from the humid room, clung to his wiry frame.

"Nah, nothing," Paul said with a wave of his hand. "Said he dug the Sade cover, that he's excited to hear some new stuff."

"Shit," Bunky said, "makes two of us." He fished a rumpled pack of Pall Malls from his back pocket, shaking one free. He could afford a lifetime supply of Dunhills, and yet here he was smoking mulch as if to prove something. He placed the cigarette at the corner of his lips and lit it, hunching against the November chill. He leaned against the side of his truck and smoked in edgy silence. The sounds of the city rushed in to fill the hush and Paul pretended like he didn't know what was coming.

For six months now, tension had been building and Bunky had begun to make it abundantly clear who was to blame for their lack of momentum. He was no longer the kid with the easy smile, the loose-limbed confidence. *Impatience*, Paul knew. That was part of it at least.

Lately, Bunky had developed a habit of showing Paul images on Instagram of friends, acquaintances, people he'd read about who were breaking through, realizing dreams. An echo chamber of success stories—*young* success stories. The woman from his class at Columbia whose play just opened at the Public with Patricia Arquette and who was already fielding streaming offers. The siblings from his Tribeca block whose startup—a wine delivery service called Grapeful that issued recommendations using a patented algorithm—was in its second stage of funding. A childhood friend of his—Carlo Bonucci was his name, a name Bunky referenced often with a hint of awe—who had been signed to a major gallery in Chelsea and whose debut show was set to open in January. And on. And on. And on. Yet it wasn't jealousy that fueled Bunky's frustration. No. Unlike Paul, he was too proud for jealousy. Paul knew it was because there was an invisible deadline looming on the horizon like a warship, barrels drawn. A Steinway suspended overhead by a fraying rope. He knew it because he felt it too.

Thirty. The possibility that his dream was dying before he'd even exited his twenties. If he failed? He went back to the Ohio Rust Belt, back to a mother and father who never had time for his music, and certainly no time for his dreams.

Paul often let Bunky's attitude slide, knowing it also festered in the tall shadow of his parents, who had reached a level of success as visual artists that he and Paul could only dream about. He knew it affected Bunky's confidence. Which was crazy because he was good. No, he was better than good. He was a beast. And everyone could see it but Bunky himself. He wanted to take Bunky by those boney shoulders and make him think back: *Don't you remember? Our first record? This used to be fun. We were, and still can be,* On. Our. Way.

"Check it out," he said as a diversion. He nodded to the space over Bunky's shoulder. Bunky craned and they clocked two ex-sorority girls in high heels and bedazzled tanks wobble across Essex like giraffes spindling through the savanna. A force field of entitlement seemed to propel them into the night, as though the city had been erected just for them, the whole cavernous maze their runway. They clopped around the corner, out of sight, and Paul's thoughts drifted to the woman he had seen in the crowd. He'd made up his mind. "Let me leave my stuff with you."

"Why?"

"I'm going back to reap the fruits of our labor."

Bunky rolled his eyes, sucked the last from his cigarette. "Fuck's sake," he said. He flipped the nub into the narrow river of grime where street met curb.

"I caught her eye," Paul reasoned, as much with himself as with Bunky. "How about a little confidence in your bandmate?"

"How about you show me something worthy of confidence," Bunky sniffed. "The fuck happened back there?"

He could have told the truth. Should have told the truth. He should have said that during the first few songs, he had, for the first time in ages, felt the thrill of creative kinship. That he was sure the show would be a turning point, get them back where they were supposed to be. Shit, he should have even been honest about Sara. That he was still heartsick and that a trick of shadow and light had tripped a wire in his brain. Because who knows? Bunky might have understood, heard the passion in Paul's voice and let bygones be bygones. Instead, he let his pride take center stage and said, "What do you mean?"

Bunky smirked and shook his head. "Fine," he said. He shoved off the side of his truck and took a step closer to Paul and looked like he was ready to take a swing. "To be honest? I don't know how long I can keep playing these bullshit shows."

"Bullshit?" Paul said, rocking back. "We're a band. We get to go on stage and play music in front of people. Isn't that enough?"

"When was the last time we made a song we were actually proud of? I mean, shit. How much did we even pull today?"

Paul retrieved the wad of money from his pocket, leafed through to count it up. Without speaking, he divided it and handed over Bunky's share.

Bunky sneered. "Keep it man."

"C'mon. Don't be like that, take your cut."

"I'm telling you I don't want it. I'll take it when I feel like we earned it."

"Don't want it? Or don't need it?"

Paul knew it was a soft spot and poked it before he'd given much thought to the words. Bunky flinched and spit a white jet of saliva onto the sidewalk.

"You really care about this music?" he said, jabbing a finger in Paul's face. "I got a suggestion: Stop moping around about Sara. She's gone. And instead of going back in there and chasing some woman that'll probably shut you down, go home and finish a beat." He unclipped his nest of keys, shaking the one to his truck. He watched a kid ride past on a skateboard with a thunderous scrape and clack. Then he turned and climbed in, shut the door and fired the ignition. Talking Heads bellowed from the stereo, "The Book I Read," Tina Weymouth—his childhood hero—kept slinky time on the bass.

Paul stepped to the driver's side, tapped the glass in desperation. "I've got something cooking," he lied, "for real. Can't wait for you to hear it. Tomorrow at practice."

Bunky cracked the window, spoke over the music. "Good luck in there," he said. "Hope you remember what to do." Then he lurched from the curb and left Paul glaring at a lone working taillight, wondering if by tomorrow they'd even still be a group.

***

In the distressed mirror that reflected a phalanx of glowing bottles, he ran a hand through his dark curls. He caught the attention of the bartender who brooded beneath chopped bangs and scratched the tattoo on the bulb of her shoulder— the stump from *The Giving Tree*—a cue, he sensed, to suggest the extent of her depth. He ordered a Jameson and took a sip, feeling the amber heat sting his throat.

The two women from the crowd emerged from a thicket of bodies and settled at the crook of the bar. He edged over, elbow-close, as the pair chatted and sipped drinks. The one he was drawn to sported a leather jacket over a floral blouse and jeans ending in scuffed-up Chucks. In proper light, it was striking, the extent to which she looked nothing like Sara. Her hair, gathered back, was the color of a dirty penny. A spray of freckles crossed the bridge of her nose. But it was because of this dissonance, not despite it, that he wanted her. He felt certain this was the course that would, if not make things right, then at least make him feel better. He leaned in, entered her perfume radius—notes of citrus, vanilla maybe—and suddenly realized he was starving. His stomach moaned. She might've heard it too had her friend not been chattering.

"Mikey? With him it's like, always doggy. Which is fine I guess. But how about some variety?"

"Is he a good guy?" said Copper Hair, restoring Paul's faith in humanity.

"Well yeah, but that's beside the point."

He toed the brink, edged the abyss. A new conversation, the potential of a different future, if only for the night. He lifted his glass, took a swallow. Then he made the leap—she turned at the sound of his voice—and he felt the earth fall away.

They didn't flee. "Why didn't you two come up closer?" he had said. Harmless enough. Warm, with a little reminder that he'd minutes ago been on-stage. The one with the copper hair smiled, but her friend, the hawk-like blonde who clutched her drink with both hands, sprang to protective action.

"Because there was hardly any room," she said flatly, in the way that stung the most. He realized quickly he was going to have to succeed despite her and offered to buy her another vodka to ease the tension. "You want to throw your money away?" she shrugged. "Happy to help."

"To be honest," Copper Hair said, "Beth and I came out to see Woolies' late show around the corner. We stopped in to kill time when I saw you guys were playing in the back room. I liked those songs you put out a few years ago. I actually didn't know you were still around."

"Woolies," Paul said sharply, a tone he reserved for bands he wasn't in.

"Cassie likes them," Beth said. "I just think the guitarist is hot."

"It's just refreshing to see a band like, rock out, you know? Actually *play* their instruments? Everything is buttons and samples and beats nowadays. I mean, who knows what they're actually doing up there."

She read Paul's expression.

"I mean, not *you* specifically. It's just … you know what I mean."

Beth snickered and slurped the remains of her drink with an emphatic gurgle. "So, what *were* you doing up there? Besides pressing play and bobbing your head for forty-five minutes."

He waved off the comment like it hadn't been a punch in the dick, cleared his throat and hit the reset button. "You know, where I'm from? We like to get to know someone before we roast them."

"Oh yeah?" Cassie said. "And where is that?"

At this, he pictured his parents and felt a twinge in his heart. He could see his boyhood home: the rancher with the unkempt yard, the rusting swing set out back. Everything he had left behind.

"Midway between Dayton and Cincinnati. Not much happening, but salt-of-the-earth people." This last phrase he hated, knew the subtext was usually *simple folk*, but he also knew it was shorthand for *decent human beings.*

"You're speaking our language," Cassie said.

The way she told it, she and Beth had been friends since childhood, had grown up together in a small town outside Bakersfield, a town not unlike his own in size and identity: the real America. She came east to Brown, then got a job in the city editing textbooks for a scholastic publisher and freelancing record and concert reviews for *Time Out.* Beth had stayed local until they finally reunited when she moved out for a gig in PR. "And so here we are," Cassie said with a little shrug, "out on the town, catching a couple shows." She touched her glass with Beth's.

In response, Paul said the only thing he felt there was to say: "You guys will have to come back here next month when we open for Feathers."

It was a long shot, but Cassie's eyes went wide. "Wait, really?"

"Dee Gallo? The lead singer? He and I go way back. He was my bandmate in high school. Then we were roommates when we first moved to the city." He stole a sip from his whiskey to keep his petty jealousy at bay. "Briefly."

"Shut the fuck up," Cassie said. She sat forward on her stool, closed the spatial gap that had yawned between them. "Seriously. Shut the fuck up. You know Gallo?"

Brown was where Gallo had gone, where he met the guys who would eventually round out Feathers. He'd been a senior when she was a freshman. Turned out they sat next to each other in an Anthro class Gallo needed when he switched his major. They saw each other in the city now and then, especially when Feathers played a local show.

At least, Paul mused, *Gallo is good for something.*

Gallo was the de facto bandleader: he played guitar—then mandolin when it became fashionable—and sang lead vocals and had reshaped his personal aesthetic to what could generously be considered Lumberjack Lite. He sported a manicured beard and a shellacked haircut—quite at odds with the shaggy mop he sported in high school—with a side part so precise you could see the white of his scalp. He was chummy and chipper and eager to be liked. And to Paul, his band shilled the musical equivalent of a rustic furniture catalog. Keywords like *classic, bespoke,* and *dry goods* sprang to mind. Nostalgia packaged as authenticity. And it was working. To Paul, every track felt tailor-made for a Coke ad, a schmaltzy HBO crescendo. Many of their songs prominently featured a washboard, which would have been fine had Gallo hailed from Appalachia. But no. He was from Southern Ohio too. And not the shabby part, the shopping mall part. Rest of the band? Jersey. Hell, bands broke through all the time. Bands Paul didn't know and frankly couldn't give a damn about. But once the blurbs started rolling in—the *Times, Vulture* and all that—Gallo moved out of the apartment they had shared in Prospect Heights and left Paul in the dust. Paul knew his jealousy was ugly. But it ran deeper than success or failure. He resented that Gallo refused to acknowledge any role Paul had played in his growth as an artist. And it killed him that Gallo, even back in high school, had always seemed to care more about his reputation—and his haircut—than he did the damn music.

And yet ... it was crazy what a common connection could do, and he observed in Cassie a new level of comfort. He bought a round to celebrate, then sunk both whiskey and pride and offered to cover their tab—and the Woolies tickets—as an excuse to follow them around the corner and into the basement of Bowery Electric.

They squeezed in amongst the gummy bodies. Paul's head began to swirl, the booze fulfilling its promise. He craned to see Woolies—four gangly guys of varying heights and ethnicities—play bouncy, angular tunes which, judging by the moving mouths around him, people seemed to know. What made them any better than he and Bunky? It sure as hell couldn't have been the music, which Modern Lovers could have played with their feet. He suspected it had to do with elements outside of his control: a squadron of managers, booking agents and publicists, components of the machine that conspired to dictate public perception.

He stood between Cassie and Beth refusing to enjoy the music, as though by submitting he might lessen his own chances for success.

"Ugh," Beth said to no one in particular, "he's so beautiful."

Paul studied the guitarist—a kid with sharp features and a tattoo peeking out of his sweatshirt's collar—who seemed transfixed by a spot at his feet, as if it was giving him vivid instructions: *Hey. Look as bored as possible.* More than once Cassie's arm brushed against his own as she swayed and shimmied with the rhythm. He pretended not to notice. Beth too swayed where she stood, though to a cadence altogether different from the one that swelled around them. Bored, plastered, she leaned across Paul to ask Cassie to join her in the ladies' room. It was code for a huddle, a conference by which Beth would make her case against him. It was with no small amount of pride then that he watched Cassie wag her head, her shoulders keeping time: she wanted to hear the band. Spurned, Beth huffed and bumped her way to the bathroom. The music rushed headlong, and the lead singer twisted his face as if each word had to be dislodged from his throat.

Time to go. Paul turned to Cassie and did his best impression of someone who knew exactly how the game worked. He asked her if she was planning to write about the show, and when she wagged her head, he said, "Then let's get out of here."

She looked in the direction of the bathroom as though weighing her options, then, to his shock, she followed. Together they ducked and weaved out of the room. Outside on the sidewalk, a loose group of solemn smokers struggled to light their cigarettes against a stubborn wind.

"Where are we going?" Cassie asked, arms crossed. "I should tell Beth. She's pretty drunk."

It was true. And part of him felt bad for ditching her. But the other part of him felt the thrill of possibility. He suggested food: a kati roll joint in the back of a bodega on Chrystie. She texted Beth; he served up a silent prayer and on they went. She knew the place, even had a favorite order, and as they sat there amidst the clink of spatulas, the hiss of oil, the manic clips of kitchen lingo, he made her laugh. A good, honest laugh that, for the moment at least, made him forget about Sara and Bunky. He sucked his cheeks, wagged his shoulders.

"Oh my God," she said, "that is *not* how I dance."

"There are meds, you know," he said. She raised a middle finger, long and elegant, and for the first time all night, he felt sure of himself.

"So," she said in between bites, "opening for Feathers. That's like, pretty big, right? I mean, are you going on tour with them?"

"We're negotiating," Paul said. He found it easier to lie if he studied his food. He let the comment linger for emphasis. "It's a big time for us."

"There's still potential in there somewhere," Cassie said, "I can see it."

"So then what about you?"

"What *about* me?"

"This is the part where you tell me about your, you know, dreams."

She demurred, swatted away the question. "Nah, that's the boring stuff."

"No it's not," he said, "that's the only stuff."

She looked at him skeptically from the corner of her eye. Reading his expression, she ran a hand through her hair and decided to believe him. "Fine," she said. "You want to know the truth? I've already done it."

"Done what?"

"Fulfilled my—*dream* or whatever you want to call it."

He must have looked puzzled because she breathed in and out and felt the need to explain.

"It's just, you know, getting into Brown from where I'm from? Moving to the city? It all seemed so unrealistic that," here she shrugged and glanced away, "everything else is a bonus."

In that moment, he felt a swell of, not love exactly, but admiration.

Cassie narrowed her eyes. "You're looking at me funny," she said.

"Any word from your friend?"

She checked her phone. "Looks like she's meeting up with Mikey."

"Do you like him?" he asked, trying to hide his relief.

"He's nice. Though for Beth I'm afraid he might be too nice."

"Nice guys finish last," he shrugged.

"Where does that put you?"

"Jury's still out," he said.

He paid for the food, tried not to think about how quickly he was flying through his cash. Out front, they kissed without hesitation: sloppy, breathless, garlicky. A group of zooted kids strode past. "Somebody's getting *laid* tonight," one of them yelled and Paul felt Cassie's lips spread into a smile.

"If she's lucky," he yelled back.

"Watch it," she said and wacked him in the arm. Then she turned and put a hand in the air. A cab veered over, brakes like a tea kettle. Paul suggested her place—his shoebox in Red Hook was out of the question—and they sped off into the night.

***

Her room—in a battered walk-up off Tompkins Square—was small, space enough for a double bed, a dresser and a little bookshelf that doubled as a nightstand. A scan of the shelves read like a syllabus—Camus, Woolf, Thoreau—the books that had recently traveled with her from Providence. Below the books were DVDs including, remarkably, the full suite of OG *Star Wars* films. He slid one out at random: *Return of the Jedi*. He squinted to steady his swimming gaze: Mark Hamill clutched a green beam of light and considered something in the distance, as though scanning for the source of a fart; Princess Leia broke the fourth wall, coy and half-naked. He'd pay good money, if he had any, to know what went through a woman's head when she brought someone back for the first time. Had she already made up her mind? Had six flights given her enough time to change it? It was the closest he'd been in ... well, *technically* since ... he shook the thought from his head.

"Still have your shoes on?" Back from the bathroom, Cassie leaned on the doorjamb. Her socks were blue with little umbrellas.

Paul kicked off first one sneaker then the other. "May the Force be with you," he said, tapping Jabba's face.

"Fuck off," she said. "You don't even know me." In a single motion she took the DVD case, cast it to the floor and stiff-armed Paul to the bed.

She climbed up and straddled him. "Would you ever make a song about this?"

"I would make a double album about this," he said, the whiskey speaking for him. "Long as you don't write a review of it."

She smirked. "Just so you know? I'm not sleeping with you."

"As if I was going to let you sleep with me," he said.

She smirked again, leaned back, put her arms in the air and he obliged. Her breasts were held in place by a black bra with lace. He closed his eyes, looked again.

The same kind Sara wore.

He fumbled with the clasp.

"Wait," she said.

She dismounted, retrieved a laptop from her nightstand. She scrolled, found their soundtrack, clicked off the bedside lamp. The alien glow of the screen cast the room in fuzzy shadows. From the laptop speakers: the even thump of a drum, a multi-part vocal harmony. Then, as she unfastened her bra, the aw-shucks thrum of Gallo's mandolin. *No fucking way.*

"Now you," she said.

He unbuttoned his shirt, balled it and threw it into the shadows. He tried to focus as his hands scanned and paused, rode ridges and curves. He felt Cassie's warm breath on his neck and as he palmed the space between her legs, her breath became halted, dire. He slipped beneath the elastic. His fingers fumbled and searched, out of practice. "Slow," she said. She reciprocated shyly at first, running her palm, hovering, grazing as it strayed south. As she worked, he lay still, trying to fight what was beginning to emerge as the cruel reality. A reality as pathetic as his inability to get over a fucking breakup.

Sensing his failure, Cassie worked faster, rougher too, irregular and desperate. "Does that feel good?" she whispered. Her lips moved against his neck.

He groaned and nodded, though once his thoughts had entered a tailspin, it was nearly impossible to rein them in, to ground himself in physicality. He began to consider his reputation, what she would think of him: that he wasn't a *man*, that he couldn't *perform*.

Yet somewhere within him, a clear thought cut through the thickening gauze: *don't let her blame herself.*

"Show me," she said.

He guided her hand, thought once more of Sara, the way she would murmur his name. Still nothing. He opened his eyes, studied the plaster ceiling, the little ridges like frosting in the glow. The Feathers song on the laptop surged toward its crescendo despite him, heart on its flannel sleeve.

"Fuck," he said at last.

"Did I do something wrong?" she said, her face twisting up, a mask of concern.

He considered lying. What was he supposed to say? *Yeah. In the low light of a music venue, you happen to be a dead ringer for the woman who broke my heart.* At least in this case there was the booze to blame and he didn't have to soft-shoe his existential dread. "Damn whiskey."

Propped up on an elbow, she looked down at him, this time with a little smile. A smile of pity, one that notched another point in the lopsided tally for women as the nobler sex. "Happens to the best of us," she said. Mercifully, she cut off the music. He clamped the crook of his elbow around his eyes. Sobriety pierced his core like an ice-cold bath. He felt her pat his chest. "Hang in there," she said. "Everyone loves a good comeback story."

***

He hadn't tried to fall asleep. The room was dark now save for a pale sliver of moonlight slashing the wall above the bed. Cassie was curled away from him beneath the sheets. His desire to rouse her, to explain and—with newfound sturdiness there to mock him—prove himself, was overruled by another more practical certainty: he had to get the fuck out of there. In the murky blackness, he groped for his clothes and quickly dressed. Without turning back, he stepped into the hall. He stopped short. On an armchair against the far wall was a rumpled heap, legs dangling over the armrest. Beth's head was cocked back, and she snored, a rattling garbage disposal buzz.

Compulsion led him to the kitchen. From a cupboard above the stove, he took a jar of peanut butter, a few cans of tuna, and loaded them into the pocket of his parka. In the living room, he spotted a crate of records. He crept across the room and crouched down. Cassie had a vinyl copy of Feathers' album, as he suspected she might. On the cover was a group of three, clad in wool vests. He slid the record from the crate, held a middle finger to the faces looking back at him and took it. He stood and turned for the door, but at the creak of a floorboard, Beth shot up and inhaled sharply as though defibrillated. Confused, she stared at Paul until the pieces locked into place.

"Oh, you *asshole*," she croaked. "I hope you fuck better than you play music."

He booked it for the door, cradling the record like a textbook.

"Look," Beth hissed, and when she did, something seemed to soften in her face. "All I'm saying is she's been really hurt in the past, okay? I just don't want to see it happen again."

Paul knew at once that he had misjudged her. And he was almost compelled to tell her the real score of what had happened in the back room.

"I hope it works out with Murphy," he said, and meant it. Though he knew Beth's opinion of him prevented her from believing it. He yanked open the door, which caught on the security chain with a thud. His failure was complete.

"It's Mikey," Beth said, "and he's realer than you'll ever be."

Paul shut the door, unhooked the latch and opened it once more. Then he stepped into the wan, sickly fluorescence of the hallway knowing she was right.

Outside, the sky was lavender, the hour ambiguous. The ghosts of Saturday hung in the air along with the stench of vomit, of which there was a pile like creamed corn at the base of Cassie's building. In Tompkins Square Park, winos stirred from their benches and lurched about. Paul could see his breath. He walked north on Avenue A. When he felt he was at a safe distance, he stopped at a corner trash can. It was overflowing with detritus. He slid the vinyl from its sleeve. At first, he'd considered taking it home, studying it for secrets, but his resentment wouldn't allow it. He held it flat like a plate and smashed it on the brim. Once, twice ... on the third smack it shattered, shards of black plastic scattered at his feet. He tore the sleeve in two, threw it on top of the heap where it slid off onto the ground. He looked north up the avenue, seeing the traffic lights flip green in dutiful succession. It felt like an omen. For what, he didn't know.

3.

HE WOKE FULLY CLOTHED, SWEATING FROM HIS NECK. HE STILL HAD on his jacket. He still had on his shoes. Check that, one shoe.

Hold up. He hadn't been that drunk. Had he? Instinctively he patted his pockets for his wallet and phone. *Thank fuck.* He glanced at the murder-red digits on his bedside clock, the impassive blinking colon; it was mid-afternoon. Lying there still, afraid to move for the pain it might activate, the thud in his chest resounded in his temples. When he smacked his tongue, it Velcroed to the roof of his mouth. He burped, tasted curry, and was relieved nothing more came up. But more than the hangover, made more acute because he had nothing—no one—to show for it, he felt that old familiar foe radiating with a steady buzz from his core.

The anxiety.

"Kill me," he said aloud. The memory of last night made him flinch. He rubbed his eyes until he saw kaleidoscopic amoebas ping behind his lids, then sandwiched his face between pillows. The cool cotton soothed him, until the dread performed its Whack-a-Mole routine and his pulse prevented him from dozing off.

He swung his legs to the floor, kicked off the remaining shoe, unshouldered his jacket and checked his phone. Nothing from

Bunky. Nothing from anyone. He absently scrolled his feed of photos until they blurred together. He tossed his phone on the bed and stood up, nearly passing out from the blood rush. His circulatory system seemed to be staging a protest, demanding better working conditions.

He shuffled to his sole window and peered through security bars into the metallic November light of a Red Hook afternoon. Down on Van Brunt, he watched a bedraggled passerby nonchalantly toss an empty coffee cup onto the lumpy patch of grass that passed for a front yard. The row house, his landlord once told him, had belonged to a single family in the early part of the prior century. It might have been a charmer too, a jewel of domestic tranquility in a quaint fishing village. But right around the reign of Robert Moses, a shrewd developer chopped it into three, just as the BQE chopped Red Hook off from the rest of Brooklyn.

He sat at the wobbly tray table that served as his makeshift desk and let his eyes drift around the room: mounds of dirty clothes, tangles of audio cables, stacks of records. And there, atop a shoebox that housed the essentials—expired condoms, loose change—was his trusty accomplice. Next to it, the pink rent slip he'd found taped to his door when he got home.

He bent down and retrieved the pipe—a bowl of carved ivory he bought on Canal Street for twice its value when he'd first arrived—and the Ziploc of green crumbs—a bag he got for half its value from the sound tech at the Farm, the only perk he could justly claim from band life. The pink rent notice he left crumpled in a ball: to ignore it made it less real. He grabbed a record from the closest stack, and atop Stevie Wonder's beaming face, began to crumble what was left of the herb. He filled the pipe and brought the torch from Lady Liberty down onto the little mound of leafy green crumbs. He drew in, listened to the pleasant crackle, held the smoke, swallowed, and blew out a thin jet of blue-grey.

He reached over and grabbed his phone from his bed. He wished he could call his parents. To hear their voices. To tell them he loved them and ask for their advice. But he couldn't. He couldn't because for one thing, they assumed he was still gainfully employed at Scrimshaw/Duff. The job his mother and father had been so stunned he'd managed to even land. He could still see the beatific look on his mother's face when he told her the news, the way she clasped her hands beneath her chin. Because all signs had pointed to him following in his father's footsteps at Amalgamated. Unlike his older brother Will, who overachieved at every step, who was now busy with his own success as a banker in Chicago, Paul had eked by in high school, got into UC because it was nearly impossible not to get into UC, paid his way by serving four years of lukewarm cafeteria slop and DJing parties and off-campus mixers, and then came within a half grade point of failing out. And he would have too had it not been for an angelic act of kindness by his communications professor—Debbie Blitz, a name he would never forget—who liked him, who knew the course his life would take, and allowed him to pass her final exam. Professor Blitz must have seen something in him, something he never saw in himself, because she then went out of her way to make some calls to a friend in New York that helped him get in the door as a low-level admin at Scrimshaw/Duff. But through it all, he could only think about the music, so when it seemed he and Bunky had a chance to break out with a self-released record, he quit his agency job. Easy as that.

He scrolled through the names on his phone until his thumb hovered over the one who could feasibly make things right.

"Is it too late?" he said when Greg answered. "Tell me it's not too late to book the show. I'll do anything." He cringed as he said it. He couldn't imagine anything of substance he could offer to make a deal. He had no money, no real skills. He was barely hanging on with the hourly wages from Dead Wax, clawing for a break that was drifting further out of reach by the hour.

There was a clipped, crackly blankness on the other end.

"Hello?" he said. He paced the shabby area rug in the center of his bedroom, feeling the scratchy weave beneath his feet.

"What'd you say, brother?" Greg's voice punched through at last. "On the train and about to leave fourteenth. Better make it quick."

"I said, we'll take the gig. Feathers. We'll take it. We want it. Please."

"Ah, no can do, brother. Already filled it. Told you I needed to know this morning. Any other time I'd say no sweat. You know I love you guys. But I'm telling you, their manager is out of his fucking mind. He said he'd have me deported if I fuck it up. And this is a warm up show."

"Greg. Please. Is there anything—"

Paul could hear the mechanical bleat of the doors closing.

"Gotta go, brother! Keep those new tunes coming!"

"*Greg*. I need this—"

The line went dead.

He stood in the faded center of his putrid rug and took in the pale, bare walls of his room, the flaking paint, the water stains at the corners. Bunky was absolutely right. He had to get over Sara. And he had to get back to work.

He sat at his desk and cycled through commands on the LED screen of his drum machine. He called up a project he'd left half-finished, a beat-in-progress with a drum pattern he'd built from two of his favorite songs: the kick from "Humpin'" by the Bar-Kays, the snare from "I Remember" by The Sylvers, onto which he'd added brittle decay until it was ready to crumble. Ninety-five beats-per-minute with a swinging hi-hat. He dug up a dollar bin lounge lizard record he'd been toying with. He stretched and chopped the warbling vocals into a melody that was a distant cousin of the original, like a puzzle with the pieces out of order. He laid it into the track, played it back.

He closed his eyes and listened and tried to find the same elements of the hip hop records that had spoken to him as a middle schooler sitting alone in his bedroom for sanity-threatening stretches of time, stacks of stolen wax establishing a sort of fortress. He was left largely undisturbed. By then, Will, with whom he'd shared his room, was off to DePaul on scholarship, for books of course, not ball. His father worked long shifts at Amalgamated, and his mother taught and tutored at the high school. It was this feeling, this loneliness, that was a driving force in his decision to pursue music: if he couldn't find a meaningful connection at home or at school, perhaps he could find it at the other end of a song. His parents would never see it that way.

This reality was made abundantly clear in his junior year of high school, by which point Gallo was the closest thing to a friend he had. They shared a homeroom, discovered a mutual love of *Ill Communication*—Paul had stenciled the Beasties logo onto his binder—and soon began jamming together in Gallo's two-car garage: Paul behind the decks, Gallo on guitar. It was something of a miracle that they got along at all. Gallo, for his part, was a charmer, a shapeshifter who could confidently slot himself amongst the athletes or the art kids. He had that elusive quality girls were drawn to, an aw-shucks grin that paired with a broad-shouldered comfort in his own skin. Paul, meanwhile, was an introvert who, for the most part, tried not to be noticed, who people seemed to like, but didn't seem to know, a reality he was perfectly fine with. But despite their differences, they clicked when it came to creating. What began with shaggy Beck covers evolved into writing and making songs. As the school year drew to a close, emboldened by the thrill of performance and the electric charge of creation, they decided to throw their hat in the ring for the damn high school talent show.

It had by and large been a cringy affair. There was the group of girls that bopped, preened, and strutted along embarrass-ingly to Destiny's Child, the acapella dweebs who squeaked out Maroon 5, the magician who sent his cards sputtering all over the front row. Then there were Paul and Gallo, who took the show enormously seriously. For two weeks, they had punched out of their after-school jobs bagging groceries at the Food Lion (for Paul the job was mandatory, for Gallo it was for "spending money") and retreated to Gallo's garage to prac-tice. There they cooked up a five-minute routine, such was the limit of the program, a medley of remixed Beach Boys tunes, which Gallo sang convincingly enough. He played the melodies on guitar overtop the beats Paul provided, which were really just a selection of De La Soul instrumentals that he pitched up or down to the right speed on his turntables, adding scratches now and then for flare. It was a mash-up before Paul even really knew what a mash-up was, and it brought the house down. Paul knew it had much to do with Gallo, who even by then had begun to develop the wholesome charisma that lent Feathers charm. But he also knew it had something to do with the fact that their performance was fucking fun. They finished their routine, and when Principal Weatherspoon called the three finalists onstage and hovered his hand over the heads of each to gauge the applause that would determine the winner, it wasn't even really close. Their classmates whooped and hollered to such a degree that Weatherspoon turned to them and asked if they'd like to play one more. Well, they didn't have one more, but they also couldn't say no, so they went back up there and replayed "Wouldn't It Be Nice" with "Stakes Is High" as the backdrop and couldn't wipe the dumb smiles off their faces. It was, up to that point, the best day of Paul's life. Until he ran into his mother in the hallway after the assembly. She looked at him with a kind of pity and his grin fell away.

"Please, honey," she said and patted his arm, "don't make things harder for yourself." Then she turned and set off down the hall for her sixth-period class.

He opened his eyes, stopped the track, and leaned back in his chair. The beat wasn't working, plain and simple. Something elemental was missing, a living core that welcomed the listener in and invited them to stay awhile. But at least he realized as much. The real danger was when you convinced yourself there was potential. He was stuck and he knew it and he didn't know what to do.

He needed some fresh air. He went on a search mission for his missing shoe and found it beneath a t-shirt by his closet. He picked it up and grimaced. Pancaked on the bottom of it was a mutilated cockroach the size of a prune. He flicked off the bug with the edge of an album sleeve. It hit the closet door and fell to the floor in a papery crunch. He put on his coat, the same one he'd woken up in, and trudged down three flights of creaking stairs.

He went into the yard and punted the stray coffee cup into the street. Something about the debris-free yard, dead as it was, made him feel, if not better, then at least pragmatic. He checked the time on his phone and as he did so, it lit up with a text. His father had recently learned the skill, though he approached the task with a goofy formality that tweaked Paul's heart.

Dear Paul, it read, *Know u r very busy with ur job. Work hard. Look fwd to seeing u in a few days for Tksgvg. Dad.*

He clicked out of the text, checked the time once more. He breathed in and shook his head, tried to rid himself of the groggy comedown, the worst part of any high.

***

He emerged at Montrose into the milky twilight.

The squat blocks of Bushwick: brick and rust punctuated by blazing murals of graffiti. Bodegas with bulletproof registers adjacent to organic food co-ops and yoga studios.

An hour to travel six miles. A snuffing bus and two trains. Twice a week he made the trip to meet Bunky for practice, or as they had taken to calling it in the early days of their partnership, "scrimmage." Paul himself had come up with the term, which he felt neatly encapsulated the playful purpose of their approach. At least it used to.

The streets were Sunday-quiet; he could hear himself breathe and felt as though he was on a death march.

Bunky.

Shit.

To think his future was bound up with a guy he didn't even know existed before he moved to New York. His message had arrived via Soundcloud, the open mic of the internet. *Found your beats and glad I did*, it read. *Let's work.* Paul had received

DMs before, mostly abbreviated gibberish from high school kids who couldn't sing or rap their way out of a wet paper bag and who wanted his stuff for free. This felt different. Google recon revealed a guy named Bunky Turan who had bounced around playing bass, who even had a few seven-inch singles to his name. Who was far and away the best player on every song Paul dug up on YouTube. And then there was the image he found from a MoMA party of Bunky in all-black, dark hair knotted in a bun, wedged between his parents: *Artists Maria and Aldo Turan*, read the caption. Smartly dressed, tortoise-shell frames, moneyed confidence. They were painters who had come of age in the eighties downtown scene, contemporaries of Keith Haring and Kenny Scharf and Jenny Holzer, and though they never reached such towering heights, their adjacency meant their work still fetched outlandish prices.

He agreed to a meeting at Flaherty's in Chinatown—a damp dive with scarred wood fixtures—and arrived early as though for a job interview. He had polished off three bottles of beer before the kid from the photo strolled in. Paul marked the controlled scan he cast about the room, the unhurried look of someone who was used to arriving late. Bunky parked himself on the stool next to Paul and extended a tattooed hand. For a while they sipped beers and circled each other conversationally, like boxers after the first bell, until Bunky looked Paul dead in the face and with an innocent smile asked the question that Paul had been asking himself for years:

"Ready to do this?"

He said it like Paul would have been a fool to say no. Like he was A&R from an influential label like Stones Throw or XL and not just some lanky kid in a black hoodie with greasy hair and a Soundcloud account. Paul deflected: "How'd you find me?"

Bunky gave the answer he had been expecting: "Sport and a Pastime." A song Paul had tried to forget about. A surf-tinged groover he and Gallo had cooked up when they'd both first moved to the city. A song that wound up in a skate film that became something of a cult classic. Gallo's cousin, an editor on the film, had used their song on a montage of slams and spills that racked up a few million views on the internet. And on the strength of their momentum? Gallo took all the credit for the song, started Feathers, got signed and moved out of their apartment one night under the cover of darkness.

As though reading Paul's thoughts, Bunky picked at the label of his beer and narrowed his eyes. "Look," he said, "I don't know what you think you know about me." Paul pictured the tasteful Tribeca loft, as featured in a *Times* spread. The parties. The access. "These hands?" Bunky raised them as evidence. On the back of each was inked a black-and-white rose, etched and shaded for depth. Tattoos that must have cost a pretty penny. "My parents would prefer they grace the keys of a grand piano. Something tasteful. Useful. They seem to think all those lessons, the fucking youth conservatory, was a waste. To say I'm a disappointment to them would be an understatement. In fact, we hardly speak. But I'd rather do it my way and fail than do it their way and coast." He gestured for two whiskies and a glaze of seriousness clicked in his eyes.

Paul hesitated. Not because he didn't like Bunky. He hesitated because to commit was to *commit*. To risk the possibility of falling flat on his face, finding out he didn't have what it took: the discipline, the balls, the thick skin, or worse, the talent. But it was the fear of regret—the image of himself thirty years hence, sitting in a shabby reclining chair, wondering what might have been—that led him to lift his tumbler of whiskey and shake Bunky's hand.

When it was time to pay the bill, Paul lifted an ass cheek to fetch his wallet and expected Bunky to do the same. No, what he expected was for Bunky to wave him off, cover the bill. Instead, his debit card rested solo on the plastic tray and the bartender snatched it up.

"Consider it an investment," Bunky said, clapping Paul on the back. He stood from the stool, circled the bar and relieved the bartender from duty. He grabbed a rag, began to work it over a flotilla of dripping glasses. "Cause I'm broke as hell right now."

Money. Everything came down to money. Yet as their relationship progressed, Paul hardly ever heard Bunky talk about it. And he never asked about it. No, he never asked how Bunky could afford to pay rent on his East Village studio—even if it was a bandbox—on a bartender's wages. He never asked about the '63 Fender Precision bass, or all that vintage gear, gear that Paul would have had to steal. He never asked because Bunky seemed as embarrassed of his wealth as Paul was at his lack of it.

Early on in their partnership, he had arrived at Bunky's apartment a few minutes before their scheduled session and heard shouting on the other side of the closed door. At first, Paul thought Bunky was arguing with someone in the room, until he realized he was only catching one side of the spat. He had put his ear to the door and listened as Bunky screamed that he would *never be enough*, that all his mother and father cared about was *how I represent the family name.* Paul had waited a few minutes for the dust to settle, then lightly rapped on the door. Bunky opened it with a thin smile and filmy eyes, stepped aside to let his bandmate enter. Without much in the way of commentary, Bunky picked up an orange pill bottle from his bedside table and shook a few free into his palm, swallowing them without water. "Otherwise, this session might go all doom metal," he shrugged, and they both set about their business as though nothing was amiss.

***

He entered the Sweatshop, a labyrinthine behemoth of brick and poured concrete that still bore vestiges of industrial function. Musty hallways lit by hanging fixtures encased in wire lattice. Steel I-beams at every turn. An utter lack of proper ventilation which, in the warmer months, made extended rehearsals feel more like boot camp than band practice, and lent the building its frank moniker. On the second floor, at the end of a long corridor that swelled with the muddy cacophony of simultaneous jam sessions, Paul stood and shored himself before a dented metal door. He couldn't help but laugh to himself: his future hanging in the balance in two-day-old underwear. He breathed in and out and shouldered through the doorway.

In the far corner of the room, Bunky sat on a stool, vamping a rubbery groove on the bass. Above him on the eggshell-colored concrete walls, loping squalls of graffiti and spray art hovered like a threat. Bunky looked up and nodded stiffly without breaking stride. He had, Paul noticed then, shaved his head down to the quick of his scalp.

"You ready?" Bunky said. He stopped playing with a resonant thump and was now scrutinizing Paul with the stern impatience of a teacher.

"Born," Paul said with all the conviction he could muster. He went to his folding table, on top of which, to his surprise, Bunky had neatly arranged his gear. He hoped it was a sign. He donned his headphones, a set of fat cans that wouldn't have been out of place in air traffic control. He cued up a bank of samples on his MPC and listened to the jagged buzz bleeding from the other side of the wall. Some band was doing its damndest to channel the sludgy, horny, rambunctious spirit of Janis Joplin.

"Somebody's drowning cats," he said, trying to make light. He looked over where Bunky was fiddling with an effects pedal at his feet. "At least we're not that." It did make him feel better that the band on the other side of the wall sucked and was enough to fortify in him at least a baseline of confidence.

"Right," Bunky said at last. He met Paul's gaze for the first time since he'd come in. "So, what are we then?"

Paul felt prickly warmth climb the nape of his neck, round his jowls and rise to his cheeks. He pulled his sweatshirt over his head and tossed it onto a ratty armchair adjacent to his table. "We," he said, "are about to make some heat. Check it out."

From the speakers standing at attention at opposite corners of the room: the warm, lived-in crackle of vinyl, a thick kick drum, an elastic snare, the soulful yowl and wobble of a Hammond B3 organ. A beat he'd been tinkering with for weeks, but which Bunky had yet to hear. Then, atop the sample loop, a voice, airy and ambiguous, diced and compressed to the distant frequencies of payphones and noir. Paul bobbed his head as he tapped out the sequence on his drum pads—he felt the need to really sell it—and watched as Bunky shut his eyes, running his hand down the fret of his bass until it found the right place. Then his tongue stuck out at the corner of his mouth and he began to play one of his greasy grooves. Paul too closed his eyes and let the beat carry him to a place where subtle shifts and changes emerged, where the guiding principle was instinct rather than thought. He listened as Bunky's bassline fell into the pocket, meandered back to every downbeat. An absolute killer, just like always. There it was: lockstep. A flash of inspiration. He could feel it.

Then the bass fell out.

"No," Bunky was saying, shaking his buzzed head.

Paul stopped playing and looked up to see Bunky glaring at a spot on the concrete floor. On the crown of his scalp was a quarter-sized patch of uneven hair, like he had passed the clippers over his head in a rush.

"What?" Paul said. "That was feeling good." He dialed down the volume, lifted his headphones from his ears and let them curl around his neck. Once again, he could hear the muffled clamor from the practice room next door: a tortured wail beset by a cascade of pots and pans.

Bunky shook his head and looked up at Paul. His expression was blank. The look of someone accountable only to himself. "No. It's all wrong."

"What's all wrong?" Paul said. He tried to steady his voice. "The bridge? We can ditch it. Repeat the chorus for another eight bars."

"No, man." Bunky let a little snuff of air pass from his nose. With the thumb and forefinger of his fret hand, he rubbed his eyes as though summoning fumes of patience. He lifted his bass and nestled its neck in the crook of the stand next to his stool. He stood and sighed and made his way to the other side of the room. He folded his arms across a ratty t-shirt emblazoned with the word DAYTONA—one of his prudent thrift store purchases—and said, "You know this isn't working, right?"

Though he'd felt it coming, Paul found himself in the position of fighting for his life. He felt if he could just buy himself time, Bunky might be willing to reason. "I told you. We can skip the bridge. I was—"

"*Yo.* It's not about the fucking bridge. You want to talk about the bridge? Fine. Let's talk about the bridge. Let's talk about how it's a Jimmy McGriff sample. How about that?"

Paul tested a brittle smile. "You got a good ear, man. I tried to sneak it by you, but you got a good ear."

"And *you* got no common sense. You know how much that sample would even cost us? I mean, we're talking at *least*—shit, it's not even worth saying it out loud. That's how irrelevant it is."

"Well, we don't have to release this one," Paul reasoned. "We could post it for free like we first did with the record. Let it happen organically. DIY like we used to—"

"I'm done with DIY, man. I'm done giving away stuff for free. I'm trying to make another album. What are *you* trying to do?"

"Make something great," Paul said, almost under his breath. It was the first honest thing he'd said in a very long time.

And Bunky laughed. "Something great." Abruptly, he let his arms fall heavily to his side, then flung them about for emphasis. "Great isn't *this*, Paul. Great isn't using the same fucking jazz samples over and over and over again."

Paul absorbed the comment like a blow. "Hold up," he said. "In case you forgot, you used to *like* my ear for samples. Matter of fact, that's why you hit me up in the first place. Isn't that what you said? You said—"

"I said I liked your stuff because I could *feel* it, okay? Now? It's recycled. Played. It's like—you gotta do better than low-rent J Dilla. You gotta do better than channeling your record collection. Nostalgia is only good if you can build on it. Take it *forward* for once."

Paul clenched his fists until he felt his fingernails dig into the skin of his palms. He swallowed a burning lump in his throat. "Where's this coming from? Far as I'm concerned? I'm doing the same shit as when you hit me up. I'm doing—"

Bunky snapped his fingers and pointed. "*Exactly.* Exactly! You're doing the same shit, Paul. We put that record out two years ago. Other artists have put out entire catalogs in that time. And for the last six months it's been the *same* shit." Here Bunky crossed his arms again, tightly this time, as though girding himself against an unseen force. "It's like, when Sara left?" Paul felt a cold flash at the sound of her name. "I swear, when she left, she like, took your fucking soul."

"Wow," Paul said with a curt laugh. "You know what I don't get?"

Bunky's eyebrows jumped, inviting an answer.

"Why are you so ashamed of what you come from? It's like, you have this idea in your head about being authentic. About being real. But honestly? You're one of the fakest dudes I know."

Bunky shook his head and smirked. "Nah," he said, "you have no idea what you're talking about."

"C'mon. You don't think I know who paid for all those fancy lessons back in the day? Who pays for your apartment? Your share of this space? You work at a *dive bar*."

"Fuck off. Where I get my money is none of your business."

"But that's exactly what it is. *My* business. This is my life, man. I don't have a fucking trust fund to fall back on. I quit my job, remember? This falls through? I go home to Ohio and grind in a factory for the rest of my life."

"Listen to yourself. You want to make it so bad? Why'd you blow off Greg? Huh?" Bunky read the look on Paul's face. "What, you think I don't know? I called him on a hunch. Shit. You're so lost and you don't even know it."

"If you knew, why didn't you book the gig yourself? What, was that a fucking test?"

Bunky thought about it for a moment, nodded. "Yeah. You could call it that. And you failed. Like I knew you would. Like *you* knew you would." He made his way to the stool where he'd been perched, lifted his bass from the stand and crouched down to pack it away. When he spoke again, the edge in his voice had smoothed, as though he'd found a pocket of peace. "You get laid at least?"

"What?" Paul said. His ears were ringing and he felt dizzy, as though he'd been punched square in the head.

"That woman you were after last night. You fuck her? Or you fail at that too?"

"No," Paul said, "I mean yeah. We—"

"Good," Bunky said, snapping the clasps on his case, "at least one of us got something out of that show." He stood from his crouch. "Can I give you a little advice?"

Paul stared, dazed.

"Stop feeling sorry for yourself. It's not a good look. So some girl broke your heart. Get over it." Then Bunky turned and made his way for the door.

"Wait," Paul said, his voice shaky. He cleared his throat, thinking of that crumpled pink ball of paper on the floor of his apartment. "Now what?"

At the door, Bunky turned. He ran a hand over his head, felt the tuft of hair where the clipper blades had failed. "Me? I'm about to go get some tacos because I'm starving. You? What you do is up to you because we're done." Then he ducked out of the room, shut the door, and left Paul to absorb the atonal squall bleeding from the room next door.

4.

A BOY'S ROOM.

The bed he was once scared to sleep in. A tattered bear long since cast aside. Walls that told a story in the fading protest language of adolescence: vicious cars, coy women, mean-mugging heroes of the music that became his life. Shoved beneath a mirror, a squat dresser littered with stickers. Stashed in the bottom drawer, a stolen magazine, rumpled and illicit.

From a low shelf, he clutched a trophy. A rigid batter chipped and tarnished. His finger traced the nameplate: Southwest Ohio Regional All-Star. He scoffed: as a boy, he'd briefly envisioned a future as a ballplayer. The freedom of adulthood. Travel. Ease. Vague, yet somehow inevitable. Time alone would ensure it. A busted wrist derailed his progress: he had never quite learned how to slide. What had begun as a temporary setback soon calcified—with the onset of aimless angst—into apathy, and cleared the way for a surging, altogether more visceral obsession. One that felt dangerous, a blueprint for disruption. The birth of a yearning for the urgency and truth that propelled the music he loved. That he'd had to steal it all made it that much more urgent. It started on a weekend afternoon, the summer after his sophomore year of high school. He had crept into a nearby housing construction, lifted a pair of circular saws he'd noticed left uncovered by a tarp, lugged them to a borrowed car, and pawned them for a pair of turntables, stunned the gambit had been so easy. Then came his drum machine, the MPC60, which at first had felt illicit sitting there on his wobbly desk. He had, after all, pilfered it straight off the loading dock at Best Buy—a crime that felt more illegal somehow—with the help of a classmate who worked there, a shifty, angular kid who was later arrested for running a black-market car stereo emporium out of his parents' garage. But soon enough, the machine called to him, and he was hell-bent on mastering it. Digging for samples became an adventure. Gallo would pick him up and drive the two of them to Dayton or Cincinnati in his boxy yellow Volvo. They'd kill a whole Saturday in a record store, Gallo lost in the rock bins seeking inspiration for his burgeoning guitar chops, Paul shuffling through dusty boxes of cheap funk and jazz. His method was to buy a few bargain LPs—a dollar, three dollars, five bucks tops—and stuff a few more records into the sleeves. The old stoner at the counter never caught on to his ruse, or if he did, was too lazy to make a fuss. The goal was to find a drum break, a horn melody, a vocal phrase, the component parts on which he could draw to craft something fresh, <u>a new world built upon the foundation other artists had laid down</u>. And when it clicked? It was unlike anything he had experienced. He remembered the first beat he ever made, a woozy chop of the bluesy first four bars of Luther Ingram's "If Loving You Is Wrong." Overtop the sample, he scratched vocal bits from Erykah Badu's "On and On." It was drowsy and infectious and, listening back to it when it was complete, gave him chills. The thrill he felt when he created a beat was a beam of light, especially when life at home could loom heavy.

On the plane home for Thanksgiving—a ticket he'd booked months ago to nab the lowest price—the dressing down he'd received from Bunky was still fresh in his ears. The pink rent notice loomed like a guillotine. Bev, his landlord, would come pounding on his door at any moment. He was, it had become clear, falling apart, and his parents had no idea. So, he had decided to tell them. He would tell them he'd long ago quit Scrimshaw/Duff. That for the last few years he'd put all his chips on the music. That Sara, the woman his parents assumed—based on what he'd told them—was the one, had left him to build her own musical career with the Los Angeles Philharmonic. His plan was to be open and honest and hope they would at least sympathize, for once deploy the kind of love and advice that would help him get back on his feet.

At the sound of his name, he put the trophy back in the perimeter of dust that marked its place.

"Come eat," his mother hollered.

From one end of the low-slung rancher to the other he went. A dusty runner muffled the moaning floorboards as he navigated the narrow hallway. On either side, fading photos of extended family that hadn't been updated in decades, maybe ever. In the cramped kitchen, his mother stood at the stove scooping lumps of potatoes onto a trio of loaded plates.

"Can I help?" he offered. He'd asked twice already, and both times been rebuffed: "If I need help, you'll be the first to know."

This time she nodded toward the fridge. "Get what you'd like to drink. There's Coke," the word she applied to the soft drink gamut, "and beer. Might have to dig for it."

From the fiberboard cabinet, he retrieved a glass. He fetched ice and ran the tap. He tended to grow maudlin if he drank in his parents' company. There was a peeling away of layers he preferred to avoid. And he wanted to be clear-headed when he spoke his mind.

His mother gestured for him to take a plate to the kitchen table. "Sit wherever you'd like." By this she meant: take the chair you've sat in since before you could cut your own food.

She had aged more visibly than he could ever remember. Since he'd seen her last Christmas, the time had been cruel. She hunched more noticeably at the shoulders and her close curls, once dark brown, were shot through with grey. The sleeves of her pilling sweater were shoved up to reveal skin that sagged and creased as she moved. She was just sixty-four—two years younger than his father—but looked a decade older, weathered by the cumulative demands of playing her role in the delicate maintenance of financial solvency, the rigors of policing rambunctious high school classrooms, and lately, by the degenerative disc in her back that forced her to retire from teaching.

She carried the two remaining plates to the table and sat. She let out a deep, weary breath and spread a paper napkin, stamped with pilgrim hats, across her lap.

"Where's Dad?" Paul said.

"Lord knows," his mother said. "He can't ever sit still." She cleared her throat, made way for indignation that was by now well-grooved. "For Pete's sake, Len. Come eat."

The bellow came from the basement: "Goddang termites. What'd I tell you?"

Paul looked at his mother. Straight-lipped, she let her eyelids fall.

A moment later, his father emerged from the door that led down a set of rotting steps to the cellar. He was breathing heavily. Sweat darkened the peninsulas of hair between ear and temple. He pushed his glasses—the same style of big, wireframes he'd worn forever—up on his nose. "Either mites or the foundation is starting to rot. Timing couldn't be worse."

"Just sit, honey," his mother pleaded.

His father smoothed the tuck of his work shirt, adjusted his belt, and sat down. "Would you look at this," he said, surveying the bounty: a basket of Pillsbury rolls, plates piled with turkey, steamed beans, mashed potatoes, and hunks of canned cranberry, ribbed and quivering. "Your mother worked very hard."

Paul dipped his head in a show of reverence, imagining his mother tidying the stack of coupons that would make it all manageable.

She offered a thin smile. "Why don't you say grace?"

Paul bowed and began to recite the words that had been drilled into his head since Sunday school: *Bless us O Lord, for these thy gifts ...*

He snuck a look at his parents. To his right, his father: closed lids atwitch behind his glasses, mouth moving silently with the words. A man who had dutifully clocked in at Amalgamated for forty years. Who had, without complaint, worked his way from ten bucks an hour as a Production Laborer, cutting, bending, and tying rebar—a job Paul could scarcely imagine—to Shift Manager, all without a technical degree. This last fact he spoke about defiantly, like a badge of honor. "Can't teach hard work," he liked to say. And sure, that might have been true. But Paul knew his title was more impressive than the forty-some grand that came with it. Not to mention that his white whale, Plant Super, would always remain out of reach because the position required a bachelor's.

Which we are about to receive ...

To his left, his mother: forehead bowed and supported on the bony knuckles of her clasped hands, sustained by the faith she clung to more deeply with each passing year. A former teacher of Language Arts at the very high school he had attended five years after Will. Had this reality sucked? Yes, it had. And doubly so: he was the subject of no small amount of ridicule from his peers, not for being the teacher's pet, but the teacher's son, a position even more loathsome in the corny pecking order; and his mother disciplined him with an iron fist to erase any suspicion of preferential treatment after Will sailed through with straight As, the golden child.

From thy bounty...

His parents. People who had sought to build a life, to live discreetly. People for whom work ethic was as much a religion as the one they professed each Sunday morning. "Put your head down and bust your butt," his father had always said. It was a mantra instilled in him from his father, who had come to the Midwest from the old country and worked two jobs during the week and another on the weekend. People worked to live, simple as that.

Through Christ, our Lord, Amen.

His parents echoed the refrain, falling quiet to their private anxieties. The clink of cutlery. His father's nasal breathing as he chewed his meal. Occasional punctuating grunts of approval.

Then: "Shame Sara couldn't make it down. Would've been nice to finally meet the girl."

Paul swallowed a lump of potato. "Mm," he said, studying his plate.

"She went home?"

"Home," he said, the right words treading water in a rising tide in his brain, "yeah."

"She's from the Northwest, right? I always forget where."

Paul looked at his mother. She raised her eyebrows as she chewed as if to say: "You're on your own."

"Uh. Tacoma."

"Right. Tacoma. Supposed to be beautiful up that way. We'd like to get there someday, wouldn't we, Deb?"

"We would," his mother said. They hadn't been outside the tri-state in years.

His father edged his mouth with a napkin.

"She got money?"

"*Lenny,*" his mother interjected, setting down her fork.

"What? I'm not allowed to ask? They been together, what, two years?"

"Not quite two years," Paul countered. "It's complicated." Though truthfully, it wasn't complicated in the least. Not anymore. Not since she left.

"What's complicated? Shit or get off the pot."

His mother rolled her eyes. "Please, Lenny. You weren't exactly Mr. Decisive."

"Well, I had a *few* gals knocking on my door."

"I'm sure you did."

"Besides, son. You're not getting any younger. Thirty soon, which is hard to believe, and—"

"Thanks, Dad," he said. "Can we please talk about something else?" This was not how it was supposed to go.

"Hmph," said his father. "Figure you'd want to talk about your lady. You were the one who showed us pictures last time. It was me? I'd put something down on it." Here he winked and grinned.

"Dad."

"Not like my mother used to say about the dates I brought home. 'She has nice ways.' Which I'll let you guess what that meant. Until I met your mother of course."

"Leonard. For God's sake, will you give it a rest?"

Paul let a laugh escape his nose.

"Suit yourselves," his father said. "Turning the page."

Fine. So, his parents thought he and Sara were still together. After enough time, they'd stop asking, or make their own assumptions. Besides, he couldn't think about that right now. No. He had to control the dialogue. He had to tell them the truth.

"How's Dee Gallo doing?" his father wanted to know now. "Did he come home too?"

Perfect. Another scab to pick.

"He's—fine," Paul said. "I don't think he came back home. His band is getting ready to head out on tour."

"*Tour*," his father said, like it was a disease. "I sure hope he has a backup plan."

"He's doing really well actually," Paul said in a defensive way that surprised himself. "I think they could be big."

"Mm," his father said, "and what does big mean exactly?"

"If things go well for him playing clubs on this tour, he could move up to theaters on the next one. Bands can make like, ten grand a night playing theaters."

His father stopped chewing. "Ten grand a night?"

Paul nodded.

Lest he allow himself to get caught up in what he surely thought was a delusion, his father chortled, took a swig of milk from a glass that had once been a Welch's jam jar. On it, Garfield stared lazily into space, cynical and heavy-lidded. "Sounds about as certain as playing the lotto."

"Well," his mother cut in, "I'm just glad you decided to move on from music and focus on real life. And I'm glad that you and Gallo stayed close. He's a good kid even if he's off in la la land. Hard to believe you two wound up roommates—"

"These potatoes," Paul cut in, growing weary of the lie, "fantastic, Mom." He shoveled a bite onto his fork and plotted his way in, the lines he'd rehearsed in his head. *Look, you always told me to work my ass off*, went his reasoning, *which is exactly what I'm doing. I got my work ethic from you two. It just so happens that I'm working on something I love. But I hit a few bumps in the road.* Here was the hard part, the impossible part really: *So, if there's any way you could help me, just a tiny cushion, just some breathing room while me and Bunky, see, he's my bandmate and ...*

"Speaking of old friends," his mother chirped again, "I told Rhona Jenks about what you're doing up in New York and all. She was *very* impressed." She chewed a sliver of turkey, eyes alight for the first time all evening. "Her son Everett just finished at UC. I gave her your number, told her you might be able to share some advice. Jobs. Interviewing. Keeping your head straight in the big city up there. Things like that."

His father picked up the baton.

"Campbell's is a good company," he said, as though issuing a verdict. "The kind of place you could build a future. I know your grampop would be proud." He speared the last of his turkey, smacked his lips as he chewed. He had inhaled his food—an unshakable habit ingrained as the youngest of eight kids—and was down to the last gelatinous shards of cranberry.

Enough. It was now or never. Paul put down his fork, wiped his mouth with his paper napkin and said, "Well, I don't think he would be too proud, because I quit."

"You what?" his father said. He leaned in so Paul could speak into his good ear.

"I said, I quit. And I never worked for Campbell's. The company I worked for was called Scrimshaw/Duff and we made ads for a soup brand called Nature's Gift. Not Campbell's at all. I just went along with what you thought because I hated the job and didn't feel like explaining what I did. I was a gopher. I made copies and got everyone's coffee. I was a bitch, basically."

"*Paul*," his mother said.

"But it doesn't matter anymore, because I quit."

Paul's father leaned back in his chair, stunned. "When?" he said.

"Like, two years ago."

"My God," his mother said. "What have you been doing for money?"

"I work at a record store."

"A *record* store," his father spat.

"And I make music."

"You do not," his mother said.

"I never stopped."

His mother cast down her eyes and shook her head. Then she shot him daggers. "So I *lied* to Everett's mother. That's what you're telling me?"

"He's been lying to us, is what he's telling us," his father said, on the verge of shouting. He crumpled his napkin and threw it on his plate.

"I'm sorry I lied," Paul said. "It was better that way."

"Better than *what?*" his mother said.

"Better than you being more disappointed in me than you already are."

"Well, if we weren't before," his mother said flatly, "we certainly are now."

"Why couldn't you guys just fucking believe in me? Like you believed in Will?"

"There are realities, Paul," his father said.

"Well, the reality is I need some money."

"Of course you do," his mother said. "You're up there wasting your life, and everything we worked to give you."

"Like what?" Paul said with venom. "What have you guys given me?"

His father looked wounded, and Paul felt ashamed. He cleared his throat.

"Well, son. You have a funny way with timing because we have no money to give. And we have a little news of our own since you seem to care so much."

"Lenny," his mother said.

"*Yes*, Deb?"

"Not now."

They shared a long glare.

"What happened?" Paul said. "What, are you guys like, getting a divorce or something?"

"Excuse me?" his father said. "No, we're not getting a *divorce*, Paul."

Despite it all, he was relieved. It would have been too much to bear. "Well, then what?"

His father removed his glasses, set about cleaning them with the edges of the same napkin he'd a moment ago tossed onto his plate. "We're getting rid of the house."

"What?"

"Leonard," his mother said, "we hadn't even decided that yet."

"We shouldn't kid ourselves."

"Will you guys please tell me what the hell is going on?" But suddenly, he knew. *Of course.* His stomach sank. "Amalgamated," he said.

Abruptly, his father stopped polishing his glasses and looked up.

"God," Paul said. He looked at his mother who avoided his gaze, then back at his father, and all of a sudden, the atmosphere around them shifted. "You were so close. Forty years."

"Thirty-six."

"Thirty-six years. Why—I mean, why now?"

His father stared at the air in front of his face. "Wasn't just me. Whole team got axed. Writing's been on the wall for a while now. Hell, the last few years? Not a week goes by the news isn't talking about some factory town or another. And they say *Rust Belt* like it's some concept. Not a place where people actually live their lives. I just hoped I could keep my head down and my mouth shut long enough to retire. Different world than the one I grew up in." He exhaled and shook his head. "So, no. We don't have any money to give you, son."

"But wait," Paul said, narrowing his eyes. "You guys own the house. Why would you need to sell it? Does Will know?" He could see it: Fucking Will in his light-flooded condo, Lake Michigan sparkling through the plate windows as he absorbed the news over the phone, he and Teri and little baby Andrew firmly entrenched in their lives. He would, no doubt, dispense advice in that measured, removed tone of his, as though he was talking to a client.

His parents stole another glance at one another.

Paul looked across the table at the empty chair. "Does he have something to do with this?"

His father sucked his teeth.

"Hold on. What happened?"

"He was trying to help." His father shook his head, dazed as he spoke.

"What did he do? Invest your pension?"

"He made it sound like a sure thing."

"Oh my God," Paul said. He stood up and wobbled as he felt the rush of blood to his head. He pulled his phone from his pocket. He scrolled for Will's number and dialed.

"Paul," his father pleaded, reaching out to grab his arm, "it's not his fault."

The call went straight to voicemail. Of course it did. Will's smug voice cut through: *You know what to do.* BEEP. Paul hung up and seethed. He slumped back in his chair.

"Not his *fault?*" he said. "That's exactly what it is."

"How do you think he feels about this? He had our best interests in mind. He's our son."

"*The* son," Paul said.

"And just what does that mean?" his mother said.

"You know what it means," Paul said.

"Will is devastated," his mother said.

"Devastated doesn't fix this," Paul said, re-routing his anger. "What's he doing about it?"

"It hit him really hard, Paul."

"Well, he should have thought about that before he—" He looked at his mother. "What are *you* going to do?"

"What do you think I'm going to do?" she snapped. "I'll go back to the classroom. And I'll tutor again on the side."

"But what about your back?"

"Okay," his mother said, balling her patterned napkin, "I've had just about enough for one evening, thank you." She shoved back in her chair and stood, leaving half her food untouched. With the unhurried simmer that had made her a watchful enigma in the classroom, she made her way down the hall.

Paul and his father were left to linger in the charged atmosphere. The only sounds were the plunk of the dripping faucet— a metronome of disrepair—and the hum of the ancient fridge. Sounds that would soon become someone else's problem. He swallowed back a surge of sadness. His father sucked his teeth again. Paul wondered what life he had once envisioned for himself, the dreams that now lay dormant, distant and faded as his youth; he wondered if he'd ever had the chance to dream at all.

"Why?" his father said, looking at him.

"Why what?"

"Quit? That was a job."

"Because I had to bet on myself. Because no one else would."

His father exhaled, then got up heavily, as though struggling under the weight of what was to come. "Son," he said, as though Paul was a little boy, "I hope things work out for you because that's a big gamble."

***

Paul leaned against the edge of his bed and fumed. He scanned the small room: the worn beige carpet, the cheap figurines and trinkets from boyhood that still populated his shelves. The corner where he'd wedged the pawn shop turntables and turned a hobby into a fixation. Tomorrow, he would head back to the city. He would never step foot in his bedroom, in this house, again. He made a conscious effort to log the moment, to stash it in the vault of his memory, a symptom of his tendency toward nostalgia for events that hadn't yet ended.

He thought of his father, the years he dedicated to the job that had cast him aside for cheaper labor. About his mother and her stubborn resilience. About Will, that mother*fucker*. And about Sara, who he'd never had the chance to bring home. He could still picture the night they met, the bar on Eldridge where he'd landed a weekly DJ gig after he and Bunky released their record. Midway through his set, she had approached the booth and, with a heavy-lidded confidence that he fell for at once, requested "Think Twice" by Donald Byrd, which had stunned and delighted him. "Play it next," she had said, "and I'll come back to request another." He agreed, and it wasn't until she left for a drink that he realized he'd left the damn Byrd record at home. He played "Paradise" by Sade next instead, and it was only when she returned to the booth and mouthed, *Ballsy*, that it occurred to him the sultry chorus could be interpreted as a reckless come-on. It had, unintentionally, worked: she wrote her number on the back of the album sleeve. It took him a week to work up the nerve to ask her out, six hours for her to text back a single word: *Sure*. At the Thai place he picked out, he had ordered prawns because he thought it sounded sophisticated, then made her laugh until she cried at the way he fumbled and cursed at the clumsy shells. Soon she began to show him her version of the city: the dusty bookshops she loved to browse, the rehearsal space she retreated to with her violin. There was the first song they made together, the day he had brought his MPC to her place on a whim. She had begun to play an aching melody, drawing her bow across the strings patiently, as though the notes would break apart if she used too much force. He improvised a bruised and fizzing beat, built around a yearning horn sample. The look on her face when she lifted her bow, clear-eyed and warm, was confirmation: their voices weaved well together. He had felt a sort of bliss, pride really, when he told people he and Sara were not only dating but creating together. Of course there were fights, which were in many ways just brooding tests of will to see which of them could set aside their entrenched stubbornness and apologize first. They were often about the direction of the music, sure, but beneath the surface, he suspected, they were really about their future.

A familiar impulse led him to his dresser. He stooped at the waste and opened the bottom drawer. Beneath a stash of old, yellowing t-shirts was a magazine that had sustained the furious urges of adolescence. Paul flipped through the magazine, the spreads and centerfolds asserting their familiarity in a reunion of glossy skin and curves. Toward the middle of the magazine, a series of pages was particularly well-worn, ink faded by sticky fingers.

He settled on an old favorite, the model's hair out of fashion in both places, when, just like an episode out of his teenage years, he heard footsteps approaching his door.

"Got a minute?" said his father.

Had it been a minute later, he might not have been wearing pants.

"*One sec,*" he said. He shoved the magazine beneath a pillow and muttered under his breath, chastising himself for his absurdity: here he was, a grown-ass, taxpaying adult, stashing vintage contraband beneath the pillow of his childhood bed. "What is it?"

His father opened the door and stood in the threshold. He blinked behind his glasses, tired. "You alright?"

"Me? Yeah. Fine. Just—I'm sorry. About all of it."

"Mm," his father said. He stepped into the room and shuffled over to the bookcase. He picked up the same trophy Paul himself had been holding less than an hour ago. "You should've kept at it."

"You can say that about a lot of things."

"Like what?"

But Paul didn't know. It was one of those things you said to your parents to keep from talking about the darker stuff. He shrugged. His father put the trophy back and stuffed his hands in his pockets as he stood there in the middle of Paul's bedroom.

"Look, I think we all said things we regret up there. Your mother has been taking this very hard," he said. "Harder than me."

Paul looked away. "I had no idea." He couldn't even look at his father as he spoke. "I just, you know—"

"Hey," his father interrupted. It was as though he knew Paul wasn't equipped to express the extent of the sentiment. He moved closer to where Paul leaned against the side of his bed. He took one of his hands from his pockets and held it out. "Here."

"What?"

"Take it," he said.

Paul held out his hand, into which his father pressed a fold of bills.

"Dad. No—"

"Go on. It's not much. This is your life. It might never make sense to us, but you're still our son. Get Sara something nice. Take her out to dinner."

"Dad, I can't."

"Put it in your pocket. Don't tell your mother."

Paul did as he was told and bit down hard on the inside of his cheek.

His father again patted his shoulder, a gesture on which he had always relied to bridge the emotional gap that hung between them, the closest he ever came to a hug. He stepped back and surveyed the room. "Some good memories in this house," he said and made his way to the door. He knocked on the doorframe as if to casually test its stability. Then he nodded. "Okay," he said and shut the door behind him.

Paul stared for a moment at the closed door. On a poster tacked to the fiberboard, two MCs crouched low before a vintage Benz. From his pocket, he retrieved the fold of weathered bills. He unpeeled the money, met the taciturn glare of Andrew Jackson, and counted forty dollars.

***

The journey back to New York gave him plenty of time to think. The East Coast was getting an early dose of snow, so his flight from Cincinnati was delayed first an hour, then three, then six. He puttered around the too-bright terminal and flipped through magazines at the newsstand. He fidgeted in his seat at the gate and tried to listen to music. He blew thirty bucks of his father's money on a watery beer and a lukewarm burger at perhaps the saddest Applebee's on the planet. He sat on the floor against the wall of his gate and couldn't shake the truth: he had to find a way to help his parents. He had to do something because a part of him felt like he hadn't done enough to keep Sara from leaving. He couldn't let the rest of his life fall apart. That much was clear. What wasn't clear in the slightest was how.

Nearly ten hours after he had kissed his mother on the cheek and left her glaring past him on the porch of the home he'd never see again, he was back in Red Hook, low-slung and snowy, climbing the steps to his apartment in slushy shoes. Despite the grueling trip, he was energized, ready to hunker down and use his desperation as the fuel for creation. He unshouldered his duffle bag and put his key in the deadbolt.

It wouldn't turn.

Shit.

He tried again, more forcefully this time. It was foolish. The key didn't work. The reality of his financial situation was made brutally clear. Standing there before his locked apartment, he almost screamed. No, what he almost did was rear back and slam his fist into the blunt aluminum door. But he thought better of it. He took a deep breath and calmed himself and trudged downstairs to the garden-level apartment.

He knocked on the door. After a moment, a moment spent cursing himself, the door swung open and a little boy of about ten was standing on the threshold. Ricky. His landlord's son. The boy wore a black t-shirt emblazoned with the image of some flexing wrestling superstar and clutched a handheld video game console. He looked up at Paul deadpan, annoyed that his game had been interrupted.

"Ricky, what's up buddy?" Paul held out a high-five for him to slap. Ricky blinked at it, so Paul pulled back his hand. "Your dad around?"

The boy rolled his eyes and ducked back into the apartment. "*Dad,*" he bellowed, "somebody's here to see you. I think it's the weirdo from upstairs."

Damn. Four years and he was still the weirdo from upstairs. Paul heard cranky floorboards give way beneath heavy footsteps until his landlord filled the doorframe.

Bev. Short for Beverly. A former longshoreman and a Red Hook lifer who bought the row house back in the early '90s and who had no intention of leaving. Ever. He loomed before Paul in socked feet, baggy carpenter jeans and a faded New York Giants sweatshirt that protruded over his keg of a stomach. His greying hair was combed down into a straight edge that emphasized the furrow lines on his forehead. His cheeks, as always, were ruddy, as though he'd just arrived from a wintry scene.

"Bev," Paul said, "my apartment is locked." As though he didn't know.

"And?" Bev said. He crossed his arms over his chest and widened his stance in the doorway.

Paul could picture it now: Bev putting him in a headlock, depositing his meaty fist onto the crown of his skull.

"And I'd like to get in?"

"And I'd like to get paid."

Paul swallowed. "Today's what," he checked a watch that wasn't there, "the twenty-ninth? I still have, like, two days."

The air went out of Bev's shoulders and he shook his head. "Paul. C'mon, kid. You and I both know two days ain't gonna make a bit of difference. I have to let you know this is real shit, aright? Not some game."

"And so, what? You lock me out the day after Thanksgiving?" He was intent on playing the heartstrings, the only move he had left. "Real compassionate."

"I figured you'd be gone all weekend," Bev said. He scratched his cheek. "But that ain't the point. You owe me two months now. You got the money, or what?"

Paul did not have the money.

"First of all, I do not owe you two months. I already gave you like, half of October. And second, I'll give you everything I've got. We can go to the ATM right now and I'll empty my account. C'mon."

"Paul." Bev ran a hand down his face.

"Please. I'll have the rest of it by the first, I swear to God. Just give me a shot."

"I've already given you a shot, pal. *Several* shots."

Paul had actually clasped his hands at his chest now. He was pleading. "Last shot then. I got nowhere to go, Bev. My parents back home are losing their house. I gotta help them. I can't be losing my apartment."

Bev's face softened a touch and he leaned against the door-jamb. Paul saw a crack in the armor and pried it open.

"My brother made some fucked up investment and flushed their nest egg down the toilet. Now they gotta sell the house they've been in forever. The house I grew up in."

"Brutal."

"So what I'm saying is—"

Bev rolled his eyes and Paul knew he'd broken through.

"Fuck's sake," he said, "I'll go get my shoes."

"Oh man, thank you. Thank you, Bev."

"Don't thank me yet," he said. "Let's see how much is in this bankroll of yours."

***

A shade over $900. That's what was left. Well, $895.11 after the ATM fee, which he'd have to pay twice since the bodega machine only allowed five hundred dollars at once. Carlito, the bodega's mustachioed maestro, the man from whom Paul had ordered his bacon-egg-and-cheese on hungover Saturdays for four years running, greeted them warmly, but fell quiet when he saw the look on their faces as Bev followed Paul to the Mini-Bank in the back by the cleaning products. It must have looked like a holdup or an extortion bid.

"How much?" Bev wanted to know.

Paul stepped aside so Bev could see.

"That's grim, Paulie."

"No shit," Paul said.

"Well," Bev said, "it's either this or you find someplace else to live. And I make it very difficult for you to call Red Hook home."

The ATM spat out the bills with wicked indifference. When it was all over, Paul had eleven cents left in his account. Plus the rest of his cash from the Farm gig and a few bucks from the forty his father had given him. He handed the wad of hundreds, twenties, and fives to Bev, who folded it and put it in the deep pocket of his carpenter jeans.

"Thanks," he said.

He said it as though Paul had closed a drafty window or given him directions. He felt empty, hollowed out. His paltry savings were gone. His hourly wages from Dead Wax, the hundred bucks or so each time he DJ'd, hadn't even been enough to let him break even. In fact, by the time all the records and gear and cabs and late nights tallied up, music had been *costing* him money. Shitloads of money.

Bev cleared his throat, as though sensing the black hole of Paul's thought spiral.

"How do I know you're good for the rest?"

"The rest?"

"Yeah, Paul. December is in two days. What's my collateral?"

Paul had been so focused on not throwing up that he'd forgotten there was more to give. He had no more to give, money or otherwise. Hell, he hardly owned anything aside from the clothes he wore and the bed he slept in and the—

"Drum machine," he said. It was the only way.

"Say what?"

"My MPC. Drum machine. That's your collateral, Bev. It's all I got. And it just so happens to be the thing that means the most to me, pretty much on the planet. So you better believe I'm going to fight to get that shit back."

Bev smirked and smoothed his sweatshirt over his belly. Paul could sense the wheels turning, there in the back of a bodega next to shelves of roach spray and Lysol.

"You are a fighter," Bev said at last, "I'll give you that." Then he nodded over his shoulder and led Paul out of the shop and into the empty night.

***

Bev stood by the door as Paul unplugged his drum machine, gathering up the cables that ran to the mixing console stationed in the corner of his apartment.

"When's the last time you cleaned up in here?" Bev said, scanning the room. He turned up his nose. "Looks like a drug den."

Paul wound the cables around his drum machine, gave it one last look and handed it over. Bev put it under his arm, loosely, like a stack of old newspapers.

"Please be careful with that," Paul said.

"I'm only doing this because I like you," Bev said, "and I respect what you're trying to do with this music thing." It seemed to Paul in that moment that Bev's ruddy cheeks grew a shade ruddier, and it was enough to steel Paul's resolve.

"I'm going to get that thing back," he said, "just watch."

"I hope you do," Bev said, "because next time I won't be so charitable." Then he handed over the new key, cast one last glance into the mess beyond, and before he had a chance to think twice, turned and took the stairs down to the ground level.

5.

IT WAS A SPARKLING LATE-FALL MORNING: GENTLE BREEZE, TOPAZ SKY, the kind of low-angled sunlight that made Bleecker Street look like a movie set. To Paul, the beauty of the day felt almost like a personal insult: the city was at its most charming when his life was at its most precarious. In the windows of cafés and bakeries, sharply dressed young couples sipped lattes and prepared for a day of shopping. Tourist families in scarves and bubble coats held hands, rosy-cheeked and smitten as they strolled the sun-kissed sidewalks. It was the kind of scene that, under normal circumstances, might have inspired Paul to create, to translate the hopeful yearning of the day into song. To take, perhaps, a lilting piano sample and let it drip like honey over a spare shuffle of drums, to channel the spirit of Billie Holiday's "Autumn in New York," add his chapter to the story. Today, however, as he made his way to work, the only thing on his mind was how to get his life back on track.

On the one hand, Dead Wax was a sanctuary. A place where the records on the walls and in the bins established a kind of barrier against the problems of the real world. On the other hand, he knew Dante and Mika would read him like a book, so, as he pulled open the sticker-caked door, he tried his best to pretend everything was peachy fucking keen.

Dante was at his usual perch behind the register dealing with a customer. He wore a grey hoodie with the hood flipped up, dreads poking out from the top, drawstring tied in a bow beneath his scabbed chin. Next to him, Mika took hungry bites from a foil-wrapped bacon, egg and cheese and flipped through a Xeroxed zine with ink-stained fingers. She glanced up, barely, as Paul passed by, and offered him a wink, magnified cartoonishly by her big red frames. He counted his blessings and rounded the counter toward the stockroom in the back.

"Aye," Dante said as Paul reached for the door handle, "we need you to settle a debate."

"Mm," he said, without turning around.

"Don't be rude, bro. Come over here. I'm asking for your opinion."

Paul obliged, set his face in an approximation of equanimity.

"Take a look at these two bad boys. The guy I was just dealing with traded them in." Dante gestured at two records laying side-by-side on the counter. One was Pearl Jam's self-titled album from the mid-aughts; the other was *The Spaghetti Incident?* by Guns N' Roses. Both hundred dollar records, easy. "Objectively speaking, which of these two has the shittier cover?"

Paul glanced at one cover, then the other. Objectively speaking? Both were atrocious. The Pearl Jam cover boasted a halved avocado floating upright against a matte blue background and situated beneath a minimalist rendering of the band's name. That was it. It was austere and absurd and seemed to have been pulled from a vegan cookbook. The Guns N' Roses cover meanwhile, was the spiritual opposite: maximalist and grotesque, a closeup of a St. Vitus dance of soupy noodles squirming in what was either tomato sauce or blood. It looked as if the photographer had simply stuffed his lens into a can of Chef Boyardee and pressed the shutter.

"Honestly?" Paul said. "You can fire both into the sun as far as I'm concerned, because neither holds any meaning for me."

"Bro," Dante said, swiping a hand down his face, "that's not what I'm asking. It's a simple question: which sucks more?"

Paul looked over at Mika, who chowed down the last of her egg sandwich and flipped through the pages of her zine as though she was alone in the bowels of the New York Public Library.

"What did Mika say?" he asked.

She didn't even flinch at the sound of her name.

"That's not important," Dante said. "I'm asking you."

"Fine," he said, and relented to the game. He knew his answer, one way or another, would elicit an explosive reaction from one of them and he was excited to witness it. "Put a gun to my head and it's not even really close. The Pearl Jam cover is worse by far. It's … an avocado."

"*Ha*," Mika squawked. She slammed shut her zine, looked up and grinned—perhaps the third time Paul had ever seen her smile—and pointed a long bony finger in Dante's mug. "If somebody as clueless as Paul agrees with me, you know it's the easy answer."

Dante swatted the finger out of his face. "Fuck out of here," he said. "That's some backwards-ass logic."

"And why is that your answer, Paul?" Mika rested her chin in her palm in a caricature of curiosity. "Pray tell."

"Uh," he said, "because the Pearl Jam feels like a harbinger for the bourgeoisification of our peer group, of which avocado toast is the perfect distillation?"

Mika cocked her head, partially impressed. "Not bad. I'll give you half-credit. The answer is this: the floating avocado, you see, is an ironic gesture, meant to tell the listener, *Look, it doesn't really matter what's on the cover. What matters is the music, which rawks, bro. Trust us.* It's a pretentious display of ego and self-regard and it makes me want to chew that avocado right off the sleeve. Our man Axl, on the other hand, presents us with an image of excess and consumption, a perfect representation of the band's aesthetic, reputation, and modus operandi. If I'm not mistaken, it's also meant to refer to the ex-drummer's coke supply, the reserves of which he kept in the fridge next to takeout containers of spaghetti. So, the GNR cover is honest, which is all we can really ask from our artists, big or small."

"But," Dante stammered, "from a purely aesthetic stand-point—"

"Mm?" Mika said, but by then, she had turned her attention to a stack of new arrivals at her elbow to be arranged and placed into the bins.

"Whatever," Dante said. He took the two records in question and set them aside. "We agree to disagree."

"Wrong," Mika said. "We obviously disagree about the extent to which we disagree. And it's good to know that all you really care about is aesthetics."

It was fascinating to watch, really. The way the two of them could take a dumb debate and turn it into an examination of personal code. But it was contagious, and he suddenly found himself thinking about the cover art he and Bunky had used for *Clockwork*. How Bunky had handed Paul his Leica—just a five-thousand-dollar hand-me-down collecting dust in his derelict apartment—and told him to *Snap something that means something*. He showed Paul how to work the aperture and shutter speed, how to focus the rangefinder eyepiece, then let him loose. But Paul didn't need to move beyond the cramped confines of Bunky's studio. He found himself enamored with the cluttered array of gear and records they had amassed on the floor in the corner of the room. Bunky's bass, a dinged-up amp, a collection of pedals, a knot of cables; on a messy desk, Paul's MPC and turntable, his headphones with worn foam earpieces, and a jagged stack of dusty 45s. That was it: the raw materials for their craft. There was nothing slick or fancy about their setup; it was, as Mika said, honest. So that's what Paul zeroed in on, went through half a roll of film snapping the assortment of equipment from different angles. The one they chose for the album cover was bird's eye, taken from a standing position atop Bunky's desk chair, a view that also caught edges of the disarray of the surrounding environment. Paul loved that image, the rich blacks and grainy contrast of the film, the way the picture seemed to say: amidst all this noise, something meaningful.

Dante was still sputtering, trying to maintain a foothold in the argument. "Well, what I was about to say, was that the real reason I called our boy Paul over here was to ask him how his show went the other night." Dante raised his fist in what was meant to be a celebratory bump, but Paul was so unprepared for the question, still caught up in the crux of the argument, that he didn't have time to steel himself. He felt his shoulders slump and stared at Dante's fist until it retreated.

"Oh shit," Dante said.

"Oh boy," Mika said, "time for a smoke." She gathered her coat and was out of the shop before Paul even had a chance to manufacture a lie.

"Shitshow?"

"I blew it," Paul said. "We had a chance to rally, and I blew it."

"I mean, like—" Dante scratched his head through the hood of his sweatshirt, trying to find a tactful way to approach the conversation.

"We were clicking at the beginning. Grooves were tight. Crowd was feeling it. The kind of set you dream about. And then, I mean—shit man, I thought I saw Sara in the crowd and I just fucking went off the rails."

The look on Dante's face said it all: he grimaced as though he had witnessed a bone-crunching slam on one of the skate videos he often watched on his phone.

"Yeah," Paul said. "And, to make things worse? Bunky's blaming me for botching a chance to snag an opening slot for Feathers."

"Those lumberjack-looking-ass dudes."

"Right."

"Your boy Gallo."

"I wouldn't call him my boy, but yeah."

"They're managed by Stevie Reese, right? That would've been big for you guys."

"Okay, you know what? Forget it."

"Look, man. You fucked up. So what? Then get your shit together. Because you know what you're not going to get?"

"What?"

"My pity."

"What it comes down to is this: you think Mika would pay me in advance?"

Dante tried to read Paul's face. "I'm sure it's not that big a deal. Why? You good?"

"Just could use a little cushion right now is all. You know how it goes."

Dante nodded, though Paul could tell he wasn't entirely convinced. "I can ask Mik—"

"Don't," Paul cut in, "don't say anything to her yet."

Dante held up his palms. "Okay. Chill. I won't say anything."

"Swear?"

"Swear," Dante said, putting one palm in the air, the other right smack in the middle of Axl's spaghetti.

In the stock room, Paul flipped on the buzzing light, took a seat, and booted up the old computer. He leaned down and tore open a box at his feet. Right away he sensed potential: a collection of Brazilian records, which often fetched a pretty penny online. Hardcore vinyl heads were always hunting for the rarest groove, the earliest pressing. He'd seen the prices on Discogs, which cataloged just about every album ever pressed on wax. Looking for that ultra-rare spiritual jazz masterpiece from 1978? Odds were some collector in Switzerland was willing to part with his copy for a cool grand. Paul flipped through the records: the cocktail bossa nova of Stan Getz and João Gilberto, the late-career folk of Milton Nascimento, a beat-up samba compilation. Good music, but not nearly rare enough to help his cause. Yet nestled toward the middle of the box, when he was beginning to sense it was hopeless, he found them: Tom Zé, Os Mutantes, and Azimuth, all first pressings. Though he could hear Mika and Dante chattering beyond the cracked door, he looked over his shoulder to be sure, and when he knew it was safe, put the records in his bag. He would just have to pray that Mika would be too busy with her daily concerns—sniping at Dante, navigating the angst of her own musical pursuits—to notice they were gone.

He took a deep breath to steady himself and moved on to a box of new LPs. He slid free one of the fresh, shrink-wrapped records and felt a jolt of recognition. The cover was a photo of Gallo and his bandmates—impeccably coiffed and bearded—seated around a bonfire on the beach. Each of them gazed at a different point just off-camera, as though considering the trajectory of a swarm of flies. Each of them that is except for Gallo, who sat elbows on knees, staring imploringly right down the barrel at you the listener. So they'd put out their second record. Big deal. What did Feathers have that They Is didn't? Besides a functioning band of course. And two albums. And a headlining tour. And press. And fans. And probably some cute women in floppy hats waiting for them after shows. *Shit.* Paul slid the album into his bag. One less sale.

He double-clicked a new spreadsheet, leaned over to open another box of records when he heard a knock on the door.

"Yeah," he said and spun around on his chair.

It was Mika and she was holding out an envelope. "Here," she said. She hooked her hair behind her ear and avoided eye contact.

"What is it?" Paul said. He reached out and took the envelope, peeked inside. It was, to his shock, a thin layer of cash. Dante must have said something. For an instant, he was upset; his trust had been betrayed. But the anger vanished just as quickly, and he felt grateful for his friend. He looked up at Mika and felt an unexpected hitch in his throat.

"Oh God," she said, "don't."

"What?" he said.

"Hug me, or whatever it is you're thinking of doing. It's half your check. You'll get the rest next month."

"Mika," he said, "I—this means a lot. You have no idea."

"What'd I say? Just stop." She looked over her shoulder into the shop beyond, where Dante was nodding along to the music. "I told Avocado Boy out there I'd think about it, which as far as he's concerned means *absolutely-fucking-not*. So don't ever—and I mean *ever*—tell him I did this for you, got it?"

"Got it," Paul said, but she was gone before the words had even left his lips.

The evening traffic slowed, and Paul powered down the whirring computer, shouldered his bag—heavier than usual—and snapped shut the lights in the stock room. He steeled his resolve: he'd march out into the night, casual as can be. He opened the door and was set to say goodnight to Mika and Dante when a familiar face appeared at the entrance across the room and caused his stomach to plummet. A familiar face whose bright eyes went wide, whose mouth slid into a grin, at the sight of him.

"Oh, hell no," Paul said aloud and instinctively made an about-face back toward the stock room.

"Hey, where you going, buddy?" Gallo said. "Long time no see."

What was he doing here? Paul stopped short, plastered his best imitation of a smile on his face, and turned back around.

"*Yo*," he said brightly. He glanced at Dante, who watched the proceedings from his stool with casual interest, at Mika, who had set about cranking the volume on a manic drum and bass record—her closing-time selection—from the stereo behind the counter.

Gallo bopped his head to the music and a strand of his lacquered hair sprung free and hung about his bearded face. He wore a crisp winter parka—forest green—over dark denim and high-laced boots. L.L. Bean made manifest. "Man, it's like a party in here," he said.

"Not a bad place to work," Paul said stupidly. He gestured to his colleagues. "Hey, you know Mika? Dante?"

"Don't believe I do." Gallo waved politely. "Dee Gallo," he said. "How y'all doing?"

Y'all?

"Fine," Mika and Dante muttered in unison. The drum and bass track steamrolled overhead.

Paul adjusted his shoulder under the weight of the records in his bag and the four of them blinked and lingered in the blank space.

"Well anyway, I was wandering by, thought I'd come in to see about an album. Try to do my part in boosting sales. Y'all got it out yet?"

"What album?" Paul said, trying not to seethe. He wanted to hear him say it.

"Aw, you know," Gallo demurred, "just this little album I heard about."

"Check new releases," Dante said. He pointed to the bin by the window.

"Thank you kindly," Gallo said. He made his way over to the bin and began to flip through.

Paul was stuck. He couldn't very well leave now. He cast a murderous glance at Mika and Dante, as if there was anything they could have done about it. Dante shrugged, like, *What's your problem?* And Paul realized with a start that he was being ridiculous. Childish. He should have been happy for Gallo. That a humble kid from his town had gone and *done the shit.* After all, Paul hadn't exactly been betrayed. If it had been him? Sure, he might have handled it a little differently, given Gallo at least a heads up that he was moving out instead of coming home after work late one night to catch him stashing suitcases and belongings into a van. But still. They were young. And being young accounted for a multitude of dumbass decisions.

Without much of a plan, he took off his bag and placed it at the foot of the counter, joined Gallo at the well of records by the window. He pretended to engage in the serious business of arranging the racks in proper alphabetical order, a task Mika had already completed with OCD precision.

"Hear you guys are heading out on tour soon," he said.

"Yeah," Gallo said, "finally doing our thing."

"Must feel good."

Gallo turned to him with something like relief.

"You know? It does feel good. We've been working our tails off. It's rewarding to know that our stuff resonates with people. It's the kind of thing you dream about as a kid. Which, you know what I was thinking about? Remember that first show we played together in my garage?"

"Remember? I hope I never forget it." He could still picture Gallo's neighborhood, where the homes were a little spiffier, the backyards a little roomier. He remembered that warm spring Friday evening—made more buoyant by the approaching summer break—as though it had happened two days ago instead of a dozen years ago. "How many people did we cram in there? Thirty?"

"Shoot, at least."

"We played like somebody would've wrecked our gear if we didn't go all out."

"Damn straight," Gallo said with a chuckle. "Greatest all-covers set in the history of high school bands."

"And I remember that brunette you made out with after it was all over."

"Shoot. Amber Darcy. She was a cutie."

"I'll be honest. That show made me realize what I wanted to do with my life."

"Naw. For real?"

"No bullshit." It was true. Nothing else at that point had struck him quite like watching the polite skepticism on the faces of those huddled in the garage slide into a sort of delighted surprise—*Thank God they don't suck*—and by the end, naked enjoyment. Sure, the last song was a ramshackle cover of "Summertime," but the way the kids in that small crowd forgot themselves as they sang along, the way they hollered and clapped when Gallo struck the final chord, made Paul believe it didn't matter what song it had been, it had been good.

Gallo registered the look on Paul's face and his grin fell away. He dropped his eyes and shook his head. "Look," he said, "that's part of the reason I came in here."

Paul waited for him to say more.

"I shouldn't have bailed on you like that," he said. He almost laughed, wagging his head at the idiocy of it all. "The way I peaced out. No way to treat a friend. I guess I just didn't want it to get weird, you know? Like, I know how bad you want this too, and—I don't know what I'm saying."

"It was fucked up. I come home from work late and it looks like you're making a getaway?"

Gallo shrugged then looked Paul in the face. "Shoot, man, I'm sorry is all."

The last thing Paul had expected when he came to work was to begrudgingly feel the warmth of a friendship rekindled. Yet he found himself sticking out his hand for Gallo to shake, and saying, "Water under the bridge."

Gallo shook his hand firmly and Paul felt, if not good, then at least a little lighter.

"Say, how are things going with you and Bunky anyway?"

"They're ... going," Paul said and ran a hand through his hair. For reasons he didn't understand, he said, "We're working on a new album."

"Oh yeah? That is the best news I've heard all day, my friend. I can't wait to hear—ah, here we go." Something caught his eye in the bin, and he lifted a copy of the record—his record—shining in its shrink wrap. He ran his hand over the cover like it was an heirloom. "I feel like a proud papa." He brought it to the register, reached into his back pocket to retrieve his wallet, and slapped a few bills on the counter. "Speaking of Bunky," he said, "Greg told me—there was some rumbling that you guys were potentially going to open for us? The Farm?"

"Oh," Paul said. He rolled his eyes in a conspiratorial way that said, *Shit, you know this industry.* "Fell through, unfortunately. Little miscommunication."

"Bummer," Gallo said. "Woulda been cool to see Ohio represent like that. But I'll tell you what. You should still come on out to the show." Here he popped Paul on the arm. "I'll put you on the list."

"Count me in," Paul said.

"Maybe even introduce you to Stevie. Put you on his radar."

"Whoa. You'd do that?"

"Of course," Gallo said and beamed. "Feels like this is just the start of something new." His bright eyes drifted to the space where Paul's bag of records slumped on the floor against the counter. "Say, what you got in there?"

"What?" Paul said. Instinctively, he shifted his weight to block it, as though Gallo might have lunged to catch him red-handed.

"The bag. I'm just curious what you're listening to." Gallo addressed Mika and Dante across the divide. "This guy always had the best taste. Obscure funk, jazz. You name it."

"Mm," Mika said, crossing her arms over her chest.

"Ah," Paul said, "nothing you don't already know." He reached down and lifted the bag and slung it over his shoulder.

"C'mon," Gallo said chummily, "let me have a peek."

"Yeah," Dante said with a smirk, "let us have a peek."

"Guys, I'd really rather not. You know. Producer's secret."

Gallo squinted and nodded and pointed at Paul. "Ah. I gotcha. Cooking up a little something special. Respect. Can't wait to hear the final product."

"Oh, you will," Paul said under a wash of guilt, "very soon."

"I'll keep an ear to the underground then," Gallo said.

With that he spun on his heels and turned for the door and Paul knew that this was just the beginning. That Gallo was at the start of a steep and fulfilling trajectory. And he felt the jealousy bubbling up once again.

***

On his way home, a track fire waylaid the F train, so he took the A into Brooklyn and waited for the G at Hoyt-Schermerhorn. On the platform, a young woman was busking, playing a cherry red guitar with an open case at her feet. A few bills lay scattered about the case, and she was mostly ignored by the impatient commuters sulking about the platform. But something about her enamored Paul. It might have been that she was singing "Fade Into You" by Mazzy Star, a haunting, mournful song that always seemed to jab him under the ribs. It might have been her voice, which bloomed like smoke in the cavernous station. Or it might have been the fact that she was, simply put, very pretty, and there was always something intoxicating about a beautiful woman making beautiful music. But no. It was more than that. Something to do with the way the young woman carried herself there on the subway platform. There was an honesty, a vulnerability—indeed a bravery—in the way she tilted her head back and closed her eyes as she sang, a red bandana keeping her dark hair in place. Paul found himself wanting to talk to her, to ask her where she was from, to say *Thank you*, to say anything really, in the hopes that just maybe, some of her courageousness might rub off on him at a time in his life when he needed it most. But she was at the height of the chorus, and he didn't dare interrupt. Then, for the first time in his life, the train arrived before he wanted it to, the G train a screeching bullet, swallowing all sound in its wake. Paul stepped on board, and as the doors closed behind him and the young woman receded from view, he knew it would be some time before the sound of her voice faded from his memory.

6.

It was nothing.

He knew it was nothing. It would take a hell of a lot more than a few stolen records—maybe six-hundred bucks worth—if he was to have any reasonable shot at helping his family. But that he had done something gave him a jolt of momentum.

He would just have to charge ahead for now without his drum machine. He thought about his MPC collecting dust downstairs in Bev's apartment, about how Ricky—that little shit—was probably mashing its buttons this very moment.

Fuck it. Maybe Bunky was right. Maybe his music was stuck in the past. With his beats, he had always sought to pay homage to his heroes. To produce only on the MPC, with no help from the limitless digital wizardry and sonic manipulation that computer programs allowed was, he had always felt, a mark of respect for the craft. It was akin to writing on a typewriter or shooting on film. But it didn't mean shit if it didn't push the art forward.

He opened his laptop. Without hesitating, he brought up a website from which he had downloaded pirated copies of just about everything—movies, music, porn ... on occasion—and searched until he found what he was after. He ripped down the program, and within minutes, had access to an interface that would have cost him hundreds of dollars if he'd bought it square.

From the corner of his table, he retrieved his trusty pipe and the Ziploc that was empty but for a thimbleful of tiny crumbs. He tapped what remained into his pipe and lit it. He worked the flame around the concave pocket of his pipe until the resin was hot enough to generate smoke. He worked the ashy bitterness around his tongue then repeated these gestures again. Resin hits: just another tick mark on his growing tally of desperate measures.

For the first time, he set out to dig for aural inspiration, the raw material for his beats, not from the crackle and dust of vinyl, but from the anonymous depths of YouTube. Vintage Folgers ads. Old cartoons. Lost episodes of *Yo! MTV Raps*. The options were vast and endless, a sonic abyss. He needed something familiar. Without thinking much about it, he typed in Sara's name and found one of her recent chamber performances, the small group she had founded as a platform for her musical exploration outside of the Philharmonic. He hovered his cursor over the title of the song, an original composition she had called "Cantilever," and clicked play.

On his screen, a trio was arranged in a loose semicircle on a darkened stage. Taking up the rear of the ensemble was a balding man seated at a grand piano in a dark suit. As his fingers danced across the keys, his chin dipped and bobbed as though it was drawing forth the notes. To the right was a younger man whose shoulder-length hair wagged and swayed as he drew a bow across the strings of his cello. And there, positioned just forward of the cellist to affirm her prominence, was Sara. She was wearing a sheer black dress that pooled at her feet. Her walnut hair was swept up in a bun. He watched as she guided the bow languidly across the strings of her electric violin. Then, as though startled from a violent dream, she made slashing motions to produce urgent notes, before resuming the gentle rocking of lullabies and dreams.

"Fuck," Paul croaked, surprising himself. His voice was low, his throat dry as sand. He ran a hand down his face. It frightened him to confront the level of his obsession. Sara lingered in his brain like a splinter.

On a day like today, he might have taken the train up to her place—a tidy one-bedroom in Hell's Kitchen—the closest she could find to Lincoln Center, as though proximity alone would make her goal more reachable. She'd open the door wearing a baggy sweatshirt with sleeves that fell over her hands and they'd fight back smiles as they greeted each other, a dumb game they played, as though neither wanted to admit how much they'd fallen for one another. They'd smoke a joint and listen to records, or lounge on the couch and put on one of those awful B-movie horrors she loved so much. She'd jam her socked feet beneath his thighs to keep them warm or put a pillow in his lap and rest her head there until she drifted off and he'd hold his breath, afraid to move lest he wake her, while the TV screen swam with slick crimson gore. He thought about how on one such afternoon, she paused the film—the violence always seemed to put her in a frank mood—brushed the hair from her face and told him, apropos of nothing, that she'd love to meet his family someday. The earnest clarity in her eyes when she said it nearly knocked the wind out of his chest.

He thought about the night—it must have been during their second month of dating—they lay in bed after sex and Sara got up, still nude, and got her violin and ordered him to sit in the chair by the window. When he asked her why, she said,

"Just do it, dummy." He sat in the chair and watched as she perched herself on the edge of the bed and placed the violin on her shoulder. She closed her eyes and began to play, drawing the bow across the strings in delicate ebbs and flows. Her hair spilled around her bare shoulders. He sat and watched in awe and thought about how lucky he was.

They'd been together over a year by the time they began to make songs together. They were simple: spare beats and violin, but their simplicity belied the excitement, the lightness he had felt as they came to life. It was a feeling that seemed to underscore the foundation of their relationship. And he knew she felt it too. Or at least he thought she did. Because what he envisioned as a natural progression of their relationship—shit, their life together—turned out to be the crest. Within a few months, she'd be gone for Los Angeles, out of his life. What killed him, perhaps as much as her absence, was that she deleted the songs before she left.

Now, Bunky articulated what he had felt to be true: that when she had left him, gone too was the warmth, the life, the—

"Oh my God," he said aloud in the stuffy radiator heat of his apartment. "Oh my God."

He stood up.

Blood rushed to his head.

He sat back down.

He started the video over, closed his eyes. He listened deeply and sought to live in the fabric of the song. He listened as if it was the last song he might ever hear.

What struck him was the space. The moments of tender silence that filled the gaps between notes. It was as if the empty air was the true mode of articulation that happened to be placed amidst the notes and melodies. It was an antidote to the messy web of thoughts that pinged around his brain. It made him stop. And think.

Ghost notes. Counterbalance. A concept perfected in *Kind of Blue*, that Miles had admired and borrowed from the soulful piano of Ahmad Jamal. The notion that empty space could be just as emotive as the notes that surfaced to fill it.

The idea simply emerged. It was not a bolt of lightning or a shock to the synapses or a moment of exhilarating breathlessness or any of the bullshit artists often articulated in self-conscious interviews. It was a logical progression. Everything he had done, from listening to producing, had led him to this point.

He could try to deny it, but it was no use: he had been at his most creative when he was with her. When she had encouraged him, pushed him. Told him he had serious potential. When they had worked together, he had been sure of himself. Her voice and her presence had drawn it out of him. Now her voice and presence would draw it out of him again. He copied the link to the video, downloaded the audio track and pulled it into Ableton's digital interface. He donned his headphones and set about listening to the song. Over. And over. And over. He went to work decomposing, breaking the song apart into its component bits.

Sara had once told him she wanted to bridge the gap between classical and popular music; to make classical cool. She talked about how it remained an unapproachable, intimidating genre, for no real reason other than the fact that listeners had no popular entrance point, no contemporary artist telling them it was okay to dig classical. No. Instead, it was a genre guarded by old heads and sniffy public radio jockeys at the lowest end of the dial. It was time to *blow the doors open*, she had once said.

Welcome young listeners with open arms. He was going to do just that.

There was no better time than right now. He had witnessed the walls separating, had seen genres crumble. There were no longer rigid borders separating the musical continents. Hell, he had found himself in bars lately—dim, filament bulb affairs accented in dark wood and wrought iron—and seen people his age, who at one time would have practically stabbed each other to be the first to discover a new band, belting along to a Top 40 hit because it now included a verse from a well-respected rapper. The doors had not only been blown wide open, but there was also no trace of doors having existed at all.

***

He posted on Discogs the three Brazilian records he'd stolen from Dead Wax and sold them all in a day. He went to the bodega ATM and withdrew the funds. He kept sixty bucks for himself, slid the rest beneath Bev's door in an envelope to pay most of December with a note promising the rest on the quick. He found Cassie on Instagram and thought about calling her. With a little cash in his wallet, he could take her out for a drink, try to rekindle the spark he'd felt that night at the Farm. Try to turn an awkward moment into a memory they had shared together. But he chickened out, convinced himself work was more important. Instead, he dialed up a number labeled Mr. Potter in his phone, and when the disheveled delivery man arrived with his suitcase of little vials, he picked the cheapest eighth. He remained high as a sloth and as unselfconscious as one too.

By day, he went to work at Dead Wax, then came home and slaved at his computer, subsisting on pilfered Pop-Tarts and stolen cans of soup. From a distance, Ableton loomed impenetrable, a cloistered labyrinth that became denser the deeper he dove. So he kept it simple and treaded the surface. He quickly learned the basics. He pulled in snippets of Sara's violin and stretched them across the musical scale so that each key on his laptop triggered a fragment of her sound. He bent and manipulated her notes to create melodies of his own. He could slow her down to make it sound as though her violin had been dragged through syrup, or speed her up to flashing squelches of quicksilver strings. He could run the violin parts through the equalizer, manipulating frequencies to render them unrecognizable, as though they had been recorded on the seafloor, or retrieved via satellite from the farthest reaches of space. It felt like cheating, to create sounds that would never be possible using only hardware. But it was thrilling too. In a strange way, it felt as though he and Sara were collaborating again.

If the internet, and life, really, was a din of overlapping, raging voices, then his new beats would be the antidote. Openness amidst the chaos. Inspired by "Cantilever," they would be built around space. They would pause for a moment. Breathe.

He had always felt that his beats were never really done, they were ready. He saw the sun go down, come up, then go down again before he felt he had something close. He listened back. The track was moody, but inviting, an understated thunderstorm, a fever nap in the dark. But more importantly, he could hear Bunky's reverbed croon soaking into the cracks and crevices with fluid ease. He sat back in his chair, checked his phone. Sunday, 2:38 a.m. on the eighth of December, and the track was nearly ready. But something was missing. A flourish. Something to carry the track from *good enough* to *what the fuck was THAT*. And as he sat there in the bunker he'd created for himself, he knew what it was.

Her voice.

He took his phone and navigated to his voicemails, scrolled to the one at the very bottom. The one he'd kept there even after he'd deleted her name from his phone, his *Break For Emergency*.

With as much detachment as he could muster, he put the phone on speaker, pressed play. For a moment, there was dead air, as though she was deciding whether to leave a message. Then her voice broke through: *"Hey,"* she said, her voice low and tired. *"It's me. Wondering if you've eaten yet or if I should wait for you. K. Bye."* It was the last message she'd leave before the end.

He emailed himself the audio file, brought it into Ableton. He clipped two words from the message, pitched them down to sludge, and brought them into the timeline as an intro over a few measures of tinkling piano. He turned *It's me* into a ghostly beckoning. Then he reversed the words so they played backwards, a brief phrase in tongues.

Nearing four o'clock in the morning, he played the song back and began to wonder what he had done. He was aware that it was strange, unsettling even. But, for the first time in a very long time, he was aware that it was good.

***

He heard them before he saw them.

He stood outside the blunt metal door of the practice space—open a crack to reveal a sliver of light within—and he listened.

The buzz and hum of Bunky's bass. Running scales. Tuning.

The sound came as a relief. He had expected to arrive to find the door closed, the coffin shut on their partnership. But Bunky was there. He had shown up. And Paul felt a tingly surge at the crown of his scalp. Hope that he could earn his way back into their partnership. Hope too that he would have the balls to follow through on what had steadily emerged as an ambitious—and criminal—plan to make more quick money.

What followed was a brighter sound, thin and icy, but somehow vibrant. Familiar. A guitar. He thought for a moment that Bunky was getting ready to play along with a recording.

The tuning and futzing gradually melded into a playful vamp that it took a second to catch. *The fuck?* Bunky—serious and sullen-ass Bunky—had begun playing the saucy, unmistakable bassline to "Brick House."

Then the vamp abruptly fell apart, the notes tumbling to a halt as if they'd fallen down the stairs. And there was laughter. The laughter of an inside joke, a shared understanding. Paul held his breath because the other laugh in the room—there was *another* laugh—was one he didn't recognize. High and full and womanly. There was someone else. Bunky had found someone else. Paul wracked his brain and felt his heart begin to race in his chest.

"Hold up," Bunky said, and the laughter ceased.

"What?" said the woman. Bright. Curious.

"Ayo."

Shit.

"Paul? That you?"

Paul stepped away from the crease of light and slid up against the wall like the world's worst spy.

"I can *see you*," Bunky said with an edge. "The hell are you doing out there?"

"Uh," Paul said. He squared to face the door, set his jaw. *Stop being a bitch.*

He shouldered open the door and stepped inside. "Aright look man," he said with a bit of bluster, "I know that—"

"Why are you here?"

Bunky was seated on his stool with his bass in his lap and his feet hooked behind one of the rungs. He was humorless and deadpan and tipped back his chin as though daring a response. His expression was somehow amplified by the steely gaze Prince wore on the t-shirt he had on beneath an open flannel shirt.

"Huh?" Paul said.

"I said: Why. Are. You. Here. There's no reason for you to be here. You interrupted us."

Us?

Paul turned to look at the woman whose laughter he had heard from the other side of the door. She was small, maybe five feet and change, and wore a black sweater over black jeans and black sneakers. Her black hair was drawn back by a red bandana that was the same color as her lips.

The bandana.

She stood there casually, weight on one hip, one battered Vans high-top crossed in front of the other. The posture of someone who seemed to have a tacit understanding that there were greater concerns than those that consumed the minute-to-minute. Paul looked at her and she looked at him and she must have read the look on his face, a look that said something like—*Please, throw me a lifeline*—because she put her guitar pick in her teeth and crossed the divide. She held out a hand and with the pick still in her mouth, introduced herself.

Except Paul couldn't quite catch her name spoken through her teeth.

"Sorry?" he said.

Without flinching she took the pick from her mouth, wiped her palm on her jeans and tried again.

"Eloise. Heard a lot about you."

"Oh boy," Paul said nervously, and she laughed. A high, full laugh and as she laughed, he noticed, *ping*, a flash in her mouth. A silver tooth where her left canine should have been.

"Not all bad things," she said, and *ping*, there was that flash again.

It was right then that he realized: the busker on the train platform. *How in the fuck?* Bunky had gone and done what he hadn't had the guts to do: invite her to play. As his replacement. Up close, he confirmed what he had felt from a distance that day underground: her whole aura was alluring. In a way that suggested she knew things you didn't. Or couldn't. Her heavy-lidded hazel eyes, even as they looked at you, seemed to be considering something in the distance. If you played your cards right, she just might be willing to share it with you.

"Listen," Bunky said, "we were about to get down to work, so—"

"Perfect," Paul said with a gusto meant to mask his bewilderment, "then I'm right on time." Without hesitating, he strutted to his folding table, set up his laptop and turntable.

"Oh for fuck's sake."

From the corner of his eye, he saw Bunky shift, set his bass on the floor with a low squelch from the amp. He stood from his stool. A shade of menace hung about his shoulders.

"Guys, *guys*," Eloise said. "You're kidding, right? Don't be so—lame."

Bunky stopped in his tracks and they both looked at her. The fuzzy low hum of gear at rest in the air. She was shaking her head and looking down at her guitar where she had begun to pick a few stray cords.

"I've known you both for like, eight seconds. Can we just, you know, play something?"

Simple as that. To argue, to *fight*, now seemed flatly ridiculous.

"That's all I'm saying," Paul shrugged.

Bunky glared at him: *This? This is not over.* He found his way back to his stool and once again shouldered his bass. "Show us what you got then."

"Brand new," Paul said. He checked his levels, scrolled through the files on his computer.

"Wait," Bunky said, "where's your drum machine?"

"Don't worry about it," Paul said. He didn't have to look up to know Bunky was rolling his eyes.

"So then, how are you—"

"Ableton."

"*Ableton*," Bunky said, incredulously. Then, to Eloise: "This kid has like a categorical aversion to technology and all of a sudden he's making beats on a computer."

"Who cares?" Eloise said. "Long as it's good."

Paul could feel her approaching his table. He looked up as she leaned over and offered a little smile.

"You know, you shouldn't feel threatened by me," she whispered, as though sensing his confusion. She glanced over her shoulder. "He told me you got chops."

Bunky spoke up. "We doing this or what?"

Eloise winked, fell back to her position, and Paul wanted to hug her.

He pressed play and the beat gurgled to life. The slurry intro of Sara's voice: *It's me.* The steady, open pulse of the lilting piano. The space. He could sense Bunky watching him, skepticism etched on his face. Waiting for the right moment to pull the plug, end it once and for all. The drums kicked in—drums engineered to rattle trunks and clubs—and with them, Sara's dismembered violin. Bunky focused his attention on his bass and negotiated the strings for the right chords. He closed his eyes, worked his tongue into the corner of his mouth and settled into a sparse, minor key bassline that landed on the ones, then escalated to a quickened pulse when the drums picked up.

Eloise craned over her guitar until Paul could see the pale crease of her scalp where the dark hair was parted and pulled tight by her red bandana. She picked clean notes that fell like icicles around the open space. Fed through the pedal she worked at her feet, the sounds were bright, almost synth-like.

A shade under three minutes later, the track faded to silence and Paul watched the two of them emerge from cocoons of creation. They stood for a moment in the buzzy quiet. Eloise knit her eyebrows.

"Hot damn," she said, "that was sweet. And not at all what I was expecting. What's the sample?"

Paul fought back a grin. "Secret," he said.

"Can you play it live?" Bunky said like a challenge. He averted his eyes and Paul understood this meant he *liked* it. He fucking liked it. Or at least he didn't hate it. It had been months since Paul had received a compliment from Bunky. This was as close as he would get. The trouble was that it was damn near impossible for Paul to play the beat live—and Bunky knew it—without his drum machine.

So he said, "Of course," and counted them off.

By some miracle of luck, focus and force of will, he made his way through. "Again," Bunky said when the song faded out. Once more, Paul laid down the beat, feeling it now, fingers dancing across the keys of his goddamn laptop. The third time through, he hardly needed to think about it, improvising now and then for swing, and all the while Bunky supplemented the rhythm.

Eloise began to feel her way around the melody, plucking chords, as though calling out into the ether to see what called back. It was clear right away that she knew her way around a song, falling in, dropping out, leaving gaps at just the right moments.

There was something happening there in the practice space, something Paul hadn't felt when it had just been him and Bunky. It was as though they'd plugged into a power source that only generated a surge when all three of them were in lockstep. He would hesitate to call it spiritual, but it was close. The hairs on his forearms stood at attention. Bunky's head bobbed as he stared at his feet, and Eloise, eyes closed, painted lips moving, mouthed words to herself, humming now and then, beseeching whatever spirit the three of them had managed to channel there in that dingy little room.

During the fifth time through, when each of their parts had begun to coalesce, to really settle into something, Eloise started to sing. Two bars in, her lips parted and out came a feathery and elusive contralto, filling the holes left in the melody just as it had filled the yawning train platform. It was a sultry cousin of the voice with which she spoke, grounded in melancholy, unbearably hypnotic. Her voice, no, *she* held a magnetic power over them instantly.

When the lights
Go out
I remember why
I turned them on
With you

She sang patiently, stretching ellipses to the point where Paul thought she might stop, or forget her place. But at just the right moment, she picked it up again, a little intake of breath leading the way, as though settling the air for the words that were to come. All the while, Bunky kept time, head bowed, unflinching. It struck Paul then, more than it ever had before, how at-odds Bunky's playing style was with his personality, as though all his anxious energy dissolved into a Zen-like trance, a force field within which he was guarded from the insecurities that drove him to perform in the first place.

The song ran its course and for a moment they stood in the pillowy quiet. Eloise unshouldered her guitar, set it against the side of an amp.

"I'd say we're on to something," she said.

Paul looked at Bunky. God, he hoped so.

"You got another?" Bunky wanted to know.

"Why don't we quit while we're ahead," Eloise said. "I'm cooked anyway."

"Up to you guys," Paul said, despite the fact that he had nothing else to share.

Bunky ran a hand over his buzzed scalp, nodded in acquiescence. "Yeah, okay. Let's break for the night."

"Yes, boss," Eloise said. She caught Paul with a side-eye, the look of a co-conspirator, and he no longer felt like an outsider in his own group.

They packed up their gear to the weightless trumpet of Freddie Hubbard, which Bunky played from his phone over the speakers. When his bass was put away, he rummaged in his backpack for his pack of Pall Malls as Paul suspected he would. He put a cigarette to his lips, then held out the pack to Eloise.

Paul prayed she would take one and join Bunky outside—after all, he had one more mission to accomplish, one that would benefit enormously from their absence—but she shook her head.

"Nah," she said, "trying to cut back. Besides, I don't know how you smoke those things. I can practically taste the cancer."

"Suit yourself," Bunky shrugged, then ducked out the door. As soon as he did so, Paul stole a glance at the mic stand by Bunky's stool that his bandmate used as a coat rack. There, dangling from one of the bolts, were Bunky's keys as Paul knew they'd be. The trick would be how to nab the key he was after with Eloise there in the room.

He played it cool, snapped shut his turntable case and zipped his laptop into its cover. He brought his bags over by Bunky's stool and placed them in a neat little pile at the foot of the mic stand. He observed Eloise, who sat crouched on her shut guitar case on the floor, pecking at her phone.

"You always been able to sing like that?" he asked.

"Like what?" she said without looking up.

"Like your life depended on it." He was not entirely kidding.

She craned to look at him. "Please tell me I don't seem that serious."

"Um. You don't seem that serious?"

"Are you fucking with me? I don't know you well enough yet to know if you're fucking with me."

"Nah, all I'm saying is—" She turned her attention back to her phone and he knew this was his chance. "You don't want to be taken seriously?" He leaned against the mic stand as though waiting for an answer and then pretended to lose his balance, not dramatically so, but enough to send the mic stand clattering to the floor, and with it, Bunky's loop of keys. "Idiot," he

118

said, and shook his head. He bent down and swiftly grabbed the keys, righting the mic stand to its standing position.

Eloise hardly noticed. "Well, of course, I want to be taken seriously," she said. "Who doesn't? But not at the expense of like, enjoying this. I mean, what're we really doing in here? Messing around? Making songs? Not like we're in here changing policy. Or doing some kinda charity work. We're having fun. At least I hope we're having fun. Otherwise, we might as well go sit in a cubicle someplace."

Paul made a show of twirling Bunky's set of keys around his finger, toying with them distractedly as though considering what Eloise had said, before freeing the one he needed—the one Bunky had once threatened to throw into the East River—and stashing it in his pocket. He returned the keys to their resting place on the mic stand.

"Having fun," he said and nodded. "That's what me and Bunky have been missing. That this is supposed to be fun."

The door opened and Bunky stepped through the threshold.

"Your ears must be burning," Eloise said with a smirk.

"You guys talking shit?"

"We were saying how much fun this is going to be. Right, Paul?"

Paul fingered the key in his pocket and thought about the absurdity of what he was planning to do. "I'm just glad there's a *we* again."

Eloise laughed, and *ping*, there was that silver tooth.

"I need to talk to you for a second," Bunky said as they hovered at the door to leave for the night.

"Oooh," Eloise said like a middle schooler, "somebody's in trouble."

"We'll meet you outside," Bunky said.

"Nice knowing you, Paul. If you die, can I have your turn-table?"

"Bury me with it," Paul said.

When she was far enough down the hallway, out of earshot, Bunky held out a hand. Paul looked down at Bunky's hand, then up to meet his bandmate's eyes.

"Well?" Bunky said.

Warily, Paul clasped Bunky's hand, and as he did so, Bunky pulled him in for a hug. He slapped Paul on the back—harder than necessary—and said, "Welcome back, asshole."

Paul pulled away, mystified.

"I can see it in your face," Bunky said. His eyes were clear. "You're with us. Present. Been a while since I've seen that look. And shit, if you have anything more like what you just played? We'll be on to something. For real."

"I guess it's now or never," he said. He nodded at the open doorway. "How did she—"

"G train."

"I know that much," Paul said.

Bunky cocked his head.

"I saw her the other day. Hoyt-Schermerhorn. She was absolutely destroying Mazzy Star—"

"Fade Into You," Bunky nodded. His face softened.

"I was blown away," Paul said.

"I'm telling you," Bunky said. He shook his head and puffed out his cheeks. "She finished the song and like, two people clapped. She just murdered this song, and no one was even paying attention. It could've been Hope Sandoval herself as far as anyone knew and it wouldn't have made a difference. So when she passed by with her little hat, I put a twenty in and told her what I thought."

"Which was?"

"That we should make music together."

"And what'd she say?"

"I wrote my number down. Told her to call me if she had any interest. And—what's today, Sunday? Friday, she finally did." Bunky shrugged. "So here we are."

Here we are.

It was an innocuous statement, a tautology, but one that ignored—or at least swept aside—the fact that Bunky had recruited Eloise as Paul's substitute, the *next phase*. He swallowed his pride and said: "Where's she from? What's her deal?"

"Listen," Bunky said, and Paul knew the meat of their conversation was over. He adjusted the weight of his bass case, clamped a hand on Paul's shoulder. "This all works out? You two will have plenty of time to get to know each other."

7.

THE LOBBY WAS HARDLY A LOBBY AT ALL. IT WAS AN ENTRYWAY AND nothing more. Yellow walls and yellow light from the fixture overhead. Straight ahead, the elevator. Paul pressed the button and the silver doors slid open.

Inside, he took a deep breath. He wiped his palms, slick with sweat, on his jeans. He clenched his jaw to keep his teeth from chattering. There were seven floors; he pressed the button marked "PH" and felt a soft jolt as the unseen gears went to work.

The elevator opened to a brushed aluminum door. Paul fished the key from his pocket, unlocked the deadbolt with a satisfying *thunk*, turned the handle and pushed the door open. It swung on its hinges noiselessly. For a moment, he stood on the threshold. From his vantage, he could see the big picture window that looked out on Church Street. It was covered by sheer curtains that softened the metallic light from outside. There was a white sectional shoved up beneath the window, a glass coffee table with a low stack of art books, and, set to the right side of the couch as Paul faced it, a tasteful brass cocktail cart stocked with colorful bottles of booze.

The elevator buzzed to protest his inertia; he had little choice but to step inside and turn the corner, taking in the open expanse of the space that stretched the length of the block. The apartment smelled of lavender and cotton. The predominant motif was white. The walls, the rugs, even the exposed wood beams in the ceiling matched the theme. A wall of white brick ran the length of the apartment, interrupted at intervals by blurry large-scale monochrome photographs: Bunky's father's work.

He made his way toward the middle of the apartment, where the stereo and turntable sat atop a long wooden console with a system of drawers. The first drawer he opened contained a stack of two-inch tape reels, but the second, third, fourth and fifth were crammed with records.

It was a digger's dream, just as Bunky had once told him: rare Blondie test pressings, Kraftwerk seven-inch singles, hand-numbered Television releases. A comprehensive collection of just about every notable punk or new wave record released in the late '70s and early '80s. Nestled in the middle of the third drawer he opened, amidst a row of early rap releases, was the crown jewel: "Beat Bop," a supremely limited proto-hip hop single released by K-Rob and Rammellzee for which Jean-Michel Basquiat did the cover art. Only five-hundred copies of the original pressing existed on earth and now Paul was holding one of them. He slid it into his bag.

He stood up from his crouch to head for the door when he remembered: *True Stories*. A signed copy of the Talking Heads record Bunky had mentioned several times and that seemed to hold deep sentimental value. He didn't know what he would do with it if he found it—he couldn't very well give it to Bunky—but he felt it was crucial to find it nonetheless. He lowered himself back to the floor and reached for the fourth drawer and heard a creaking floorboard. He held his breath in the ensuing silence, convinced himself it was the sigh of a radiator or some other mysterious utterance of an ancient building. He pulled open the drawer and began to flip through and there it was again, the whine of wood fixtures giving way, more pronounced this time, and followed by a woman's voice from the hallway in the back.

"That was fast."

Fuckfuckfuck. What was she doing here?

The open floor plan prevented him from finding a hiding spot, so he ducked low to the ground beneath the sightline of the sectional couch. He could hear the woman approaching, feel the animal magnetism of a looming presence.

"Aldo?" she asked. "Did you forget somethi—"

She stopped behind the couch and Paul turned on his haunches and looked up to face his fate. He looked, he knew, like a total fool.

"Oh," she said, taking him in. Her eyes widened a touch, but she was not startled. She reacted as though someone had shown up a little early to a party. She wore her dark hair, greying at the edges, cropped fashionably close. Atop a pair of trim black leggings, she wore a flowing grey hooded sweatshirt, the kind of thing you might wear to yoga class. She was pretty in a refined way and looked as though she had just woken up from a nap or knocked back a few glasses of wine. She was stylish and slim and wealthy, but nothing about her appearance screamed *artist*. He had watched Bunky's father leave the building, so Paul hadn't expected to run into either of Bunky's parents, but he had always envisioned the encounter involving a pair of disheveled loons with pockets full of Xanax.

Bunky's mother crossed her arms over her chest and narrowed her eyes.

"Well? Can I help you?"

"Um," Paul said. He stood from his crouch and cast an inadvertent glance at the open drawer of records. He reached into his pocket and held the key in his palm. "Bunky sent me."

Bunky's mother looked at the key like she had never seen such a thing in her life. "He *sent* you? And who are you again?"

"I'm his bandmate." He gave his name, and because there was little else he could do, he took a few cautious steps in her direction, wiped his palm again on his jeans, and extended an arm over the back of the couch.

For a moment, she studied him, as though deciding whether he was worthy of her trust. She blinked, broke her gaze, and held out a hand.

"Maria," she said. Her grip was cool and firm. She nodded at Paul's open bag on the floor. It was full of records. "Find what you're after?"

Despite the heat that ringed Paul's neck, he tried to remain in control. "Most of it. He sent me to borrow some of Aldo's records. You know, inspiration. That kind of thing."

"Mm," she said, "I thought he might have woken up from this little punk rock dream of his by now."

"Yeah, well. There was one he wanted that I can't find. A signed copy."

Maria narrowed her eyes, so he continued.

"He told me all about this one show. A Talking Heads show you'd taken him to as a kid? I think the memory means a lot to him. Kind of set him on this course, you know? And so. I think maybe he wants that record back as a memento or something."

He hadn't realized he was after the record as a sincere gesture to Bunky until he said the words that set the truth in motion. But once they were in the air, he stood firm despite the absurdity of it all.

Maria pursed her lips and shook her head. "There were a lot of shows." She crossed her arms once more. "And if this thing means so much to him, why didn't he just come and get it himself? I haven't seen him in—I can't remember the last time I saw him."

"He'd prefer to be here," Paul said, finding himself in the bizarre position of intermediating—falsely—on Bunky's behalf to his own parents. "I'm sure of it. But I think he thinks you guys are ashamed of him, that—"

Maria screwed up her face. "*Ashamed* of him? That's ridiculous. He's my son."

"That maybe you feel he should be doing something more," he rubbed the tips of his fingers together as though to conjure the right word, "important."

Maria unhooked her arms and batted away the comment with the back of her slender hand. "Oh please. He can do whatever he wants. It's his life."

Paul detected the tension that underscored her words. "I think he feels like he needs to escape your shadow, you know? Or at the very least, just make you guys proud." The words came naturally to him now, because in many ways, they reflected his own truth.

Maria looked at the floor, and for a moment, Paul thought she might cry. He prayed she wouldn't cry. He was afraid that the sight of someone crying might set in motion the rusty gears of his own waterworks. But she didn't cry. She looked up at him and set her jaw. "I think I know the album," she said. Then she turned and made her way down the dim hallway in the rear of the apartment.

By the time he caught up, she was standing in the middle of Bunky's bedroom, which did not seem like a child's room in the slightest. Beneath the window that looked out onto Chambers was a sleek desk, notebooks and ephemera arranged neatly at sharp right angles. Against the opposite wall was a single bed, white sheets crisply made. The walls were blank. Paul couldn't envision Bunky growing up in this room and he realized he wouldn't trade his childhood for any of this. His attention drifted to a framed photo on Bunky's desk, the lone personal touch. It was a photo of Bunky as a boy—he might have been nine or ten—with his arm around a friend. They were seated at a table in a restaurant; in the foreground was a gleaming birthday cake, candles glowing. Bunky and his friend smiled widely; the photo radiated with lightness and ease.

Maria noticed Paul noticing the photo. "Bunky and his friend Carlo," she sighed. "He's become quite a successful artist. I wish Bunky had some of his discipline."

Paul felt compelled to defend his bandmate, to tell her how much Bunky wanted it. But before he could string the right words together, Maria went on.

"Anyhow, I would imagine the album you're after is somewhere down there." She pointed to a little shelf unit in the corner by the desk, the bottom row of which held a slouching row of records. "Help yourself."

"Thanks," Paul said. He went to the shelf, bent down, and found it immediately: it was the first record in the row. There was the bold cover: *TRUE STORIES* stamped in tabloid letters, red and white blocks of color, and positioned at the corners, four looping signatures in black Sharpie. He held it up. "This is the one."

Maria nodded. "I remember now. I took him to their last show at the Ritz." She seemed on the verge of smiling but held herself back. "Bunky had such a little crush on Tina. She was all he talked about for weeks after that."

"She inspired him to take up the bass," Paul said. "At least that's what he told me."

"So I have myself to blame then," Maria said flatly.

He wanted to laugh, to deflate the tension that still hung around Maria's shoulders, but he simply could not tell if she was joking. Instead, he followed her to the sitting area, shouldered his heavy bag and made his way to the elevator.

"Sorry I snuck up on you like that," he said as Maria saw him out. "Bunky assumed you wouldn't be home, since, you know ..."

Maria opened her mouth to speak but paused for a moment as though deciding how much to divulge to a stranger. "You can tell him Aldo and I are trying to make a go of it," she said finally. "I'm sure he'll roll his eyes."

"I really don't think so," Paul said.

The elevator doors opened, and he stepped in.

"Tell him to pay us a visit sometime soon," Maria said as the doors were closing, and for the first time since she had discovered him there on the floor of the apartment, she looked vulnerable.

***

Outside, Paul took hungry gulps of air. He felt lightheaded and dizzy and not altogether aware of where he was. A construction crew was thundering away at the asphalt on Church Street and the bloated combination of adrenaline, earsplitting noise, and overwhelming relief made Paul feel nauseous. He listed up Church and turned the corner onto Reade. He nearly ran smack into a man turning the corner in the other direction, a familiar man in sunglasses and a baseball cap.

"Watch it," Bunky's father said, gruff and impatient, and it was this encounter that sent Paul over the edge. He lurched to support himself against the northern wall of the building, palmed the gritty brick for support, bent over at the waist and vomited right there on the street.

8.

THE GLOWING RED HAND FLIPPED OVER SO HE CROSSED THE STREET, fell in behind a queue outside the Farm. Before him, a group of kids chatted and sucked vape pens, cast exaggerated billows of smoke into the early December air.

He was drunk. Very nearly smashed. He'd had no choice; it was the only way he could bear what he had done. He had come home that afternoon, his shoulder bag crammed with purloined wax, the acid taste of bile still biting the back of his throat, and very nearly had a panic attack. What the fuck had he been thinking? He had been *caught*. He pictured Maria giving Bunky's father the blow-by-blow as soon as he walked in. That some kid had just been there, some friend Bunky had sent. In her retelling of it, she would realize how strange it all was, and all it would take was Bunky's father opening one of those drawers, seeing what was missing and calling Bunky ... or the cops.

To quell his needling nerves and whirling thoughts, Paul had gone to Carlito's and purchased a pair of cheap forties. Back at his apartment, he uncapped the beers and drank them methodically, one right after the other, alone. He unloaded the stolen records and laid them out in a neat grid on his bed. He looked up their value online and tallied close to ten grand. Then he began to play them, one by one. Something about the ritual made him feel better: removing the wax from its sleeve, laying it onto the platter of his turntable, placing the needle on the groove. Those first pleasant seconds of crackle and static before the music started in.

It took him until the end of *Power, Corruption & Lies*—an original copy he took for his own collection—to finish the beers, by the end flat and warm like dirty dishwater. He wiped his mouth with the sleeve of his hoodie and grimaced: this was what he was doing while his mother and father were busy packing their lives into moving boxes. He had to sell those records, fast. But first he had business to attend to.

Inside the entrance of the Farm, a woman with blue hair was perched at a podium scanning tickets and checking names. She found his name on a clipboard and stamped his wrist. He pushed his way into the crowded bar and could hear the opening band playing in the performance space in the back. The band that should've been him and Bunky.

Behind the bar was the woman with *The Giving Tree* tattoo. She seemed to recognize him with the nod she cast in his direction.

"Jameson?" she said.

"How'd you guess?"

"I remember you. Drooling over that girl a couple weeks back. How'd that work out?"

He grimaced, caught his reflection in the mirror behind the bar. He looked worn, tired. Bags hung like heavy bruises beneath his eyes. He knew Cassie would likely be there tonight, and though part of him was excited to see her, the other part dreaded it. He tried to fix his face into a grin.

"Magic," he said.

She poured his drink and slid it over.

"In that case," she said, "abracadabra." Her eyes flicked to a place beyond his shoulder.

He felt a little tap at his back as he swallowed the whiskey. He turned and sure enough, there was the copper hair, the fade of freckles across the bridge of the nose. He was startled by how great she looked. Her mouth broke into a smile.

"*Hey,*" she said and came in straight away for a hug. She pressed close and there was her scent again: sweet and fresh. She pulled back with concern. "Are you okay? You look—terrified."

"I, uh—I'm just happy to see you." He made a conscious effort not to slur his words. "Are you here to review the show?"

"No," she smiled, "just here to support."

"Well, you look—you look lovely." *Lovely?* He'd never used the word before in his life.

She scrunched her shoulders. "Aw, why thank you. And you don't look too bad yourself." Even through the fog of alcohol he knew it was a lie, but he was touched by her kindness. "But," she went on, and he knew what was coming, "shouldn't you be—I mean, weren't you—"

"Long story," he said sheepishly. "We just couldn't get our shit together in time."

"Bummer," she said, with a look of what seemed to be genuine sympathy. "Next time." It was, he realized, not unlike the pose she struck the last time he had seen her, there in her bed, quite literally naked with shame. If she was feeling any of the same awkwardness, she was doing a hell of a job hiding it. And he loved her for it. "Nice of you to come support anyway."

"I'm proud of him," he said, and meant it. "It's his time to shine."

"That's sweet of you to say. I know he's worked really hard for this." She reached across the space between them and squeezed his forearm and he thought he saw in her eye a glimmer. A spark. A look that suggested maybe, just *maybe*, she'd give him another shot.

But then, as if on cue, as if they had teleported to the sound-stage of a bad sitcom, one where Murphy's Law prevailed for the wicked delight of the laugh track, Gallo emerged from the scrum around the bar, approached Cassie from behind, slid his arms around her waist and planted a kiss square on her cheek. She knew right away who it was, and the look on her face opened the trap door in Paul's gut through which his heart, his stomach, his underlying desire to view the universe as a generally good and righteous place, plunged into the abyss. She looked joyous, thrilled. She looked—

"Hey, babe," she giggled. *Babe?* "Look who's here."

Gallo's eyes flashed wide. "You *made* it. Man, I'm happy to see you." He spread his arms and Paul had no choice but to step into a hug. When he'd been freed from the embrace, he repeated the words he'd uttered to Cassie a moment ago, though they were harder to spit out this time around: "Proud of you, Dee."

"Means a lot coming from you," Gallo said, and Paul could tell he was sincere. Not that it made things easier to swallow. "Wish that was you guys doing your thing back there. But you'll get your due soon enough. Especially when that new album's done."

"New album?" Cassie said, impressed.

Paul's face burned red and he demurred.

"Oh, c'mon," Gallo said. "Don't be so modest. Be confident in the music. I know you got it in you."

"Hate to interrupt the love fest," Cassie said, checking her watch, "but shouldn't you be getting ready?"

Gallo shrugged and smirked. "What're they gonna do? Start without me?" He turned to Paul and fell serious. "Look. Stick around after the show, alright? I'll introduce you to Stevie. I think you two will hit it off."

At this, Cassie arched her brows and dipped the corners of her mouth as if to say, *See? There's hope for you yet.*

"You're the best."

Gallo winked and popped him on the shoulder. "Anything I can do to help." He spun Cassie around to face him square and kissed her on the mouth for *one, two, three,* and then he was off, ducking through the crowd to the door at the back of the room.

The space between Paul and Cassie prickled with his absence. For a moment neither of them spoke.

"So—"

"Yeah."

"That happened quickly."

"Well ..." She looked at her feet. It was possible, he knew— no, more than possible, likely—that her previous encounter with him had led her to find solace in the waiting arms of a close friend. "Can't fight something if it's real, I suppose." She shrugged and crinkled her nose and Paul found her more desirable than ever.

***

The back room was full, a sea of silhouetted heads, bopping and swaying, set against the stage lights. A potent mixture of weed, stale beer and sweat stung Paul's nostrils and grounded him. There, up on stage, leaning into the mic, was Gallo, his low voice filling the room, the words he sang shouted right back at him by the most devoted. He thrummed a steady riff from a smart blue Gibson, a riff that bounced off the walls, bounced around the skulls of the kids in the crowd as they bounced where they stood. Gallo was flanked by his rhythm guitar and bass, two lean guys in slim sweaters and slimmer jeans, both making the silly faces of focused creation. Off to the side, topped by a felt and feather hat, was a chunky young man in a flannel overshirt scratching rhythms on the washboard. Behind them all sat the drummer, his face a shifting mask of strain as his arms worked the kit. "Listen, we get it," went the piece in *New York*, "being earnest isn't *cool*. But hear us out: what separates Feathers from the, er, flock is frontman Dee Gallo's penchant for penning jouncy melodic earworms that'll have you humming along on your commute and at your cookout." Paul had read the blurb several times over when Gallo's post popped up in his feed. It was the lead piece in the magazine's Nightlife section, topped by a large press photo—Gallo and the gang on the roof of a building, a water tower rising behind them. "Flock together," read the caption. "NYC's Feathers play a tune-up gig on Saturday before embarking on U.S. tour."

Gallo and his band tore through songs, and after each one clattered to a close, he looked out beneath his shellacked coif and acknowledged the volley of woops and whistles with an understated, "Thanks." Paul couldn't tell if he was just playing it cool or if he genuinely hadn't expected such a reaction.

Paul looked to his left where Cassie wagged her head, eyes closed, smile-singing along with every word. And, though he knew it spelled the death knell for his chances, he was touched.

Halfway through a triumphant number driven by Gallo's mandolin, Paul watched him jump down onto the floor amongst the crowd. The froth absorbed him, and he was lit up by a glow of phones. Cassie grabbed Paul by the arm and yanked him toward the scrum. She got on her tippy toes, and he did too, and there in the center of the packed perimeter was Gallo, leading the room in a four-on-the-floor clap, stomping along, a broad grin plastered on his face. Did Paul ache to know how Gallo felt? Of course he did. But something in him began to melt away. Maybe it was the booze, maybe it was the joy on Cassie's face, but he submitted. He submitted and closed his eyes and let the tide of collective energy take him.

He opened his eyes and Gallo was back on-stage saying goodnight as his band wound down with a cacophonous jumble. Gallo slipped off his mandolin, leaned it against an amp, waved and exited stage left. He was followed by his mates, who, one by one, laid down their instruments. But the crowd never waned in its applause, coalescing into a rhythmic *thump, thump, thump,* and within moments, there they were again, the five of them striding back on stage, beaming, Gallo taking up the caboose. He donned the mandolin once more and bowed, absorbing the adulation. "Wow," he said, "you guys ..." He shook his head. "There's nowhere else we'd rather be than right here with you."

They played an encore, a campfire take on "Won't Back Down," and it was, Paul had to admit, perfect. They were poised—the motherfuckers—for what awaited them. The tour. The press. The wave of momentum that would carry them toward the zeitgeist. They were sharp, they were handsome, and they were relatable, and when they disappeared once more backstage, there was something charged in the air, as if everyone in that room knew they had witnessed something special, a night they would talk about again and again.

"Wow," Cassie said as the house lights faded up. She shook her head and her copper hair quivered around her face.

"They're ready," Paul said. "The son of a bitch is ready." He knew it, and he knew Gallo knew it too.

***

In a makeshift green room behind the stage, what felt like an oversized boiler room—slabs of painted cinder block, exposed squiggles of pipe—an after-party had gathered. Friends and girlfriends of the band, drunk on proximity to fledgling fame. Leather jacket-clad label lackeys, conspiring to roll out *the next phase*. Skittish hangers-on, hugging the perimeter, utterly failing to blend in. Coils of joint and cigarette smoke mingled overhead. A couch with ragged plaid upholstery was pushed against the far wall. A folding table supported an array of cheap food—bowl of Doritos, stack of pizza boxes, a cake, untouched on its platter—and a flank of liquor bottles. Beneath the table, an aluminum tub of beer on ice. It was ungodly hot in the room and Paul could feel prickles of sweat breaking out on his hairline.

He stood in a loose circle with Cassie and Greg, sipped warm bourbon neat from a clear plastic cup and tried to appear as sober as possible. He listened to Greg explain what had drawn him to Feathers in the first place, as if he alone was responsible for their trajectory.

"Sometimes you just *know*," he was saying with a flourish, page boy hat askew atop his flushed, meaty face when a collective cheer rippled through the party and Paul turned to see Gallo making his entrance with a performative stage bow.

"Did I miss the encore?" he said, and the room erupted in laughter, relieved that he had said anything at all.

Paul watched Gallo work the room with a beer in his hand, pocket to pocket, smiling, gesturing, listening intently, whatever the circumstance called for. More than once he placed his hand over his heart and dipped his head in a show of humility. Paul caught snippets of Greg's exchange with Cassie—she was being a good sport and listening with what seemed keen attention as Greg expounded on his dream to open a string of clubs in Cuba—as Gallo made his way over. They were next in the rotation; it was as if Gallo was a brand-new groom.

"Finally," he said, clapping a hand on Greg's round shoulder, "the gang I've been waiting to see all night." At this, he leaned over and kissed Cassie on the side of the mouth as she beamed.

"Hell of a show, boss," Greg said. He lifted his fist for a dap and Gallo indulged him and then some, drawing him in for an embrace.

"Appreciate everything you've done for us," Gallo said, muffled against the heft of Greg's chest.

He pulled back and exhaled and took a swig of his beer.

"Man," he said. "Man, man, man."

"You guys killed it," Paul heard himself saying.

"You really think so?"

"Without a fucking doubt."

"Okay, break it up," said a nasally voice over Paul's shoulder. "You jerk him off too hard he'll start to chafe. Tour hasn't even started yet. Need him fresh for all those groupies."

"Aye!" Gallo said, eyes alight. "Get in here, man."

Paul stepped aside to let the newcomer join the fray. He was short—the crown of his skull barely crested Paul's shoulder—and wore his blonde hair cropped close. He swam in a faded jean jacket set off by a scarf that hung in loose coils around his neck. He clutched the neck of a tequila bottle in one hand and a stack of plastic cups in the other. His cheeks were flush with the booze and the stifling heat of the room.

"What's up bitches," he said, scanning the faces in the circle. His eyes fell on Cassie first. "To what do I owe this pleasure?"

"Stevie," Gallo said, "this is my girl, Cassie."

So this was the one and only Stevie Reese: manager, industry player, and, if Paul played his cards right, lifeline.

"Your girl, huh," Stevie said, eyes narrowing. He stuck the stack of plastic cups under his armpit and extended a hand. "Lovely to meet you, Cassie. Keep an eye on this fucker, will you? I've seen what that haircut can do."

"Yeah?" Cassie said gamely. "And what's that?"

"Gallo, how's that collection of stage bras coming?"

"*Stage bras?*" Cassie said, twisting her face. "Yeah, right. He hardly knows what to do with mine. Do women even still do that?"

"He's just fucking around," Gallo said, pulling Cassie close. Red splotches had begun to bloom on his neck. He was smiling. "Don't blow this one for me, man."

Stevie stood up a little straighter. "I apologize. I have a real potty mouth. Scout's honor I am absolutely, one-hundred-percent messing arou—oh hey, what's up there, Greg? Glad I didn't have to deport you after all. How's that back sweat? You must be dying in this room."

On cue, Greg turned around and lifted his arms to shoulder height. A continent of wetness darkened the broad side of his back.

"Holy shit, that's disgusting," Stevie said. "Somebody get this man a towel."

He turned to Paul as if for confirmation of his comedic chops and, scanning him from head to toe, said, "And who the fuck are you?"

"I'm—"

"Stevie," Gallo said, slapping Paul on the back, "you gotta meet Paul. Close friend of mine from way back. Beatmaker, producer. Super talented dude."

Paul reached out for a handshake, but by then Stevie had transferred the plastic cups from armpit back to hand and didn't seem interested in juggling again. A flint of seriousness flickered in his eye, the poker face of boardrooms and negotiations.

"Solo?"

"Nah. A group. We're called They Is. Three of us—"

"They what?"

"They Is."

"The fuck kind of name is that?"

"It's from a—do you know Tobias Wolff? He's this author, right? And he wrote this incredible story my bandmate Bunky loved and so—"

"Dude."

"And so—"

"Please stop. You're making my head hurt. Gallo. Is this kid on the spectrum or something? My Lord."

Gallo laughed sheepishly and said, "Paul, stop being such a weirdo. What's up with you tonight?" And when Stevie was no longer looking, preoccupied with filling the cups with tequila, Gallo shot Paul a glare that, if looks could kill, would have eviscerated his family tree.

Stevie passed around cups of booze to their little scrum and hesitated at Paul before handing him a cup.

"I'm giving you the smallest one because I don't want to interfere with whatever meds you're on." He cleared his throat, raised his cup. The rest of them followed suit. "To Gallo—"

"Hang on," Gallo said, scanning the room. His eyes flicked across Paul as though he wasn't there. "Where are my guys?"

"We'll get to them," Stevie said. "For now? Here's to a successful tour, a successful career," here he smirked, "and a mountain of stage bras."

At this they all tipped back their cups and the group gradually dissolved into the pulse and thrum of the room and Paul found himself alone.

***

He should have left. He should have gone home and jerked off and gone to sleep. Woken up the next morning and come up with another plan. But no. He hovered next to the drink table and filled cup after cup of cheap bourbon from a plastic bottle, grinning dumbly at the other faces around him like an usher or a caterer. In his mind, he was going to get one more shot to talk to Stevie Reese. To tell him he was involved in something really special. That a new girl had joined their band and she was dynamite and just *wait* until you hear her sing.

Instead? Instead, his lids began to feel like heavy wool and he lost track of time. He glanced about the room and couldn't tell if the party was still full or if he was seeing double. Either way, he didn't see Cassie and he didn't see Gallo and he didn't see Stevie. The room started to tilt on its axis and his stomach lurched.

He put down his cup and snaked his way through the remaining bodies, through peals of laughter and weed smoke, through the bright synth textures of—did somebody put on Billy Ocean?—and through the empty performance space. There were still some people mingling in the bar, it was Saturday night after all, but by some miracle there was no line for the bathroom. He shouldered his way in and felt a bubble in his throat so he opted for the stall to be sure. He pushed the stall open, and the door hit something solid and somebody—some*bodies*—yelped.

"Sorrysorry," Paul slurred, but his stomach wasn't so polite. He burped and it was urgent. He slurred *Sorry* again and shoved his way in and when he saw who it was on the other side of the door, he stopped short, stunned. It was Gallo there wide-eyed and saying, *Oh shit*, and the girl, blinking with her dark makeup smeared in the dingy, graffiti-covered stall, wasn't Cassie at all. It was—he didn't know who it was—and she had her top pulled down and there was white powder on her right breast. She was saying *Oh shit* and then Paul said *Oh shit* too as he wedged between them, doubled over and emptied his guts into the toilet.

***

He woke to a string of panicked texts from Gallo. His thundering hangover made reading the texts with any kind of focus damn near impossible, so he chugged glass after glass of water, swallowed a fistful of Excedrin and smoked an ashy bowl to quell the cottony pressure in his head and mellow the frayed ends of his anxiety. But reading through those texts brought it all roaring back. Fuck's sake. Why did people feel the need—conscious or otherwise—to dig themselves into monumental canyons of shit?

It was this question that he pondered while laying on his back on the floor in a set of old sweats while *Blue Train* spun on the platter of his turntable. It had, he knew, something to do with pride. With misconstrued concepts about the nature of success. That people refused to quit while they were ahead—or at least not terribly far behind—to accept their lives as enough. Shit, he had a stack of stolen records weighing down his desk to prove it. As Lee Morgan's trumpet untangled itself in bright spirals around the loose spine of "Lazy Bird," he found himself feeling sorry for Gallo, knowing that despite his onrush of success, there was, somewhere deep inside, a hole that might never be filled.

Hey buddy how u feeling this AM? read the first, exploratory text. The timestamp on the message was just past seven in the morning, so Gallo couldn't have slept much, if at all. He was probing, testing to see what Paul remembered.

Hell of a night last night lol, read the second, *Can't do it like we used to!*

By virtue of being asleep, Paul hadn't responded, so Gallo had grown desperate, by degrees.

Was really good to see you, man. We need to hang out more.

After a gap of a good fifteen minutes, the cresting wave of panic:

Look dude not sure what you saw in that bathroom but let's keep it between us, cool?

Then: *I would REALLY prefer it stay under wraps, ok? Please don't tell Cassie.*

Finally: *Can we meet? Maybe would be best to talk face to face.*

After nearly an hour of indecision about what he could possibly text back to address the situation in any kind of productive way, he invited Gallo out to Red Hook to talk.

He was still on the floor, too incapacitated to do anything about the rhythmic click that marked the end of the Coltrane record, when the door buzzed. He'd barely pressed the buzzer, barely lifted the needle from the record to let the tonearm rest in its cradle, when he heard feet skipping up the stairs.

There was a soft, polite knock.

He opened the door to see Gallo, out of breath, hair askew, forcing a crooked smile.

"Hey, buddy," he said, looking past Paul into the cramped space beyond, "can I come in?"

There was something mangy and feral about him, which caught Paul off guard; he was usually as bright and cheerful as a golden lab. "Of course," Paul said and stepped aside, allowing Gallo to amble through the threshold.

His friend moved to the middle of the room because there was really nowhere else to go. He looked around—the piles of dirty clothes, the flaking walls, the bedsheet that served as a makeshift curtain—and appeared somewhat stunned.

"This is where you live?"

Paul laughed at the question and Gallo smiled nervously in return. Paul went over to his turntable, crouched low to sift through a leaning column of records. He was after something mellow and settled on Ben Webster. He lowered his weight onto the edge of his bed as Webster's horn descended on the room like a sigh.

"This is it for the time being."

"You moving?" Gallo asked. He seemed relieved.

"Not if I can help it."

"What do you mean?" Gallo said and scrunched his brow. Something on the floor caught his eye. "Wow. Never thought you'd have a copy." He bent down and picked up his new record and turned it over in his hands like he was studying it for the first time.

"Of course," Paul said. "Have to support the cause."

Gallo looked up and tested a smile. His eyes were baggy and bloodshot. He wore his hangovers hard. "I appreciate you, man," he said.

Paul waved the comment away and steeled himself against sentimentality. He had, after all, stolen the record, and just the other day sampled one of the tracks without Gallo's permission, taken those heart-on-sleeve strings and buried them deep in reverb, stretched them into an eerie melody over the thump and rattle of drums that Eloise's voice would weave through like syrup.

He told Gallo to take a seat. "Relax, man. You're making me nervous."

Gallo looked around.

Paul nodded at the tangled nest of wires and cables that occupied the metal folding chair at his makeshift desk. "You can move that shit to the floor."

"Look, no offense," Gallo said, "but can we like, get out of here?"

Paul couldn't tell if Gallo's wobbly unease stemmed from the fact that Paul's meager living situation forced him to confront the blunt manner in which he'd left Paul in the dust, or if it was simply that there was, quite literally, no room for the both of them.

He led Gallo on a walk south on Van Brunt toward the water's edge. It was, for December, a mild day. Occasionally, the sun broke through a fast-moving blanket of clouds and warmed their faces. On another day, they might have been two friends who'd fallen out of touch and who were now, at long last, making up for lost time. Which in a way was true. Except, as Paul walked along, a half-step in front of Gallo, and as the shuttered grates of industrial buildings slowly gave way to wine shops and stationary stores as they neared the curve of the East River, he was suddenly aware that he and Gallo would never be friends in the same way again.

They found an open bench in a little wedge of a park that faced the river. Lady Liberty, several hundred yards in the distance, jammed her fist to the sky. The grass at their feet was worn and patchy and yellow, and the steady beat of chopper blades—the sound of the privileged descending on Lower Manhattan—sliced through any real sense of quietude. Still, it was, for New York City, as close to an idyllic scene as one could hope for. Gallo tilted his head back against the lip of the bench and closed his eyes in a fleeting beam of sun.

"Not bad," he said. "Not bad at all."

He was, Paul realized, a man in some kind of crisis. The staging ground for an internal war.

"Look man," Paul said, "I'm all about appreciating a good view, but I'm guessing you didn't come all the way out here to reflect on the beauty of the East River."

Gallo's eyes clicked open, and he sat up straight. He blinked, but he didn't turn to Paul. It seemed easier for him that way.

"You can't tell her," he finally said.

Paul sighed. "She really likes you. I can tell by the way she looks at you."

Gallo wiped a hand down his face. "I know man. I *know*. You're not helping."

"C'mon, it's not that big a deal. So you blew coke off a random girl's tits in the bathroom. So what? At least you didn't fuck her, right?"

Gallo looked away.

"Well, shit," Paul said, "what do you want me to say?"

"That you won't tell her, dude."

"How long you been seeing her? Couple weeks?"

"Doesn't matter how long. I *like* her, okay. I really like her. And," here he wiped a hand down his face again, "I don't know."

"What?"

"It's just. I always thought of myself as like, a good guy."

Paul had to keep from rolling his eyes. He studied Gallo. The way the breeze, which had found its strength, lifted the loose strands of hair that hung around his forehead, ruffled the collar of his plaid coat. He waited for Gallo to say something else. But he didn't. He just looked out across the water and watched the blocky orange ferry push its way to Staten Island. He believed it. He actually thought he was a good guy. At Dead Wax, Paul nearly believed it too. But this was who Gallo would always be: the guy who took credit for the songs they'd made together. The guy who bailed on Paul and started Feathers. The guy who cheated on Cassie.

"Well," Paul said, "have you ever considered the idea that maybe you're not?"

"Not what?"

"A good guy."

Gallo turned, hurt. "You don't think that do you?"

Paul didn't answer right away. He looked at Gallo, the way he hunched his shoulders, the way he seemed to be bracing himself against some unseen force, and felt something soften within him. "Look, why would I say something to her? I have no stake in this."

Gallo looked at Paul to gauge his sincerity. Then he exhaled, relieved. "Thank you, man. You're a good friend."

"Let me ask you a favor then," Paul said. "You know, as a friend."

"Of course. What is it?"

"Introduce me to Stevie Reese."

"But I did introduce you," Gallo protested, "at the after-party. And you fucked it up."

"Don't give me that. You weren't exactly sticking up for me. I'm talking about a real introduction. You know, put in a good word for us."

Gallo slumped back against the bench. "I can't do that, man. Stevie is a weird dude. I'd really be sticking my neck out there, you know? Putting my—"

"Reputation on the line?" Paul said. "Right." He paused, cleared his throat, and said, "Well, at least it's still early enough to win Cassie's trust back."

"What's that supposed to mean?"

"Let me tell you something, my parents are in trouble. I'll spare you the details, but not only did my dad lose his job, but my brother royally fucked up their finances. Suffice it to say I'm trying to help them however I can."

"Kills me to hear that," Gallo said and shook his head. "I feel for your folks, I really do, but ... what's it got to do with me?"

"Your pops still running things at NuWaves?"

"I mean, yeah," Gallo said, "but—"

"How about you ask him to give my dad a call? See if there's a role for him."

Gallo narrowed his eyes. "C'mon. That's a lot to ask, don't you think?"

"I don't like being this way," Paul said, "but at the moment, I don't really have much of a choice."

"Shit," Gallo said and looked off in the distance again.

Just then a young couple walked into the park with a small dog off its leash. The dog—some kind of jittery terrier—made a beeline for the bench, raised a shaky leg, and took a leak right near Paul's left sneaker. The young woman, bundled in a knit scarf and beanie, scampered up, flushed and embarrassed. She pointed sternly at the dog. "Atticus, no. No." She looked at Paul and covered her mouth. "Oh my God, I am so sorry."

"It's okay," Paul said. "Really."

The young woman glanced from Paul to Gallo and back, and sensing the tension, bent down to pick up the dog and briskly fled the scene. When she and her boyfriend were out of earshot, as though it mattered, Paul spoke again. "And another thing. Actually, two more things. One, I sampled a song off the new record for a beat I'm working on."

"You *did?*" Gallo was clearly flattered. "Which one?"

"The one with the blues guitar," Paul said. "I don't know the title."

"'Angel,'" Gallo said proudly. "Wow. You liked 'Angel'?"

"I did like 'Angel.' And I'd like you to give me your blessing to use it. It's a good beat. I think Stevie will like it."

Gallo shook his head as though working through some messy calculus. "Do you have more to show him?"

"We'll have some new songs done soon. We're a trio now by the way. Her name's Eloise and her voice? Really something special."

Gallo pulled his collar close. "This little … negotiation seems a bit lopsided, don't you think? All of this so you don't tell Cassie?"

Paul steeled his resolve though it filled him with guilt. "I guess it depends how important she is to you."

"For fuck's sake, man."

"At the end of the day, this is one of those things where you need some help and I need some help. So. It's really about doing the right thing."

"The right thing," Gallo said distantly.

Like a beacon, the sun broke through the clouds once more and again Gallo tilted his head back to bask in it. For a moment, he didn't move. He opened his eyes to the sky and squinted. "So you won't say anything?"

"Don't even know what you're talking about," Paul said.

"Fine," Gallo sighed. "Consider 'Angel' payback for the way I bailed on you. I'll talk to my dad too, see if he's got any jobs open." Here he turned to look Paul square in the eye. "Just know I'm not doing it for you though. I'm doing it because I respect the hell out of your dad. And, as long as you promise not to say a word to Cassie—about any of this—I'll see what I can set up for you with Stevie." He raised himself up from the bench. He looked out at the Statue of Liberty, the Jersey skyline beyond. "You better have your stuff ready. Because he doesn't like to waste time."

9.

HE NEVER THOUGHT IT WOULD BE SO EASY. HE FIGURED HE'D BE LIVING with the looming, guilt-ridden specter of Bunky's father's records for weeks. That they would lay there, mocking him, reminding him of the shitty person he'd turned out to be. Actually, what he thought would happen was that he would be evicted before he'd even be able to sell enough to pay down his December debt.

When Bev had come pounding on Paul's door demanding the rest and once again threatening eviction, he had managed to talk his landlord off the ledge by showing him the stash and the accompanying values on his computer. Bev had whistled, impressed despite himself, said something like, "For a bunch of fucking records"—though in his mouth it came out as "rekkids"—and agreed to give Paul the end of the week. He insisted on payment with interest and pledged complete ignorance on where Paul had got his hands on *all that crap*, his way of acknowledging the stolen goods. In three days' time, Paul had kept his word. To a collector in Germany, he sold off a trio of rare '80s rap singles for nearly five hundred a pop. He had undercut the lowest seller, but not so much as to arouse suspicion as to their condition or authenticity, and had the money deposited to his account. He went downstairs, handed

Bev a check for both his December balance and an advance on January, and in return, Bev handed him back his drum machine.

He tried hard not to think about just what it was he was doing. That he was selling off someone's personal history. Like any other collectible, records marked memories, stages of life. Though his own collection couldn't touch Bunky's father's in terms of breadth and value, he knew that with each record came a story. A faceless customer could buy the wax for a few hundred or a thousand dollars, but the story itself was priceless.

By the following Friday, he had sold half of the records, including "Beat Bop," which went for a shade over two grand. He watched his bank account climb to six thousand dollars, which was more money than he'd had in years. By day, he clocked in at Dead Wax, nabbing a record here and there, less for money than for sport. By night, he delicately packed the stolen wax in bubble wrap, shipped it off to new homes in Kansas City, Copenhagen, Paris. Somehow, the phone call he expected—from Bunky, from the police, from anyone telling him the jig was up—never came. And it crossed his mind more than once that he might have a future in this kind of thing.

Instead, the only communication he received from the outside world was a text from Eloise—in which she explained that Bunky was down for the count with the flu, that they should cancel practice this week—and a phone call from his parents. A phone call that was preceded by a series of photos that his mother had texted along without commentary. He hadn't heard from her since Thanksgiving, so the images were enigmatic, either an olive branch or a sort of accusation. Still, they put a lump in his throat. They were of the empty house, each picture a snapshot of a different room, stripped bare but for moving boxes. The living room where they'd gathered to watch TV movies when he was a kid. The kitchen where they'd shared every meal until Will moved out. And his bedroom: the posters, the books, the bed, all of it gone.

He cleared his throat and answered and had to hold the phone away from his ear. His mother always spoke on the phone as though shouting down a well.

"Hello?"

"Yeah, Mom, I'm—"

"Paul? Hello? Is he there?" She spoke away from the receiver. "I don't think he's there."

"MOM."

"Oh. Oh. You're there. Well. There must be something wrong with your phone because I can barely hear you."

It was entirely possible. His phone was several generations old, as the Apple cult would tell him, the same phone he had been issued when he started at Scrimshaw/Duff. When he quit, he simply strolled out the door with it, and thus far they hadn't bothered tracking him down.

"The photos, Mom," he said, "I'm sorry."

"Well, like you said to us over Thanksgiving, sorry doesn't fix this."

He leaned back in his chair, picked up his pipe, considered lighting it, thought better of it, put it down again on his desk. He closed his eyes and tried to picture her, but had a hard time envisioning her face. He considered telling her that help would soon be on its way, but he decided it would be better left unexplained.

"You know what you can do for us?" she said.

Paul sat up straight in his chair.

"Come to Chicago for Christmas. We're going to visit Will. At least we could all be together."

For a moment, he said nothing. It was impossible. To leave New York was to halt his progress, and to do so felt very dangerous, to both his momentum, and to Will, who he would strangle. That his parents could even bear to stay with him said everything Paul needed to know about their capacity for resilience, if not love.

"Hello?"

"No," he said and shook his head as though she could see him.

"No, what?"

"I can't be there."

"Why not?"

"Because—I have a lot of work to do."

"Work," she said and sighed. "I suppose it's probably best that I don't know what it is you're doing. I would ask you about money, but I'm afraid I don't have the energy to worry about you right now."

"You don't have to worry," he said. "I'm figuring some things out."

"I hope you are," she said. "I really hope you are."

She paused.

"You know," she said. "This will be the first Christmas we won't be together."

He rubbed his eyes. It would also be his first Christmas away from the house he grew up in, the house they could no longer call their own.

"They were never big but at least we were together."

"They were always nice, Mom," he said. Growing up, Christmas had always been a time of familial peace. The kitschy decorations his mother labored with to brighten up the house, the Advent calendar with the punch-out boxes that hung on the basement door, the card games, the sense of comfort and safety and familiarity.

"Well," his mother said, sounding weary, "what will you do? Will you at least see some friends?"

Friends. He imagined Bunky and Eloise. Were they, strictly speaking, his friends? He had no idea. "Yeah, I'll probably get together with some friends. Maybe go out to dinner."

"At least you won't be alone."

"How's your back? Are you really going to go back and teach?"

"I'm taking the holidays to rest. Then I'll go back early next year as a sub. The kids won't know how easy they had it while I was gone. And Will got me a shiny new cane, which helps a little bit. You should see me now. I almost look fancy."

"Mom, plea—"

"Stop it."

Paul sighed. "Well, then how is Dad? Any luck finding work?"

"I'm sure he'd prefer to tell you himself. Hang on. He's right here."

"Okay. Bye Mo—"

"Paul, how are you?"

"Mom showed me the pictures."

"I wish she wouldn't do that," he said. "We should be looking forward."

"It's got to be hard."

"Life is hard, Paul. You'll find out soon enough."

"Have you started looking for work?"

"You know. The funniest thing happened yesterday. Phil Gallo, out of the blue, calls me the other day. What was it, Monday? He calls me Monday and says he's got an opening, and would I like to come in to discuss it."

"Get out."

"Hand to God. He didn't tell me what it was exactly, but I figure I'll go hear him out. Could be something."

"That's great news."

"The universe works in strange ways, Paul. I'll tell you that. Hadn't heard from the man in years." He was quiet a moment and there was the familiar sound of his father letting a tuft of air whistle from his nostrils. "I get the feeling you're not coming to Chicago," he said.

"I can't," Paul said.

"Look," he said. "I could holler and tell you to wake up, or grow up or buck up and be a man. But I know it won't do any good. So what I'll say is: you're on your own."

"I always have been," Paul said.

"You can think that if you want. And you can think that your mother and I don't believe in you, or don't love you. Maybe that motivates you, I don't know. But we can no longer help you. We have enough stress as it is."

"You don't have to help me. I can do it on my own. And I'm going to help you guys. I promise."

"Mm," his father said, disbelieving. As if searching for lighter territory, he said, "How is Sara? Will you two be together at least?"

"She uh, no. She has to go home."

"That's too bad."

"Besides, I have too much work to do."

"Work," he said. "I'm glad you see it that way."

The conversation petered out as it always did, and they said their awkward goodbyes. Paul hung up, shoved aside the guilt and shame that threatened to weigh him down and instead focused on the success of his negotiation with Gallo, the trajectory of his virtual pawn shop, and set about channeling that energy into making music.

For three days, he came home from Dead Wax and stayed up until sunrise finishing another pair of beats. He rode the wave of inspiration that had led him to the track he had built around Sara's voice and violin and decided to borrow from the other voices in his life. He completed the track for which he had lifted samples from "Angel," Gallo's song, a saccharine blues guitar number that revolved around phrases like, "You're heaven for a devil like me," and, "You got me bedside on my knees," which were quite ironic in the context of Gallo's recent indiscretion. He took two wordless measures of the guitar and sped them up in a way that called back to the tempo of the tracks he and Gallo once made. For the second beat, he deconstructed a voicemail his parents had left him last February for his birthday. It was not for sentimental reasons that the message remained on his phone; he had simply forgotten to delete it. But in the context of the track—a slurry thumper that dripped with tension—their voices sounded plaintive, ghostly. *Hello, son*, his mother said, as though she was on the verge of losing him. Paul took the phrase and passed it through several filters until it was poised to dissolve, and used it as an intro. *Keep up the good work*, his father said to close the message, so Paul made *work* the operative word, bending and stretching it and dropping it in between kick drum thumps.

When the sun rose on that third day of manic creation, the sixteenth of the month, Paul had sold the rest of the stolen collection. The only record he held onto was Bunky's signed copy of *True Stories*; he simply couldn't bring himself to flip it. He had just under thirteen thousand dollars in his bank account. He decided to keep a couple grand as a float for the next few months that he would steadily pad with his wages from Dead Wax. Then he wrote a check for ten thousand dollars addressed to his father, and with more pride than he had done anything before in his life, put it in a crisp envelope and dropped it in the mail.

He tried to arrive for practice early, much as he had the day he met Bunky that very first time at Flaherty's. His aim was to show renewed commitment, a workman's ethic, undeniable and true. He also wanted to beat Bunky there to give himself a little solo time to think, not to mention figure out how to return the stolen key. But Eloise was already there. He pushed open the door to find her perched on a tall stool, her Stratocaster, the same cherry red as her lips and bandana, strapped around her torso. Her head was bowed, and she was plucking crystal-line chords and vamps that eventually coalesced into snatches of "Maybelline," a lick from "Hey Good Lookin'," then some caffeinated blues chords that wound into a raucous stomp.

He watched her for a few moments, found himself admiring how comfortable she seemed, so at ease in her own skin. Everyone he knew always seemed so aware, so rehearsed, that to encounter someone so open was a reminder that such an approach to life was possible.

She felt his gaze, blushed, and stopped playing with a slap of the strings. She looked up and tipped her chin. "Take a picture."

He snapped away his glance, made his way over to his folding table and began arranging his gear. "Sorry, I was just—"

"Oh man," she said and rolled her eyes. Her lips curled into a wry smile that revealed her gleaming tooth. "Y'all have got to lighten up. That's it. That's my mission."

"Y'all?"

"Yeah, *y'all*. Bunky's tight assed as a jackrabbit too."

"Nah, I mean—you know, I never really got where you're from."

"Down south," she said and for the first time, looked off as she spoke. "Louisiana."

"You leave your accent at home?"

"Well," she said, her smile returning, "I can dial it up or back depending on the—*sitchiation*." This last word she stretched and spat as if it was made of putty.

"That where you learned to play all that rockabilly?"

"You would've thought Elvis was a member of the family," she said. She absently ran her thumb over her strings. "The way my dad had pictures all in the living room. He fancied himself a bit of a greaser I guess. It's what I grew up on. Ate it up with my breakfast. Records always playing and so on."

"Sounds like a fun way to grow up."

Eloise looked down at her hands, shifting her weight on the stool. "Had its moments."

Paul sensed a touch of unease, felt he was on the verge of trespassing. He backed off, trying a new tack.

"Busking," he said with a glint of awe, "takes balls."

"Ah," she said and smiled, "you get used to it."

"I always thought buskers were like, drifters."

Her smile remained as she said, "Not far from the truth."

Paul looked at her, but didn't probe, letting her chart the course.

"I just had to get the hell out of there," she said. She turned on her stool to face him more directly, unshouldered her guitar and propped it against an amp on the floor. She let a little laugh escape her nose. "You wanted to get to know me," she said.

"Only if you want to be known."

She shrugged, a look that said, *I got nothing to hide.* His life, by contrast, seemed to revolve around hiding, or at the very least, obfuscation.

"My brother died last year," she said.

"Oh shit," Paul said, "I'm—"

"Don't," she said and raised a hand. "The hospital's the one should be sorry for pumping him full of shit after he had the accident. Course he got hooked, couldn't control it. Mom found him one morning on the floor, curled up and blue."

"Jesus."

"Messed us up. No more Elvis around the house after that. It was just so easy to get, that was the problem. Kids could visit another planet for five, ten bucks." She uncrossed her arms, hooked her thumbs into the pockets of her black jeans. "Of course I had to try it, you know? See where my brother had gone, thought maybe I'd understand him better. Well, let me tell you, I almost ended up right there on the bathroom floor myself."

Paul's eyes flicked to the crook of her arm and she caught it.

"None of that," she said. "I left before I got that desperate. Rode the train all the way up."

"Hopped it?"

"No, dummy. I had a ticket. Burned my money," here she snapped her fingers, "like that. Wound up in some hour-hotel up by the bus station, which, I've been in some sketchy spots, but I've never felt more uneasy than I did the two nights I holed up there. When my cash ran out? I spent a few nights in the park, which sucked because one of those nights it poured, so then I crashed beneath some scaffolding. And by crashed I mean I didn't sleep at all. And then—well, I ran into Bunky on the G train."

"Wow," Paul said, "I had no idea."

"How would you?"

"So Bunky waved you down and that was that?"

"Well," Eloise said, straightening her bandana, "I guess I can't lie. I noticed him noticing me. It was a thrill to be approached like that cause you never know if anyone is actually listening. Most folks refuse to acknowledge you like you're a leper or something. And it didn't hurt to find out he could really get down on the bass."

"You want to know something?"

Eloise cocked her head.

"I saw you too."

"What? You *did?*" Color rose in her cheeks and she looked away. "Oh my Lord."

"Not that day. At Hoyt-Schermerhorn. You were on the platform?"

"Eesh," Eloise said with a wave of her hand, "that was a mistake. That's a tough station to play."

"No," Paul said, "it was incredible. Your voice filled the space. People notice. They're shy. They're busy. They're pissed at the train. But trust me, they notice. And if we keep working together, a lot more people are gonna notice."

"You think so?"

"I know so. And I know I'm glad Bunky put his number in your hat."

"I am too. If I'm honest, I figured I'd last up here a couple months, do a few odd jobs until I got tired of running, or at least until the universe made it clear to me this whole music thing was just a lovely dream. Then I'd head back to Louisiana where I was supposed to be all along. This'd be a blip, something I'd think back on now and again." She shrugged. "And that all could still happen. Hell, I bet it *will* happen at some point. But for now, this feels like a start."

"I think it's more than that."

Eloise looked at him with a knowing smile and he feared he had been too earnest. "So. Tell me: why didn't you say something?"

He felt the heat of shame creep up his neck. He wanted to believe that he had been in a hurry. "I mean," he sputtered, "I would have, but I was coming home from work and everything—"

"Take it easy, buddy," Eloise said. She shook her head and giggled. "I'm just busting your chops. I get it. You just happen to have very high standards is all."

"Something like that," he said, embarrassed that he couldn't pick up on a joke. "Is that where you just came from?"

Eloise blinked.

"Like, busking or whatever?"

"Oh, no. Work actually. Little coffee shop in Fort Greene. Saw a notice in the window. Cute place. And the manager's nice. Laetitia is her name. Czech, I think. I'm staying with Bunky until I figure out a different ... *sitchiation*."

Paul smirked. "Hope you convinced him to straighten up his shit. His place is a mess."

"Let's just say I'm starting slow."

Paul pictured the two of them in Bunky's cluttered studio, sharing the same bed, but stopped short of what came next, though he was certain of it. Because of course they had. And he longed for something like it. The physicality sure, but more importantly, the companionship.

"I'm not sure slow is in Bunky's vocab."

Eloise demurred, hesitated, as if she had more to say on the subject, but right then, as if a director off-stage had given him the cue, Bunky pushed open the door of their room and at once the molecules in the air around them seemed to quicken in their orbit.

He stopped short just inside the door, as though he could feel the charge in the room.

"Did I interrupt something?" He arched his eyebrows self-consciously and his grey eyes fell first on Eloise, then on Paul.

"You got a knack for it," Paul said. He tried to speak slowly to offset the pounding in his chest as he scanned Bunky's face for clues. "Eloise was just telling me about her love of rockabilly."

"Yeah?" Bunky said. He crossed the room to his usual position. "News to me."

Eloise lifted her guitar from its place on the floor. "Sometimes I skip chapters in my life story," she said. "You gotta know your audience."

"I don't know if I should be grateful or offended," Bunky said. He set about removing his bass from its case, crouched low to plug it in and as he did so, his pale knees pushed through the holes in his black jeans. He fastened his Fender Precision around his torso, laid waste to any further chit chat and said, "I added a verse."

It took a moment for Paul to even realize what he was talking about. And it was with a wave of relief that he understood Bunky had yet to speak to his parents. Or if he had, nothing had seemed amiss.

"I think it's really working," Bunky said. He looked at Eloise. "Could use some overdub of your guitar." Then at Paul. "The vocal samples work. Nostalgic without being cloying. Think you finally found that sweet spot."

"Yeah, cool," Paul said, trying to focus, trying not to be taken aback by Bunky's tone. Outright compliments were not something he had been trading in lately.

"So," his bandmate said with a grin, "you guys want to hear it?"

"I'm nervous," Eloise said. "I've never heard my voice recorded properly before."

"Nothing to be nervous about," Bunky said, "trust me." He connected his laptop to the speakers and pressed play. The familiar beat bumped to life: Sara's distorted voice, the violin sample, and then Eloise's vocals, sultry and warm, a come-hither beckoning.

When the lights go out, I remember why I turned them on with you
On her heels came Bunky's croon.

Darkness ain't so bad ... Darkness reveals the truth
If Eloise played the enchantress, Bunky played the cool suitor. They'd taken Paul's beat and made it a sweeping come-on. And it worked. There was a tangible chemistry amongst the three of them at play that hadn't existed when it was he and Bunky: the bass grounded the beat, Eloise's guitar gave it a spark, the tandem vocals brought it swirling to life.

Sure, it was one song. But Paul could feel it and judging by the expressions on the faces of his bandmates—Eloise's broad smile with its glint of silver, Bunky's measured nod—he could tell they felt it too. Eloise plugged her guitar into the module that ran straight into the workstation on Bunky's laptop that would record her take. She donned headphones so she could hear the track, and when she was ready, peppered in well-placed spikes from her Stratocaster, her slender fingers sliding along the fret as she worked the ones. Her eyes were closed, her lips tucked inward as she concentrated. In that moment, Paul found it remarkable the extent to which a person's playing style reflected a yin and yang between body and sound: where Eloise's playing was deliberate and precise, her words and actions were loose and organic. He watched Bunky, who observed Eloise with a look that struck him as protective. Eloise. Their band-mate. Bunky's ... well, Paul wasn't entirely sure what she was to Bunky, but he knew he'd never been the third wheel quite like this.

Eloise finished her overdubs and let the headphones curl around her neck. Paul clapped; she gave a little bow over the body of her guitar.

"Money," Bunky said, and Paul could tell he was trying to contain his enthusiasm, trying not to get ahead of himself. "Couple parts I'll tweak in the mix, but I'd say we've got our first song in the books."

"Let's keep it moving," Paul said.

"You got more?" Bunky asked.

"Don't sound so surprised." He found the files on his MPC and nearly forgot about the circumstances that had allowed him to retrieve the machine. "Who do you think you're dealing with?"

Bunky smirked. "A lazy motherfucker."

"Been working on two new bangers."

"Gross," Eloise said. "Please don't ever say *bangers.*" She made a face like she'd tasted something rotten. "You sound like a douche."

"Two? As in more than one?"

"When it's flowing, I can't turn it off."

Bunky rolled his eyes.

Eloise arched her brows. "How about you shut the hell up and play them?"

"Now there's an idea," Bunky said.

It had been a long time since he'd felt lightness in that room. It was with a wave of giddiness then that he scrolled to the file on his drum machine and played the beat he'd crafted around his parent's voicemail: a slower, patient groove, a beat he envisioned rattling trunks from Houston Street to Houston, Texas. A subterranean 808 kick drum threatened the integrity of their shitty speakers. The beat was open and spacious, held together by a ticking high hat and colored by a squelching synth, punctuated at intervals by that single word: *work.* Paul couldn't help but bob his head and Bunky did the same.

"Nasty," he said, screwing up his face.

Eloise bit her bottom lip. Still plugged in, she began to vamp an arpeggio on her guitar.

Bunky pointed at her and nodded. "Yes."

Paul felt a swell, the kind of rush that could only come from the feeling of three distinct individuals existing—however fleetingly—on the same wavelength. Bunky slung his bass over his shoulder and thumbed an intermittent line. Intuitively, he knew the track didn't need much; the drums carried most of the weight. The track trailed off and Bunky spoke at once.

"Okay. We're going to lay that down just like that." He eyed Eloise. "You and me will think on vocals." He made a twirling motion with his finger. "Next."

Paul obliged, queuing up the beat that he'd crafted from camouflaged samples of Gallo's record.

"Damn," Bunky said, listening intently, "talk about a one-eighty."

"Just give it a chance," Paul said. A foreign feeling had begun to creep into his chest: confidence. After a few measures, the pulse of the track quickened, the kick and snare weaved together into a spare, four-on-the-floor breakbeat.

"Makes me want to double-dutch," Eloise said and rocked her shoulders.

"Or like, bust out a square of cardboard and start breaking," said Bunky. "Never thought you'd have a dance track in you."

He absently thrummed a worming, infectious bassline and cocked his head, curious. "What's the sample? Cello? Sounds so familiar. Like Arthur Russell or something."

"Don't worry about it," Paul said with a grin. He didn't feel like going into the means by which he had cleared the sample with Gallo, didn't want to risk disrupting their delicate momentum.

Eloise began to play jangly chords and stepped closer to her mic stand. She closed her eyes, nodded her head, and began to test vocal melodies.

Never know ...

For a moment, she opened her eyes and let them drift around the room as if scanning for a foothold. Just as quickly, she closed them again. She started to sing, smoke and honey:

You'll never know ...

What your eyes do to me

Bunky found the pocket of the beat, laid down a steady groove, and picked up where Eloise left off.

I can't stand it ...

When you look right through me ...

And on they went, riffing and trading couplets. Occasionally, Paul laid in some scratches, but mostly he observed, watching a beat he had constructed out of loneliness and desperation bloom into something real. When the track faded out, they were quiet. Unsure, perhaps, about whether to trust the magic they'd managed to conjure. That it might escape them, vanish into the stuffy atmosphere of the room.

"Tell me you were recording," Paul said, breaking the silence.

"Always," Bunky said. Then: "What did you eat today?"

"Why?"

"Because whatever it was, you should have it every day."

"I haven't eaten all day."

"Then stay hungry."

***

Afterwards, they sucked back bottles of water and toweled off. Even in the winter months, the Sweatshop earned its billing. Eloise had put in an order for delivery Thai food, and they sat around waiting for it: Eloise on the cement floor, legs outstretched, beat-up Vans crossed at the ankles, Bunky seated on an amp, Paul on the arm of a battered chair with shit-brown upholstery.

"Welcome back," Bunky said, raising a bottle of water in Paul's direction. "What you been up to besides cranking out beats?"

Shit. Where to even start? He shrugged. "Dealing with some family bullshit."

"Like what?" Eloise said.

"I'll spare you the details."

"I'm all ears," she said. "I gave you my sob story. Least I can do is listen to yours."

"Fine. Long story short? My brother gambled my dad's pension on an investment he thought was a lock. The better part of their savings went down the toilet and they lost their house."

Eloise's face fell. "Shit."

Bunky was shaking his head. "Fuck, man. What're you going to do?"

"I don't know," Paul said. He couldn't look at Bunky. "All I can do is keep doing what I'm doing, I guess. Hope that maybe somehow this," he gestured widely as though their little powwow, their musty practice space, was the nucleus of break-through potential, "works out."

"So, like—" Eloise had drawn her knees to her chest and tiptoed around the subject, "are you guys going to try to save the house?"

"No," Paul said, "it's gone. Saw the pictures the other day. All boxed up and empty."

"Ugh," Eloise said and hung her head. "Brutal."

Bunky nodded. "Gives us another reason to bust our asses." He looked Paul in the eye. "And look, Eloise and I both know what it's like to have family bullshit."

"Amen," Eloise said.

"Makes you feel any better? It's been like six months since I talked to my parents."

And there it was: confirmation. But it certainly didn't make Paul feel any better.

As if on cue, Eloise's phone blared: "Toxic" by Britney Spears. "Food time," she said.

"Christ," Bunky said, "that's your ringtone?"

"Fuck yeah, it's my ringtone. It's Britney, bitch." She ducked out the door.

Paul and Bunky were quiet for a moment until Bunky broke the silence.

"Hey, look," he said, "I'm sorry about some of the shit I said a few weeks ago, you know? It's just," he shook his head, "you know my deal."

Paul looked at his bandmate and it was difficult not to spill his guts, to tell Bunky that his parents were trying to make it work, that his mother wanted to see him. But to do so meant unraveling everything. He stayed quiet, made as though he was considering the weight of what Bunky had said.

"I get it man. I feel the pressure too."

Eloise came back in carrying two sagging plastic bags over to Paul's DJ table. He got up to help her clear space. They divvied up their meals and settled back into place with their plastic containers of food. Bunky jammed an auxiliary cable into his laptop, studied his screen and scrolled until wispy and modulated tones began to bleed from the speakers: an album of ambient piano by Harold Budd. Bunky had always been a fan of ambient, and it had grown on Paul too. The hushed airiness, the subtle shifts in melody. Music you could disappear into. A balm for anxious times.

They ate amidst the swell of lush keys. Then, before he had much time to think about the consequences, Paul said: "Ran into Gallo the other night."

"Who's Gallo?" Eloise said.

"Kid I grew up with. We recorded some shit back in the day. Now he's got this band Feathers—"

"Oh, I've heard of them. They're getting pretty popular. Horrendous band name though."

"I went to the warm-up show for their tour." He looked at Bunky, expecting him to cut in, make a snide remark.

"What? I didn't say anything."

"We were supposed to be the opener, but I fucked it up."

"You said it, I didn't."

"Wait," Eloise said with a mouthful of food, "what happened?"

"It's … complicated."

"It's not that complicated," Bunky said. "Paul got laid instead of securing the gig."

"That's … not entirely true."

"Priorities," Eloise shrugged.

"Something like that," Paul said.

"So you saw Gallo," Bunky said. "And?"

"And he introduced me to Stevie Reese."

At this, Bunky stopped chewing the food in his mouth.

Eloise glanced from Bunky back to Paul. "Who's that?"

Bunky swallowed. "You met Stevie Reese?"

"Yeah. They had a little after-party and he was hanging around."

"What'd he say?"

"Can one of you *please* tell me who this is? Should I know?"

"Stevie Reese," Bunky said. "Up-and-coming manager. Name an acclaimed young act and they're probably with him."

Eloise gave no sign of being impressed. "Okay, so you see this big shot manager guy, and what, he offers to take us on right then and there, right?"

"Well," Paul said. He pretended to arrange the rice in his bowl with his chopsticks. "Not exactly."

Bunky set aside his container of food. "You're making me nervous. What'd you say to him?"

"Right there in the moment? Nothing. The after-party was loud and crowded so me and Stevie shook hands and went our separate ways. But. I managed to convince Gallo to set up a proper meeting for us."

Bunky arched a brow. "A meeting? With Stevie Reese?"

"You heard me."

"That's—I mean, shit." Bunky sat up a little straighter against the wall, his grey eyes alight. "That's legit. When?"

"So this is good?" Eloise said.

"This is good," Bunky said.

"Gallo is going to get back to me on timing. But ... soon."

"And so—what's the catch?"

Eloise stuffed another shrimp in her mouth. "I am thoroughly enjoying this."

"I'm telling you: there's no catch. I told Gallo we were working on new songs. That there's three of us. That Eloise is the truth."

At this, Eloise twirled her chopsticks in a kind of curtsy.

"Okay," Bunky said, for the moment appeased, "and Gallo— what did he say?"

"He said he'd tell Stevie. Put in a good word."

"So when does Stevie want to meet to discuss these new songs of ours?"

"Like I said: soon."

"Paul, I'm starting to lose my patience. How *soon*?"

"If I had to guess? Top of the year. Stevie's going on the road with Gallo for the first couple dates until Christmas."

"As in next month?"

Paul nodded.

"As in, like, a couple fucking weeks from now?" Bunky closed his eyes, took a deep breath, letting it out slowly. Then he opened his eyes and leveled his gaze at Paul. "You can't go making decisions like this without us."

"Dude. You're missing the point. What I'm saying is he wants to hear our shit."

"And what I'm saying is we don't have any shit for him to hear."

"Hell yeah we do." Paul pointed in the direction of his drum machine with his chopsticks. "We've got three songs. Three songs we knocked out in two sessions. You got to start having some confidence, Bunky. If nothing else, this should be moti- vation for us to get to work."

At this, Bunky seemed to come around, but his perfectionism wouldn't let him concede. "No. We've got *maybe* one song. And like, two skeletons."

Eloise cut in. "You know what I think?" She held a shrimp between chopsticks and bit surgically just before the papery pink tail. Then she spoke while she chewed. "I think if this kid wants to hear some music? We show him some damn music. What's the worst that could happen?"

"Uh, he laughs us out of the room?" Bunky said, like it was the obvious answer to a math question.

"Okay," Eloise shrugged and slurped an unruly noodle until it disappeared into her mouth. "And?"

Bunky's eyes darted around the room. "And? That would fucking suck. We'd've blown our chance at something big. Chances don't come around that often, believe me."

"Sure. It would suck. But you know where that would leave us?" Eloise patted the hard floor on which she sat. "Right where we are. Which, if you ask me? Ain't that bad. I hate to break it to you kids," she included Paul in her shifting gaze, "but what we're doing isn't exactly solving the world's problems. Shit. I'm not even sure we're capable of solving our own problems." She looked Bunky dead in the face: "What are you so afraid of?"

"I told you: he could laugh right in our faces and—"

"You know that's not what I mean."

It was a question—in so many words—Paul had wanted to ask Bunky for a long time, though he had always had his own suspicions. If things didn't work out with Stevie Reese, a real shot at proving himself, Bunky would have failed once again, failed to move out of the shadow of his family name. Failed to make his parents proud of him, failed to earn their love.

Bunky picked up his carton of noodles and stared into it for a moment. "Fine," he said, as if resigning himself to something that was far beyond his control.

Paul and Eloise shared a glance.

"Fine what?" Eloise said.

"Let's do this. Let's get to work." Here he looked up with a focus that seemed to be turned inwards more than it was directed at Paul and Eloise. "But we have a lot to do. I want these tracks to be as perfect as we can make them. I don't want this dude to have a fucking choice. If we're going to do this, we need to do this."

Eloise nodded and looked at Paul who nodded back.

"Deal," Eloise said.

"Deal," Paul said.

They chewed their food, letting the implications of the decision linger in the stuffy musk of the room.

"I'm glad that's settled," Eloise said, "because I just made another decision for us. We are never ordering from this spot again. Ever." She made a show of gnawing, as if on rubber. "I don't even want to know where this shrimp came from."

"Gowanus Canal, probably," Paul said. He looked at Bunky to see if a smile had registered, but his bandmate's face was newly aglow from the screen of his laptop.

As they packed their gear and prepared to leave for the night, Bunky palmed Paul's chest. "Hold up," he said. He turned and spoke to Eloise's back. "We'll catch up."

"K," she said over her shoulder.

Bunky took a half-step closer to Paul. This time his jaw was set and his lips were a tight hyphen. He exhaled through his nose. Paul could smell the Kee Mao.

"I know what you're up to," he said, his voice so low that he sounded like someone else.

Paul felt the color plummet from his face. Here it was. "What do you mean?"

Bunky shot a look over his shoulder to the door, then back at Paul. "Playing these power games. Trying to show me up in front of her."

It took a moment for Paul to understand what Bunky was saying. And he nearly laughed with relief at the ridiculousness of it all. "Dude. *What?* Show you up? We're a band now. Shit's gonna come up when it's three of us."

"Yes. Three people. Her and me. And then you."

Paul felt the blood return to his cheeks. "Fuck that," he said, "I thought we were past all this shit. Without me, there's no us."

"That's true as of right now," Bunky said. He'd begun to shoulder his gear bag, grip his bass case by the clutch. "I just hope you're ready."

10.

THE NEXT MORNING, PAUL PULLED OPEN THE STICKER-CAKED DOOR to Dead Wax and found himself abutting the back of a line of bodies that queued to the register.

The fuck? It was never packed this early.

He squeezed himself past the people in line, shimmied alongside a rack of records as the feverish horns of Fela Kuti squelched brightly from the speakers overhead. By the stockroom, he found Mika, bent at the waist, slicing open a box of records at her feet. She clocked him approaching and stood up straight. Her blood-red glasses set off her chopped red bob, her black leggings, black racer boots, and black t-shirt. She glared at him, icier than usual, and wielded the boxcutter in such a way that didn't quite close the door on the possibility of using it on him.

"Careful with that thing," Paul said, forcing a chuckle, "I'm fragile."

"Make yourself useful," she said and handed it over. Then she set about filing rows of records in the cubby-like space for extra stock beneath the bins.

He opened the box and saw what all the fuss was about. A batch of shiny new Radiohead records. "Surprise pre-Christmas release?"

Mika said nothing, which meant he was right.

"Pay-what-you-please?"

"A buck," she spat.

"A dollar? What's the point?"

Again, Mika was silent, dutifully setting about her business as though Paul wasn't there. He'd never seen Mika in a *good* mood exactly, but she'd never given him the cold shoulder quite like this. He looked at her, the way her butt looked in those black leggings. Then he looked up at Dante behind the register, who refused to be rushed despite the chaos at hand. Paul shrugged performatively like, *What's her deal?* Dante nodded sympathetically like he knew.

After Paul had unloaded the remainder of the new boxes, he joined Dante at the counter, feeling he'd earned a respite from Mika's chilly disregard. Dante was scanning and bagging records with a methodical mellowness that only he seemed capable of. Occasionally, he had to gently scold a buyer for attempting to skirt the *One-Per-Customer* sign at the door. "Don't tell her I told you," he said, "but her demo got rejected."

"I didn't even know she had a demo," Paul said.

"She keeps it quiet. She sent a track to this label she likes. Black Diamond. They put out a lot of dark ambient shit she's into. They asked for more songs, which got her excited of course. She sent them more and got flat-out ghosted, bro. Like, not even a response. She was crushed."

"Damn," Paul said. He looked over to where Mika had begun chatting with a customer by the bins. She listened intently, her arms crossed over her chest. She guided him to the racks for Experimental and rifled through, slid out a record and handed it to him as though she was assigning homework. It was hard to believe she was even capable of being hurt by something as above-the-surface as a rejected demo. "Well," he said, channeling what Eloise had said yesterday at the Sweatshop, "she's back to where she started. Nothing wrong with that."

"You go tell her that," Dante said.

"Somebody will bite on it," he said and was struck by an idea: the somebody would be him. He would bite on it, just not in the way Mika would have preferred.

"One *per customer*, man," Dante said, at last losing his cool. A heavy-set man with long hair and a wispy mustache had tried to break the rules. Dante sat up a little straighter on his stool, cupped his hands around his mouth. "*Listen.* Anybody else comes up here with more than one of the new Radiohead shits gets *zero. Nada.*" He shook his head and muttered.

"Want me to take over?" Paul offered.

"Nah, but what you can do is give me a count." He slid a leather pouch along the counter. "Stacks."

Paul took the pouch and weighed it in his hands like a fish.

"That's what happens when you sell your record for a buck. And you know what? Half goes to charity, half goes to the shop you bought it from. Support-your-local-record-store type thing."

"Wow," Paul said, impressed. "Credit due."

"Plus the label sent us a bunch of stuff from their catalog. B-sides and demos and all that. So that's been selling like crazy too. Might have to retract my ill will towards Mr. Yorke."

Radiohead. A band that took its name from "Radio Head," track two on side B of the very same Talking Heads record that Bunky held so dear. As Paul went to work counting and logging sales in a spiral notebook—a charmingly archaic system that Mika refused to let go of—he felt as though there was something to be drawn from all of this, some cosmic symmetry that would help guide him, or at least gently suggest next steps.

But he shook the thought away. The money in his hands, the line out the door, the consumerist chaos, the marketing machine, the rollout plan, the mansion in the English countryside where Thom Yorke was sitting cross-legged sipping tea, the fact that there were hundreds of shops around the country right now weathering this exact same storm: all of this made him feel silly for thinking the cosmos was even remotely aware of his existence.

***

The three of them managed to survive the morning surge, which quieted during the lunch hour, only to pick up again two-fold in the afternoon. To handle the crush, they established a system: Paul's assignment was to maintain the line, which filed past a rack where he would dole out a single copy of the new record. He would then filter customers past a bin of catalog material and then on to Dante who handled credit and debit purchases, or to Mika who took cash.

It was the single most profitable day in Dead Wax history, and it wasn't until evening, near closing time, when the crowd had at last slowed to a crawl, that the three of them were able to relax, aglow in the exhausted fulfillment of a job well done. Even Mika seemed to have thawed a bit, or at least she no longer looked at Paul with murderous intent.

To celebrate the day—and to tamp down the creeping shadow of guilt—Paul offered to make a run for beer and burgers. He pooled together their money, hooked a right on Thompson, strode up to a new, minimalist, vegan, can't-believe-it's-not-a-burger joint where the dinner rush was in full effect. The line extended three-deep out the door, four when Paul took up the caboose. He had just spent eight hours feeding a line, now he stood in a line waiting to be fed. The city and its lines. Lines for food. Lines for music. Lines for taxis. Lines for any number of bureaucratic procedures: post office, DMV, ConEd. Hell, he wouldn't have been surprised if there were lines to die. Cemeteries around the city for the particularly well-to-do that made customers wait their turn, promising hand-made, locally-sourced caskets, and vitamin-rich soil with active cultures in which to chuck them.

He trucked it back to the shop clutching a grease-splotched sack of un-burgers and fries in one hand, a bodega six-pack in the other. He wiggled free an index finger and reached to swing open the door, but it held fast, and he nearly toppled backwards with his misfired momentum. Locked. He stooped to peer through the thin slivers of glass left between the smattering of stickers. The lights were still on, and he could hear music, but he didn't see Dante and Mika.

He pounded on the glass.

Nothing.

He stole a handful of fries before they got cold. He pounded again. And again. And again.

Until at last, he could see Dante's shape emerge from behind the counter. He unlatched the door and swung it open.

"What the fuck man," Paul protested. "You guys left me hanging out here. It's freezing and the food's getting cold."

Dante wore a sheepish, sly grin and Paul knew immediately. "No way."

The tell-tale mug of the freshly laid.

"I fucking *knew* it," he said again, and couldn't help but grin right back.

Dante raised a finger to his lips. "Chill, bro. Don't make a big deal of it. Fuck around and ruin a good thing for me."

"Wait, this isn't the first time?"

Dante smirked.

"You son of a bitch."

Paul carried the bags of food and beer and rested it on the counter. From the speakers, Kate Bush yelped "Hounds of Love" from a mixtape of pouty eighties tunes Mika had cobbled together. He couldn't help but wonder if this was what she liked to listen to during sex. He was unloading the food when she emerged from the stock room. She tugged on the hem of her black t-shirt, smoothed it with her palm. She avoided eye contact; this time he knew why.

"Thanks for the spread," she said, nearly whispering, and palmed a burger. It was the first time she had thanked him for anything.

Dante seemed to make an effort to stay as far away as possible from Mika while still sitting at the same counter to eat. For several minutes, the three of them sat and ate and drank quietly as New Order's "Guilty Partner" thrummed overhead.

"Guys," Paul said at last, "stop making this awkward. What are we, in middle school?"

Mika paused mid-chew, spoke through her food without looking up. "Whuhyoumean?"

It was a futile attempt at ignorance: her cheeks bloomed a shade of red that nearly matched the frames of her glasses.

"Just tell me this: am I going to find any surprises on my chair back there?"

"On the chair?" Dante said. "Nah."

Mika crumpled a napkin and chucked it, hitting Dante squarely in the face.

"*What?*" he said. "I said *Nah!*"

"Asshole," she said. "Don't push your luck."

And then, by some divine alchemy, the opening chords of "Shout" by Tears for Fears rang out from the speakers and something about the bombastic goofiness of it made Paul, then Dante, and finally—despite herself—Mika, begin to laugh until the corners of their eyes were wet, and Dante had to unload a ball of chewed food into a napkin lest he choke.

It was, Paul knew, the perfect time to ask.

When they'd regained their composure, he started in: "So listen—"

"Uh-oh," Dante said, "here we go."

"I haven't even said anything yet."

"But you look all earnest. And that's always been dangerous."

"We might be getting a meeting with Stevie Reese."

Mika and Dante looked at each other, then at Paul.

"For real?" Dante said.

Paul nodded. "Catch is, he needs to hear a batch of songs, which we're working to put together as fast as we can." He felt a rush of momentum and possibility as he spoke. "And, you know, I've been working on some new stuff, right? Sampling the voices in my life, almost like I'm making music with the people I'm closest to. And I was thinking that, you know, it could be cool to sample some of your guys' stuff. If you'd give me permission of course."

Dante looked at him funny, almost skeptically. "That's it?" he said.

"What do you mean?"

"You were looking like you were about to ask us for a kidney."

"Is that a yes?"

"Hell *yeah* that's a yes," Dante said. He reached out a palm for Paul to slap. "And when Stevie Reese pauses the track to ask you who's the kid with the flow? You tell him King 'Te is willing to negotiate."

Mika was shaking her head.

"Aw c'mon Mika," Paul said, "I've always respected the hell out of your music. I know you're bummed about your demo and everything, but—"

She shot daggers at Dante. "You fucking told him *that* too?"

Now Dante wasn't so pleased. "Bro, what did I say?"

"That tape is good, Mika. It'll find a home. All I'm saying is I think I could make something special with it. And you'd get final approval of course."

But Mika still couldn't look at him, and suddenly the lightness they'd achieved had vanished.

"What?" he prodded. "What's the deal?"

Mika wiped ketchup from the corner of her mouth with the edge of a napkin and took a swig from a can of beer. "Look. You want to know the truth? It's not even about my music, Paul," she said after finding her calm. At last, she looked at him, her eyes even and cool behind her red frames. "You know I like you, right?"

"No you don't. You hate me."

"I do not *hate* you. Don't take things personally. It's who I am; you should know that by now. I don't know how to say this. In fact, I spent all day thinking about how I *would* say this. But I'm being very honest when I say: I can't trust you anymore."

Paul felt as though he'd been punched in the chest. "You what?"

Dante echoed the question: "You what?"

"I said I can't trust him anymore." She took her glasses off, rubbed her eyes and put them back on. "I know what you've been doing."

Fuck.

He looked at Dante who squinted in confusion.

"The fuck's this about, bro?" Dante said. He turned to Mika. "The fuck's this about?"

"At first, I thought I'd let it slide, you know? That it might just be a one-time thing. But dude, c'mon. From the shop you work at? I mean, what were you even thinking?"

Paul swallowed, hard. The first thing he wondered was: Which record tipped his hand? The second thing he wondered was: Would he get his last paycheck?

"Don't look at me like that," Mika was saying, "all sad and pitiful. This can't be a surprise."

"How did you—"

"That grip of ambient records that came in not too long ago. I remember looking through and seeing Jon Hassell, the *Possible Musics* record, which I'd always heard people go on and on about but had never listened to. Next day, I went through the bins to put it on? Not there. Which was strange cause I thought for sure no one had bought it yet. So the thought occurred to me then, but I figured *No way he's that dumb*, so I chalked it up to shitty memory."

"The fuck is she saying?" Dante said. He looked hurt.

Mika went on: "But it bothered me. And I'm no snoop, but I kept an eye out, you know? Then the same thing happened a few weeks later with some Ben Webster. And again with Os Mutantes. And then *again* with a comp of Sardinian folk."

"Why were you looking for a Sardinian folk record?" Paul protested, foolishly.

The reality of the situation seemed to have dawned on Dante and he flailed his arms, nearly sending his beer tumbling over the edge of the counter. "Bro, you *stole* a record of Sardinian folk?"

Mika crossed her arms. "Thank you," she said.

Paul scrambled for justification that wouldn't sound utterly pathetic. "I took it because—because—" Well, because he'd used some of the jumpy strings as texture for the track he'd built around the sample of Gallo's band. It had worked in the mix, but he knew it wouldn't work as justification for his idiocy.

"And then as Dante and I found ourselves back there," Mika gestured to the stockroom, "your bag was right there, and—"

"You mean when you found yourselves fucking at my desk?"

"Stop it," Mika said, "you brought this on yourself."

"Why didn't you just fire me when you knew?"

"Because," Mika said, "we needed the extra hand. Especially today."

"So then—what now?"

Mika shrugged, relieved the hard part was over. "You stop coming in? Guess we can't stop you from like, shopping here, though it might be awkward. Just don't, you know, steal shit."

Dante ran a hand through his short dreads and looked pained, offended. "I can't believe this," he said.

"I'm sorry, Dante," Paul said. He looked at the floor. To look Dante in the eye was much too painful. He felt worse for tarnishing his friendship than he did about losing the job. "I don't know what to say."

"Don't say shit," Dante said. He shook his head and glanced away for a moment. He seemed to have decided on something and glanced back. "I just can't believe this whole time, when I was trying to *help* you, to give you advice and all that? Convincing Mika to give you your pay up front? You were going behind our backs? Is that what friends do to each other?" He balled up the wax paper that had contained his burger and stood from his stool. "Fuck out of here," he spat. Then he rounded the counter, averted his eyes, and made his way out the door.

Paul was gutted. But for now, he had to risk further shame in the name of survival. "Speaking of checks ..." he said.

"You're kidding," Mika said.

Paul said nothing.

"Consider us even now," she said.

To twist the knife, Talk Talk was belting "The Party's Over" on the stereo as he packed up his things. He was thankful at least that Mika had not made his firing a show of melodrama. He headed for the door, for the anonymous void of the city streets, and let the door close behind him.

***

He woke early, restless and jittery, a spiky unease running beneath the surface of his skin. He felt as though a looming abyss hovered one step behind him and that the only way forward was to avoid looking back. He sat before the grid of rubber drum pads on his MPC. Voices. He was beginning to understand that by sampling the voices in his life—and in the cases of Sara, Gallo, Mika and Dante, the music that accompanied them—he was attempting to breathe life into relationships that were flatlining. It was a gesture of urgency, an act of reaching out. And he knew that for now, it had to happen on wax until he was man enough to enact it for real.

Guilt drove him to Dante first. He called up his friend's Soundcloud page, clicked through the songs on display. When Dante focused, he could really rap. Paul had always felt it, had long tried to encourage Dante to make a serious go at it. But Dante was too grounded to reach. He let things come naturally. His attitude matched his music: his was a wavy flow that perfectly suited the brittle beats he produced himself. Dante treaded his tracks lightly, seeming to hover above them like smoke.

Paul found himself drawn to a recent song called "A Humble Rebuttal (To the Machine in All of Us)" and was touched when he realized quickly it was an ode to Mika, a response to her personal credo. The song began with a spoken word intro that was a single phrase repeated a half-dozen times: *I follow the light I find in you I follow the light I find in you I follow the light...* It was difficult for Paul to imagine Dante issuing those words, letting his guard down in such vulnerable fashion, but it was unmistakable. The beat lurched to life, built upon clattering percussion that sounded like a drawer full of loose bolts and screws being dumped on the ground. Accenting the metallic drums was a whining melody that resembled a dying vacuum cleaner. Mika. It was undoubtedly one of her Drones tracks that Dante had sampled, chopped, and rearranged.

Overtop, he rapped in lilting phrases:

Acting like your heart is black
We both know there's more than that
Under a blood-red moon
I decipher the cracks
in your porcelain skin
where the light gets in

Paul couldn't believe the self-aware openness of the lyrics; they were the best thing he'd heard Dante rap because they were true. He wondered if Mika knew about it, and if she did, what she thought about being the subject of a love song. He ripped down the song, fed the spoken word intro into his MPC. He took the loop Dante had created from Mika's song and left the melody as it was. Then he punched up the drums until they thumped from his speakers and let Dante's spoken words dance over the track.

Next, he searched in his email for a note he'd received from Will several years ago. This was back when they had begun to grow tentatively close before Will had retreated into his own success. His older brother had gone about digitizing some of the family's home movies and sent around the results: shaky snapshots of their small boyhood birthday parties, the Fourth of July parade that used to clamber down Main Street, the special dinner—roasted chicken with yams—Mom had made when Will got his scholarship. The video Paul wanted was taken shortly after he was born and brought home from the hospital. It was the first time Will had been introduced to his younger brother. Their father held the camera and trained the lens on young Will—at that time about six—who sat on the couch in the old living room in wide-eyed anticipation. From frame left came their mother, decked out in a teal sweatsuit and big hair to match, cradling young Paul, pink and ruddy and wrapped in a yellow blanket.

"Here he is," their mother said softly. Their father prodded, "Are you excited to meet your new brother?" Paul could hear him smiling behind the words. Will, who even then had a big dome of black hair, nodded in awe, but didn't say a word. Then their mother lowered the baby into Will's arms, and he held Paul delicately, now and then looking up to his mother, then into the lens, as though to make sure he was doing it right.

"What do you think?" their mother said. "This is your brother, Paul." To which Will simply said, "Paul." After a moment, as the reality of the situation settled in, young Will turned up to the camera and asked as hopefully as he could, "Will we grow up to be friends?"

Paul added decay to Will's question and slowed it down until it was a voice calling out from beyond. It was haunting and sweet in equal measure, and he set it over a slow burn of a beat. Working on the track made him wistful and nostalgic and he had a sudden urge to talk to his brother for the first time in months. Still, it was hard not to think about all the times his parents had shown favoritism to Will growing up and had expressed just a little more brightness with their older son. Every report card was a celebration, every honor roll an excuse for Will's favorite meal. There was the spring day—the day he and Gallo had won the talent show—that Will announced his job offer in Chicago and the signing bonus that came with it. Their mother nearly fainted when she heard the sum. Their father actually clapped.

"See?" he said, glancing in Paul's direction. "Hard work pays off." But Paul couldn't blame his parents; they were merely behaving practically, putting their eggs in the more promising basket.

He fetched his phone, dialed Will's number, and put it on speaker. He listened and waited and envisioned his brother standing in a stainless-steel kitchen, decked in slacks and loafers and a pressed Brooks Brothers shirt that billowed a little around the waist.

"Hello?"

It was Teri.

Somehow, he hadn't prepared himself for the possibility. He heard little Andrew's giggle and coo, the papery swish of Teri adjusting her hold on the phone.

"I *know*, babe," she was saying brightly to the boy, "I *know*." Then, in her skeptical, adult voice: "Yes?"

"Teri, it's me."

"Paul, I mean—jeez. How's everything?" To Andrew, who had begun to squeal: "*Shhh*, babe. It's Uncle *Paul*. Say *hi*? Say *hi*?"

"Gubb," Andrew said. "Bfffff."

"Hey *buuudddyy*. How are *you?*"

"OMMOMMOMM," Andrew said.

Paul had never met the child—Teri was waddling around with an enormous stomach when he saw her and Will in Ohio last Christmas—but he pictured a tiny version of his brother: black hair, dark, expressive eyebrows and a wide mouth that would someday get him into trouble.

"Sorry about that," Teri said, taking back the phone. Andrew squealed again, piercing and shrill, ruing the end of his time in the spotlight.

"How old is he now?" Paul said.

"Ten months."

"Already."

"And more of a handful by the minute."

"Mm."

"Yes you *are*. Yes you *are*."

"So is—"

"Yes. Right. You didn't call to babble with Andrew, did you? Let me see. I know he was doing some work."

Work. At the sound of the word, Paul clenched his teeth and his goodwill soured. *And what work would that be?* he wanted to say. *Researching ill-advised investments? Squandering someone else's nest egg?*

"Look," Teri said, as though she could smell the fumes of his rage over the line, "he's been a mess over this whole thing, Paul. I've never seen him like this. It's eating him up."

And for the first time in his adult life, Paul felt sorry for Will. He had always been the smart one, the successful one. The one for whom things came a little bit easier. And now?

Teri sighed. "I just thought you should know. Let me get him for you."

He heard her set off to find him, thought he could hear a muffled conversation that seemed to stretch a bit too long—Will did not feel like speaking to him, no doubt—before his brother's voice at last broke through.

"Hey."

"Hey."

He could hear Will taking the phone out of earshot, the click of a door shut. "What do you want me to say?"

"I just want to know what happened," Paul said.

"What happened? What happened, Paul, is that I made a fucking—" Will lowered his voice to a hush. "I made a *mistake*, okay? I was trying to help them, you know? Do you know what that means? To help someone? Do you know what it means to think about someone besides yourself for once in your life?"

Paul was taken aback by the desperation in his brother's voice. He tried to remain diplomatic.

"What was the investment?"

"You wouldn't understand."

"Sounds like you didn't quite understand either. That was Dad's pension, Will."

"It wasn't just Mom and Dad."

"What do you mean?" Paul said. But it dawned on him. "Does Teri know?"

"I don't think so." Will was all but whispering now. "But she's going to start to suspect something is up."

"What are you going to do?"

"I'm working on it. But it's going to take some time."

"What are Mom and Dad saying?"

"It's brutal," he said. "I'm surprised they didn't disown me. Or at the very least stop answering my calls."

"They always loved you more," Paul said. He said it without judgment or emotion; it was simply the truth.

"Stop."

"And they forgive you, Will. They told me so over Thanksgiving."

"That's the thing. They say it's going to be okay, but I can tell they don't believe it. It's in their voices. I'm afraid they've given up."

Paul found himself in the position of trying to buoy his brother's spirits. His older brother, Straight A's Will, who always had his shit—and everyone else's so long as they were willing to listen—figured out.

"They haven't given up. We'll fix this."

"How?" Will asked with an edge.

Paul swallowed back a swell of irritation himself. What he almost said was: *Now you're out of answers?* "I sent them a check."

He heard Will scoff. "You what?"

"I said I sent them a check. For ten grand."

"How? You don't have that kind of money."

"I do now. Or did."

"Shit, I don't even want to know how you came up with ten thousand dollars. You don't even have a job."

Paul flinched. "Yes, I do."

"Making music? Working at a record store? That's not a real job."

"You sound just like Mom and Dad. And how did you know—"

"They told me, Paul. But I already knew. Right before this all went down, a client of mine in New York was looking to staff up a new agency. And I thought of you. So that's when

I checked Scrimshaw/Duff's website and lo and behold, your face was no longer amongst all those smug little personal bios and black-and-white headshots. Do I even want to know how long it's been?"

"Look, why can't you just be in this with me instead of being a dick because it wasn't you who came through for once? Why can't you just say, *Hey wow Paul, well done,* or—"

"Is that what you want? Congratulations? You sent Mom and Dad a check to feel better about yourself?"

"Get the fuck out of here," he said, though he felt a pang of truth. "I sent them that money to prove to them that I'm not a total fuck up. And because I want to show support."

"You really want to show support? Come here for Christmas."

This was not how he hoped the conversation would go. He had called Will in a moment of brotherly compassion. Now, as usual, he found himself fighting back anger. "I can't, Will."

"Can't? Or won't?"

"I have work to do."

"And how's that going for you? Huh?" Paul heard Teri's voice in the background and Will spoke away from the phone. "YEAH. *One sec.*"

"I just sent them my whole bank account for God's sake. Let's not forget that the reason I even had to do so is because *you* fucked up their money."

Will inhaled and exhaled and Paul could practically hear the stress eating him from inside out. "Look," he said, "that took balls, okay? I know they'll sure as hell be surprised."

In that moment, Paul pictured his mother and father in their old Explorer, backing down the driveway one last time and he shook away the sting in his eyes.

"But," Will went on, "you know what means more than money? Your presence. Look at it this way: when they're gone, what will you regret?"

The line went dead.

11.

SIX IN THE MORNING, ANOTHER PHONE CALL, THIS ONE INCOMING, unexpected. So unexpected Paul nearly didn't pick up. But a sense of unease made him check to see who it was, to lift his phone from the stack of books by his bed and squint into the glow.

Home.

His parents.

They never called this early. This frightened him and his brain was jarred from the fog of sleep to a wash of worst-case calculations: his mother had fallen, his father's heart had at last succumbed to stress, they'd yet to find a place to live and were on the verge of being out on the street. With a sharp intake of breath, he sat upright in bed, cleared his throat, and answered.

"Dad? Everything alright?"

"What the hell were you thinking?"

"What are you talking about?"

"The check, Paul. What in the hell were you thinking sending me that check?"

"What was I thinking?" Paul got out of bed, rubbed the gunk from his eyes and began to pace around his room. "I—I thought I could help."

"You think I need charity? Is that it?"

"What? No. Of course not. I wanted to make sure you and Mom were okay, and—"

"I've worked my whole life without help, Paul. And now I've got one son making my money disappear, and another sending me a pity check. Where the hell'd you get that kind of money that you could just give it away?"

"I—I don't know what to say. I just thought—"

"Stop." His father took a deep breath and let it out and Paul could hear the air whistle through his nose.

There was a pause.

And then the distinct sound of paper being torn.

"*Dad*," he said.

"There," said his father, "now neither of us has to be concerned with this. Ten thousand dollars. And what did you expect that to fix exactly?"

Paul was stunned. He closed his eyes. "I—I don't know. I hoped it would be something. A cushion. At least until you guys got back on your feet. I just wanted to help."

"A cushion," his father said, as though he'd never heard the word.

"I just don't get it," Paul protested. He looked out his window as purple dawn spread on the low blocks of Red Hook. "How can you be so pissed at me but forgive Will like he didn't just flush your life down the toilet?"

There was another pause, one that underscored the emotional gap that lay between father and son.

"I'm just trying to do what's best."

Paul didn't trust himself to say the right thing in return, so what he said next was: "What does Mom think?"

"Your mother?" his father said. His voice evened at the thought of her. "She doesn't know anything about it. And I'm not going to tell her. She's still asleep. I'm in the basement. What's left of it. Sold off just about everything. This time next week, we'll be gone."

"I know," Paul said. "She sent me the pictures. But that's why I thought the money would—"

"I'll tell you what else. I went into NuWaves."

"And?"

"It was a goddamn insult. Phil Gallo all but asked me if I wanted to be a janitor. Manager of Custodial Services is what he called it. How about that? Your old man pushing around a mop?" At this, he allowed himself a brief burst of laughter. But it didn't sound like him at all: it was high and wheezy and bitter. And it scared Paul.

"Dad?"

"I'd better go before I wake your mother. Then I'd be in real trouble."

He hung up.

Paul stood atop the worn area rug in the center of his room and didn't know what to do. He clutched his phone as though it might provide some answers. It was too early to call anyone— soft light had begun to spill through his grimy window—and who would he even call? Certainly not Will. Not his bandmates. Not Sara or Cassie or Gallo. For a moment, he thought Greg, of all people, might have some words of encouragement, but he feared showing cracks in his armor to anyone who might help the band move forward. Shit, what would he even say? That he'd risked the band—his entire self-conception, really— on some half-baked scheme to kick his parents some money? That he'd stolen a heap of records from his bandmate's family? It all sounded so ridiculous now, so foolish. He could still hear the sandpaper scratch of the torn check and he was surprised to feel a sort of pride in his father for doing it. That at last he'd shown a little anger about the whole mess.

He was too tired to work, too abuzz to sleep, so he began to get dressed. He put on his shoes, coat and hat and went downstairs. Outside, the sun had crested the buildings on Van Brunt and cast long shadows onto the cracked asphalt. A grey layer of frost coated the brown grass of the front yard and Paul could see his breath. He set off in the direction of the water and witnessed the neighborhood stirring to life: the auto body shop down the block hoisted its metal grate with a roiling clang; a cement truck idled with a deep growl, coughing a plume of dark exhaust.

He found himself standing outside of Carlito's and figured he might as well go in and liberate a few items for breakfast. A roll of powdered donuts, maybe a small bottle of orange juice: items that were compact and easy to slip down his pants. He'd never stolen from Carlito before. After all, it was his backyard bodega, and the old man was a sweetheart. No matter what time of day, no matter who walked through his jingling door, he would ring you up and send you off with a grin and his patented phrase: "It's your day, boss."

Paul swung open the door and passed by the counter where a man in a puffy red coat stood ruminating over which scratch tickets held the best odds. Carlito waited patiently, now and then tearing off a ticket from the glossy, colorful spools that adorned the register. Paul went straight to the aisle of snacks opposite the row of refrigerators. Carlito's place, like most bodegas, had two security cameras—one in the rear corner behind a large convex mirror, the other above the door—and the back half of this aisle was a blind spot. Paul knew this because he had made enough legitimate purchases to study the pair of grainy closed-circuit screens behind the counter. The aisle wasn't exactly a cornucopia—mostly bloated bags of chips and sweet treats—but it was better than nothing. Paul eyed a couple of packets of mini donuts: one powdered, one chocolate. He reached for the clear plastic wrapper, and as he did so, the sound of Carlito tearing off a scratch ticket made him stop in his tracks. *Wait a minute.* The hell was he doing? He didn't have to steal anymore. He had more than ten large in his bank account. A giddy laugh bubbled in his throat and before he thought much about it, he snatched up four packages of donuts, a box of coffee cakes and a honey bun. Then he turned and opened the fridge and plucked an orange juice and a peach Snapple. His arms were full, so he deposited his bounty on the front counter where the man in the puffy red coat was fingering crumpled dollar bills to pay for his stash of scratch tickets. Paul nodded a greeting to Carlito before doubling back to the middle aisle for a half-dozen packages of Top Ramen. He wanted to buy more, just because he could, but he was out of ideas, so he grabbed a lavender-scented candle because why the fuck not. Satisfied, he went back to the counter just as Carlito was telling the man in the puffy red coat that the day was his, boss. Carlito turned his attention to Paul, tallied up his stash: a shade over forty bucks, the most money Paul had spent in one place in forever.

"You having a party, boss?" Carlito wanted to know.

"Something like that," Paul said.

Carlito hoisted the plastic bag over the counter, and as he delivered his buoyant refrain, Paul had reason to cautiously believe him.

He made his way to the water's edge, Valentino Park, the same bench where he'd sat with Gallo. He was suddenly ravenous and knocked back two packs of donuts and a coffee cake as he watched the ferry carry a batch of early commuters across the shimmering river into the bowels of the Financial District. Gallo had followed through on his end of the deal. But the same pride that had led his father to tear up the check had led him to view a janitorial position as a wicked insult.

Ten thousand dollars. Money that he could use to help the band. Money that could propel his vision. He just had to figure out a way to use it without arousing any suspicion as to its source. For now, he washed down his saccharine breakfast with bright, pulpy juice. He let his attention fall to the rhythm of the river as it lapped gently against the rocky edge. He attuned his breath to the kiss and retreat of the water, a liquid metronome, a whispered song.

***

Back at the Sweatshop, in the humid funk of their little room, they set to work adding vocals and guts to the bones of Paul's beats, fine-tuning and polishing.

But not *too* much. They left a dash of rawness, a sliver of vulnerability and by the end of the week they had five tracks. Bunky was so focused on the music that he seemed to have forgotten his frustration with Paul. Either that or it was his frustration that drove his focus and resulted in some of the best playing Paul had ever heard from him. He was none the wiser about the stolen records, and the more time passed, the more Paul was convinced he was in the clear.

He was also convinced Bunky and Eloise were sleeping together—she was staying at Bunky's place after all—but if they were, they were careful not to tip their cards. Their evasion hung tension on the edges of the song they called "Lights Go Out," like the fray of a torn love letter. Even in the closeness of their practice space, they avoided eye contact as they traded couplets, enhancing the ambiguity.

On "King Kong," the rumbling slow-roller colored by synth tones built from the shards of his parents' scrambled voices, Paul let the EQ bleed into the red, letting a hint of menace creep into the dreamy textures. Bunky's croon swirled over top for the verses and Eloise picked up the chorus, which took the shape of a warning to shit-talkers, nay-sayers and boastful dilettantes:

You're King Kong. What could go wrong?

They called the up-tempo song, the one assembled from rear-ranged shapes of Gallo's emo-folk, "You'll Never Know (What Your Eyes Do To Me)." The steady pulse of the beat was held together both by Eloise's spiky guitar and the come-ons she exchanged in verse with Bunky. Their words told the tale of a missed connection, two lovers passing each other like ships in the night on the dancefloor.

The fourth track remained an instrumental, a song they called, "Friends," the one that featured Will's boyhood voice. Paul built the beat around a toy piano sample and plunged it in watery reverb. Bunky added a low-end pulse and Eloise thrummed crystalline accents that gave Paul chills.

The fifth song was all crumble and clutter, a trip-hop beat run through a blender, inspired by the spare drums of "Beat Bop," which Paul had listened to again and again before he'd sold it off. The glue of the track was the sample of Mika and Dante—an end-of-the-world drone dappled with Dante's voice—to which Paul added layers of decay until it was rusting at the joints. He peppered in skittering drums and warbling, pitched-down record scratches. The result sounded as if it had been recorded from the depths of a slow-moving iceberg.

And Eloise loved it.

"It sounds like Portishead on codeine," she said.

She took the whole song for herself, not because she asked for it, but because it couldn't have been any other way. She closed her eyes.

Skip town on the back of an alligator
drag my blood in a paper sack
Black tracks clatter after hours
slide by towns and won't look back

Her lips brushed against the mesh spit guard of the microphone. Like syrup, her voice oozed into the spaces and cracks in the beat and she damn near knocked the wind out of Paul's chest. Her voice was irresistible. There was a jagged edge around the contours of her words that let him know she sang from a place few would get to. He wondered how much Bunky knew.

She went on, cupping her hands over her headphones:

Aching veins and bleeding streets
lead to outskirts of dirt and bone
Trust the trodden earth inside me
on this journey all alone

Find myself a dusty mirror
the desert of an empty room
This roaming soul you love about me
keeps me from loving you

The room fell quiet as the song came to a close. Bunky was hunched over his laptop, unfazed as a cat, toying with the mix.

"Damn, El," Paul said, "don't go breaking my heart."

She lifted the headphones from her ears and looked at Bunky. "Again?"

"No," he said and met her gaze, "it was perfect. What should we call it?"

"Crescent Line," she said. Color rose to her cheeks, and she looked at once elated and relieved.

"Goosebumps," Paul said. Yet more than the meadow of little bumps that really had sprouted on his arms, he felt the unmistakable heat of connection blooming between his bandmates.

***

He sat with them at a booth at Flaherty's. Bunky had invited him and Eloise to the staff holiday party. Red and green streamers hung from the ceiling. People milled in groups and drank and sang along to old-timey Christmas songs.

Paul raised a glass, a tumbler of pale whiskey on ice. "I'd like to propose a toast," he said. Bunky followed suit, raising his tumbler. Eloise raised a soda water. "Here's to me," he said and grinned. Bunky rolled his eyes, in on the joke. They had, after all, completed five tracks under the gun. Five tracks they were happy with—even Bunky seemed lighter on his feet—and proud of.

"I'm just saying," he went on. It was his first drink, so the words were still sharp. "If I hadn't lit a fire under our asses, we wouldn't be toasting to half an album."

"Keyword: half," Bunky said. "And by lit a fire do you mean stumbled ass-backwards into a meeting—I should say a potential meeting—with Stevie Reese?"

"Better backwards than not at all."

"This is the worst toast I've ever heard in my life," Eloise said, holding her glass aloft.

"I'll fix it," Bunky said. "To *Eloise* for quickly becoming the glue that holds us together."

"Aw," Eloise said bashfully, "don't make me get all emotional. To you guys, for welcoming me into your family."

"Dysfunctional family," Paul said.

"Wouldn't be family if it wasn't," Eloise said.

They drank.

Then they picked songs from the jukebox. They ordered more drinks and played Big Buck Hunter, and Eloise whooped them both bad. They went downstairs to a low-ceilinged stage and sang karaoke. Bunky picked Joy Division, performing an exaggerated version of Ian Curtis's robotic, dead-eyed spasm. Paul, several whiskies deep by then, butchered "Kiss from a Rose"—he whiffed horribly on both the highs *and* the lows— and was booed off stage. Then Eloise sang "Have You Ever Seen the Rain," and blew the doors off the song and when she finished, the room fell quiet for a moment before someone yelled *HELL YEAH, BUDDY,* and everyone hollered. And no one else went up to sing after that because there wasn't much of a point anymore. But as the clock swept on past midnight, she grew quiet and seemed to withdraw into herself. Bunky didn't notice because he was busy chatting up a blonde at the bar, but Paul noticed, first because he wondered if Eloise was going to say something about it, but then because she hardly said anything at all.

The Christmas songs got louder, and people got drunker, and at one point, the bar went *Ohhhh* when a guy wearing reindeer antlers face-planted on his way out the door. Bunky had his arm around the girl at the bar, so Paul asked Eloise if she wanted to step outside and get some air. She half-smiled and said, *Sure.*

The cold air felt good on their faces after the stuffy closeness of the bar. Eloise withdrew a pack of cigarettes from the pocket of her black parka and plucked one free. She put up her fur-lined hood, hunched and lit a cigarette.

"Picked it up again?" Paul said.

They had wandered halfway down the block and perched on a rail that ramped up to a shuttered storefront. Eloise shrugged, pulled on the cigarette, and let out a plume of smoke that shifted and curled before dissipating in the sharp winter air.

"Figure I gotta indulge in something," she said. She looked away from Paul, down the block, and smoked.

It caught him off guard. His thoughts were whiskey-logged and muddy and hard to parse. This was the first time he'd seen Eloise outwardly struggle. Gone was the lightness in her face, the clarity in her eyes.

"You okay?" It was all he could think to muster.

She flipped her half-finished cigarette into the street where it bounced on the asphalt in a little spray of sparks. She turned to him, jammed her hands into her pockets and shrugged.

"Sure."

He lifted himself up on the rail so that his feet rested on the lower rung. "Is it about Bunky?"

She cocked her head. "How do you mean?"

"You know. Like," he nodded his head toward the bar, "that girl—or whatever."

Eloise squinted. Then it registered. "Ohh. *That?* No. Why would I—no. He can do *whatever* he wants. Trust me."

"No, I mean. Yeah, I was just wondering if, like. You know."

Eloise chuckled and shook her head. At least he had made her laugh a little. But the smile was gone as quickly as it had come, and she sunk her head into her hands as she perched there on the rail. Paul looked at her, helpless. He reached out a hand, then withdrew it. He couldn't see her face, shrouded as it was in the hood of her jacket.

"Hey," he said, as delicately as he could.

Passersby, drunk and loud, cast a side-eye in their direction on their way to clubs and after-parties. He and Eloise must have looked like any other couple, inebriated and sulking over some private grievance.

"I mean, can you tell me what's—"

Eloise lifted her face from her hands and looked at him. Her cheeks were slick with tears.

Paul felt an ache begin to swell through the hazy sponge in his skull. She had always seemed so grounded, so sure of herself, that it rattled him to see her this way.

"It's just, I hate the holidays," she said. "The nostalgia. The fresh starts and all that shit." She wiped away tears with the cuff of her sleeve and sniffed. "My brother, you know." Her bottom lip began to tremble. "He was at some party around this time of year with folks he didn't know too well, and, when you relapse or whatever... he didn't know the stuff he was taking, you know?"

Paul slid closer. He put his arm around her, and she rested her hooded head in the crook of his shoulder.

"I hate the holidays too," he said. And though he wished he had something more profound to offer, it seemed like enough. She nodded against his shoulder.

They were quiet for a moment. Somewhere down the block, a guy hollered, "MERRY FUCKIN CHRISTMAS!"

So Paul drew in and yelled back, "FUCK *OFF*."

Which in turn yielded a big, "FUCK *YOU*."

Eloise laughed a little and the tension in her shoulders seemed to deflate a bit. Paul felt it was safe to ask: "What was he like?"

"Stubborn as fuck," she said. "And to be honest? A total pain in the ass. I remember when I was little and he was in like, junior high, he was always getting nabbed by the cops. He used to run with this crew of little turds—that's what my dad used to call them—graffiti, shoplifting, all that stuff. I guess he got comfortable with it too because when he got really sick, he started stealing stuff from my parents." She shook her head. "That totally killed me. I have *no* respect for people who steal." When she said it, Paul's ears got hot, but he nodded along. "But he was really warm too, you know? He was good with people. His dream was to own a restaurant. And he always looked out for me."

"What was his name?"

Eloise shook free another cigarette, lit it, and took a puff, and Paul could tell she did it to keep herself busy lest she lose herself again. "Robert, but my parents always called him Slim growing up. Because he was like a string bean," she held her cigarette up as a visual cue, "and because my dad thought it was some kind of homage to the blues: Slim Harpo, Guitar Slim, Lightnin' Slim. I think my dad secretly wished he had been a musician. Probably why I'm sitting here next to you."

"Bunky and I are lucky," Paul said.

Eloise shook her head. "You don't have to say that."

"It's true. No chance we'd be together if you didn't come along. We probably would have killed each other."

Eloise glanced at him from her periphery. "He would have killed you," she said dryly.

"Nah, I'd hold my own."

She looked at him skeptically.

"I *would.*"

"Mm."

Her lips slid into a smirk and Paul knew she was feeling better.

"Let me ask you something," he said. "You and Bunky really aren't together? Because I could've sworn—"

She rolled her eyes like she'd explained it a thousand times. "No, Paul. Me and Bunky are *not* together. He's a good friend and bandmate, but I don't see him that way. And you want to know something else? I don't see *you* that way either. Or him. Or him." She began to nod around at passersby, at the small scrums mingling outside the bar. "Or *him.*" Then she looked at Paul, arched her brows and shrugged. "You know?"

The gears began to whir in his brain until they locked into place. He must have looked like a fool because Eloise laughed again.

"You look like I just told you there's no Santa Claus," she said. Then her smile fell away. "You don't like, have a *problem*, do you?"

Paul snapped up with a jolt. "What? *No.* Absolutely not. It's just—you know, when you think about someone a certain way and—"

"And how did you think of me exactly?" Eloise flipped away the nub of her cigarette with a flourish, folded her arms tightly across her chest.

"Um. I don't know. That you were pretty and cool and—"

"Oh my Lord, Paul. Confirming for me once again I'm not missing out on a damn thing."

"Shit. That didn't come out right. You *are* beautiful and cool and—I mean, whoever she is? She's going to be lucky and—you know what? I'm just going to shut the fuck up."

Eloise brushed the hair back from her face beneath her hood. "I think that's probably smart."

"Let me just say this," he said, desperate to tell her how he really felt. "You're like, the kind of person I want to be."

"Paul, stop."

"For real."

The wind began to pick up and with it, the stench of trash from the piles on the sidewalk.

"What about you, then?" she said. "Got anybody?"

He shook his head. Hell, how deep did he want to go? "Not at the moment."

"But there was somebody?"

He nodded.

Eloise gestured with a hand that she'd tucked inside her sleeve for warmth. "And?"

"And she left. For L.A. She got a big opportunity out there."

"Why didn't you go with her?"

"I'm not so sure the door was open."

"Well, shit. Did you tell her you wanted to go?"

He shook his head.

"Did you love her?"

He paused. Then he nodded.

"Did she *know* you loved her?"

For a moment, he sat there on the rail, hunched against the cold, and thought about why he never told her. Why he had been afraid to go after the only thing he ever really wanted. It was easier, he knew, not to risk hearing she didn't love him in the same way. It would have been unbearable.

He shook his head.

"God, Paul. You're breaking my fucking heart, and somehow, I still have no sympathy for you."

"Listen, I'm dying for a drink," he said and meant every word of it. "You want to head inside? See how Bunky's doing?"

"I would love nothing more," she said.

They shoved off the railing. Paul jammed his hands, pink and stiff from the cold, in the pockets of his coat. "Look, I'm—"

Eloise shook her head. "Don't get all mushy and apologetic or some shit. We're fine. Okay? You're drunk and I'm emotional, and this time of year is always a disaster anyway, so, if anything, I should thank you for keeping tradition. Wait, what are you—"

Paul felt a surge of something like faith in that moment. He looked at Eloise and was *certain* they were going to make it.

He went in for a hug.

At first, Eloise was rigid, as though a big dog had begun to slobber on her face, but Paul didn't budge, so she started to relent, relax, and laugh. She patted him gamely between the shoulder blades.

"Okay. Alright. Okay. Paul? That's good."

He pulled away and followed her inside.

Somehow the bar was more crowded than when they had stepped out. The music was louder, the atmosphere muggier. Paul went straight to the bar and ordered a whiskey, drank it quickly, then ordered another. He and Eloise shouldered through the crowd, craning their necks in search of Bunky. It gave them something to do together that wasn't talking. They looked in the photo booth. They looked downstairs. They looked and shrugged and acknowledged what they both knew to be true: he was gone.

"At least one of us is getting laid," Eloise said over the music. "Guess I get the bed to myself tonight."

"Same," Paul said.

Eloise laughed, and he did too, and when he felt the shadow of pain begin to peek around the corner, he laughed harder to chase it all away.

12.

PAUL SPENT A FEW DAYS HUNKERED DOWN IN HIS APARTMENT, ADRIFT in the temporal molasses of pre-holiday December. He listened to records, futzed with samples, and talked to no one, until his bubble was punctured one evening by a phone call from Gallo.

"So did you say anything?" he wanted to know.

"Zero."

"Oh, thank God," Gallo said. The clamor of sound check bubbled in the background.

"I'm curious though. Why do you care so much? You didn't like, kill anyone."

Gallo sighed. "Because that's not what I'm about. And besides, it's not a great look if my fans find out the guy who wrote 'Your Heart is the Home I Want to Live In' is, you know, blowing lines off half-naked girls. Or fucking over friends or stealing credit for songs."

"But you did do those things. And you're a rock star now."

"Nah," Gallo said, though Paul could tell he was saying it through a tempered smile, reveling in the possibility.

"Where you guys at?"

"D.C.," Gallo said. "Just got here from Philly. Boston before that. After this we take a short break for the holidays."

"How's it all going?"

"Surreal, man. All sold out so far. And we just got news that 'Angel' got picked for one of Spotify's top playlists."

Paul knew most of this of course, because the kid couldn't help but share it all over Instagram. The band loading up the tour van. A selfie of Gallo drawing all over his guitarist's sleeping face as the world whirred by out the window. An image of the marquee in Boston, FEATHERS looking even goofier up there in big block letters. *Truly humbled*, read the caption on the post. A screenshot of "Angel" nestled amongst a bunch of other schmaltz on a playlist dubbed, *Fauna*. Whatever the fuck that meant.

"What about Stevie? Any news?"

"He really digs the songs you sent me."

Paul stood up at his desk. "Get the fuck out."

"He wants to meet you guys."

"Don't fuck with me."

"Swear on my life."

"When?"

"Right after the New Year. His office."

Paul pumped his fist like he'd just nailed a deep jump shot. It took everything he had not to leap onto his bed and jump up and down. "Fuck, that's *massive*. Bunky is going to shit. He liked the songs?"

"That's what he told me. Straight up."

"This could be big, Gallo. Huge." He paced his room like a giddy kid.

"It will be big. But listen, I need to roll. D.C. awaits."

"Good luck tonight."

"Appreciate that, brother. Hey, did your dad—"

"Yeah." Paul stopped pacing.

"And?"

"The offer was ... it was to be a janitor, Gallo."

"And?"

"What do you think? My dad is in his sixties."

"Look, I did what I could. Really."

"I know," Paul said, "I know. And I appreciate it."

"Anything for a friend," Gallo said.

***

Two days later, it was Christmas.

He'd slept fitfully, tossing and turning, now and then waking up with a thin collar of sweat ringing his neck. His body was abuzz, his brain awhirl, not unlike how he had felt as a kid waiting to bound into the living room to see what Santa had brought. But in place of innocence and joy was a murky haze of emotions. On the one hand, he was thrilled, riding high on the Stevie news and Bunky's reaction to it. As soon as he had hung up with Gallo, he texted Bunky. The reply had been a string of a dozen exclamation points. This time, his plan had worked. On the other hand, it was Christmas, and he was away from his family. His father was furious with him. And his parents were no closer to digging their way out of financial collapse. He had never felt farther away.

During a soggy cereal breakfast spent absently thumbing his phone, he received a text from Eloise inviting him to a *Big-azz Xmas feast* with Bunky at a Sichuan joint in the city down on Pell Street. He agonized over his reply—simple decisions became paralyzing when his anxiety reared its ugly head—and in the end decided to pass. Today he just wanted to be alone.

Eloise was right: the holidays sucked. For him they always seemed to descend with a wan feeling of inertia, of sadness, a feeling that happiness and wonder was just out of reach. It was a gummy, foggy feeling, and the only cure, or really, the only stopgap, was work.

He'd settled into his metal folding chair and begun to cycle through some unused samples when his phone rattled again.

Will's number.

He braced for impact and answered.

"Merry Christmas, love."

It was his mother. She sounded tired, but she also hadn't called him *love* in years.

"Merry Christmas, Mom."

He waited for her to address the check, his father's lingering resentment.

"Everyone here misses you," she said instead, "even little Andrew." Andrew shrieked and whined somewhere in the background, and he could hear Teri's melodic calming shush. "A lean Christmas for all of us I guess."

He absently set about straightening the clutter on the surface of his desk as it occurred to him: his father hadn't mentioned a thing.

"Have you and Dad found a place?"

There was a pause. "We move in at the end of January."

"And you're with Will until then?"

"Mm. I never thought we would be renting again."

"Where's the place?"

Another pause. "It's Christmas, Paul. Let's talk about something else. What are your plans today?"

His instinct was to push, but a part of him was afraid to find out, to dive too deep into his parents' frustration. To do so would be to acknowledge that life could still find ways to let you down well into the autumn of your years. That things didn't get easier just because you'd been doing them longer.

"Going to dinner with my ... friends," he said. "A place in Chinatown."

"Chinese on Christmas. That sounds pretty good."

His next instinct was to tell her about the band, the progress they'd been making, the meeting with Stevie Reese. That things were finally turning a corner. But he simply couldn't bring himself to say any of it. It was Christmas, after all. Instead, he told his mother he loved her, told her he'd see her soon, even if he didn't believe it was true. She went off to find his father and Paul waited tensely on the line for his voice to break through, but Will picked up the phone instead, and Paul knew that his father didn't want to speak to him.

"You should be here," Will said.

"C'mon, Will. It's Christmas."

"Exactly."

"Well, at least Mom seems to be in fairly good spirits."

"All things considered."

"How's Dad?"

Will breathed heavily into the receiver. "He's been in a rough mood. I think the reality is starting to sink in."

"He tore up the check."

"He what?"

"I said he tore up the check. The one I sent him. He called me the other day, like six a.m. and tore it up with me on the line."

"Brutal."

"Yeah. He was furious."

There was a pause, and Paul could see Will pinching the bridge of his nose, trying to think.

"Look," he said. "You think he's pissed at you? Imagine how he feels about me. He looks me in the eye and tells me he forgives me, but how could there not be anger? It kills me. But I'll tell you this: more than you or me? He's angry with himself. That he'd ever put himself in the position to even need financial support from his kids. He feels like he failed. Failed himself. Failed his family. For Dad, it's like, shameful, you know? A knock on his manhood. His ability to provide. Shit. Is he stubborn? Of course. But guys like Dad? They get a picture of who they're supposed to be drilled into their heads as kids. That's got to be tough, maybe impossible, to shake."

"But it was ten grand."

"You're not listening to me. What I'm saying is that he'd never be able to forgive himself if he took it. You remember the time he took us to Riverfront to see the Reds? Those seats we had?"

"Of course. Dad almost knocked himself out diving for a foul ball. How could I forget?"

"You know how we got those tickets?"

"I mean, he said he splurged a bit."

"No. His boss gave them to him. Told him his boys deserved to see a little baseball with their dad."

"How the hell do you know that?"

"I heard him telling Mom. I'll never forget it. He didn't want to take the tickets. What he wanted to do was tell his boss to shove it and stay out of his business. But Mom convinced him that A) it would not be the smartest career move, and B) that we did deserve to see a little baseball with our dad. You were young so you probably don't remember, but he said like five words that whole trip. But even then, I knew it wasn't about his boss. It was about himself. You understand?"

"Why wouldn't Mom tell me where they're moving?"

"She's embarrassed."

"Tell me where."

"A one-bedroom off Girard. Near the old library."

"That's not a great area."

"There's not much of a choice."

"Fuck."

"Well, you know what you can do? Be here to help them move."

"I don't know, man. I don't know if I could bear it. And besides, this music thing is starting to pick up. Hopefully by then we'll—"

"Paul. Think hard about what you're doing."

"Trust me. I have."

"No. I mean really take some time and think—" Somewhere in the background, Teri shouted Will's name in a way that demanded his attention. "Shit. I gotta go. Andrew just spit up all over the carpet."

"Merry Christmas, Will."

"All I'm saying is: God knows I've made plenty of mistakes, so I can't tell you how to live your life. Just know that you don't have to prove anything to anyone except yourself. Merry Christmas."

13.

Bunky approached the intercom and mashed one of the buttons. After a moment, a woman's voice crackled through: "Reese Management."

"Yeah, They Is here for Stevie?" Bunky's voice rose an octave as he spoke, as though he was asking for permission. Paul couldn't remember the last time he'd seen his bandmate nervous.

"I'm sorry. They what?"

"Is."

"Is?

"They Is. That's the name of our band." Bunky shook his head in frustration, but for Paul the angular pretension of their name was pulled into sharper focus.

There was a yawn of staticky silence.

"We're here to see Stevie Reese? We have a meeting? He told us to come here, so we're here."

"One minute."

Bunky shrugged as they waited, and the three of them stood about wordlessly, trying to huddle against the cold in the little doorway alcove. Paul nodded west, down Fourteenth Street and they watched a family of tourists, a mother, a father and two young girls, shoulder their way toward the elevated park of the Highline as the vicious wind whipped off the Hudson. He couldn't help but think that he and his bandmates were something like tourists in their own right.

"You're allowed up," crackled the voice, and with a cell block buzz, the door unlocked and Bunky yanked it open.

At the top of a narrow staircase, the young woman who'd buzzed them in held open an enormous aluminum slab door, set on rollers, as though summoning them into a bank vault.

"Hi," she said, sleepy and expressionless. She wore her hair gathered up on top of her head with a pencil jammed through it. Her flowing black blouse left her forearms exposed. On one of them, a block of text was inked in cursive on her dark skin. Paul tried and failed to read it as she ushered them in and let the aluminum slab roll closed with a metallic clunk.

"Have a seat," she said without introducing herself. She pointed to a sleek bench with white leather cushions in the little anteroom. "Stevie will be with you in a sec." Then she disappeared behind a partition into the high-ceilinged open space just beyond.

The three of them were quiet, as though waiting at the doctor's office for a diagnosis. Bunky pumped a leg up and down. Eloise nibbled at a hangnail. Glitchy electronic music trickled like half-frozen water from the speakers overhead. The murmur of office chatter. The faint clack of typing. The tonal pulse of ringing phones. All of it unseen from Paul's vantage. Occasionally, an employee passed by the threshold—decked in the dark hues of the creative class—and eyed them with profound disinterest. Then Stevie's voice grew nearer.

"With all due respect, Mitchell," he was saying, "fuck you. We won't do it for less than forty-per-cent. If it's a no-go, you just say the word and we'll happily book the Gramercy where they'd bang a dolphin to get us." Paul exchanged a glance with Eloise.

"Yeah, you do that. Have a think and get back to me. Happy fucking New Year." Stevie turned the corner as he hung up his phone and slid it into his pocket.

"Knob," he muttered to himself. To the three of them, as though they'd all been on the line together: "Those fascists at Downtown Live think they run this fucking city." He shook his head. "Hnh nh. Nah."

He wore a blue oxford with the shirtsleeves doubled back to reveal sleeves of ink. A chrome watch occupied his wrist. Crisp Nikes blessed his feet. Paul knew his story. The one he read in *New York*. Until recently, he had still lived at home. Home just happened to be an airy Brooklyn Heights brownstone his parents bought during the wave of deregulation in the eighties. They were both financiers—hedge-funders—and had put up the money for their son's fledgling project. Since then, Stevie had managed to become something of a tastemaker and had amassed a roster of dozens of creatively adventurous bands, and a small handful that paid all the bills.

"I've been looking forward to this meeting all morning," Stevie said and rubbed his hands together.

Paul stood up. Bunky and Eloise took his cue. "Stevie, this is the crew," he said.

Stevie stepped toward them and extended a hand. "Eloise, I presume. And you must be Bunky. Where the hell'd your parents come up with a name like that?"

Bunky flinched. "Long story."

"Save it," Stevie said. Then: "Dee Gallo spoke very highly of you guys."

"Gallo's a good friend of mine," Paul said.

Stevie snapped his fingers and pointed. "And that right there is *exactly* why I maintain a healthy amount of skepticism when my artists recommend shit. Last time I saw you, you were drunk as a lord. But Gallo's such an angel I'd be surprised if he's ever told a lie in his life."

Paul let the comment linger in the air before Stevie clapped his hands to break the silence. "Well fuck," he said. "Follow me."

He led them into an open and spacious work floor. The windows on the far wall of exposed brick looked down onto Fourteenth. Skylights in the ceiling cast long rectangles of sun onto a distressed concrete floor. The room was impeccably stylish; large-scale black-and-white concert photos were hung about in tasteful white frames: rappers, rockers, crowd-surfers. A cluster of brushed aluminum desks were spaced evenly around the room. The individuals who sat at them looked as though they had stepped off the slides of a marketing deck about the target demo: young men and women of all colors and creeds, piercings and tattoos, beards and flannel, chopped hair and angular clothes, each of them pecking at slim MacBooks. They hardly acknowledged Paul, Bunky and Eloise as Stevie led them to a conference room. He slid back a glass door to a room with a rustic wooden table around which funky, mismatched chairs were positioned. In one of them sat a man with long, straight hair, a stubby beard, and ice-blue eyes.

"Here they are," Stevie said to the man as he slid shut the glass door. "Or should I say, here They Is." He snorted, pleased with his own joke, and instructed them to sit down. With a nod, he introduced them to his lackey. "Kids? Meet Malcolm. He keeps this place humming. Without him, the gears would jam."

"It's true," said Malcolm, humorlessly and with the faint burr of Eastern Europe.

"As you can tell, he's got the personality of a spatula. But he also happens to be my eyes and ears."

"I enjoyed your songs," Malcolm said without the slightest hint of a heartbeat.

Paul clocked Bunky turning red, flattered. Stevie took a seat at the head of the table and popped his open palms on the wood. "I gotta admit I only listened to two of those tracks. But I liked both of them. Malcolm, which ones did I like?"

"'Friends' and 'Crescent Line'."

Stevie pointed at his assistant. "What did I tell you about this guy? Thank you, Malcolm-san." He looked at Paul. "You got the goods?"

Paul gestured toward Bunky, who dug in his backpack for the disc he'd burned—this under special instruction from Gallo—and handed it to Stevie.

Stevie weighed it in his palm. "Feels heavy," he said. "Your boy Gallo said there's some goodies on here. Hope he's right. Shall we?"

"Long as you're ready," Bunky said with fresh resolve.

Stevie looked at Paul, thumbed at Bunky. "Kid's got cojones. I like that." He handed the disc to Malcolm, who in turn placed it on a tray that retreated silently into a sleek black console built into the wall. At this, Stevie cupped his hands around his mouth and shouted, "*Miranda*." In an instant, the music coming from the speakers in the main room faded down.

The familiar bump of "Lights Go Out" jumped from discreetly inlaid speakers above. Eloise's icy guitar. The jigsaw horns. Bunky and Eloise exchanging vague come-ons. Through it all, Stevie sat with his eyes closed, fingers a steeple beneath his nose. Malcolm stared at a point on the opposite wall. Paul stole sideways glances at Bunky and Eloise, who themselves sat still, jaws set. Was this really how fates were decided in this business? In conference rooms? He set about making music to get out of conference rooms. It all seemed so tremendously bizarre. Stevie there swaying as though to a shaman's chant. Malcolm boring a hole through the wall with those chilly blues.

The first song faded out. Stevie opened his eyes, looked first at Eloise, then at Bunky with a sly grin. "You two are fucking, aren't you?"

Bunky and Eloise traded looks.

"You know what? Doesn't matter. Whatever it is, keep doing it."

Before he could dig any further, the liquid stomp of "King Kong" cut him off and his eyes were closed again, and his head slid forward and back on his neck.

Paul's head swam. Was this going well? Who the hell knew? "King Kong" faded out, "You'll Never Know" faded up, and then, in less than twenty minutes, the disc ended.

Again, Stevie's eyes clicked open, and he searched their faces, one, two, three.

Then he slapped the table with his palms and the three of them jumped.

"Malcolm. Get the disc."

Malcolm obeyed, handing the disc to Stevie, who palmed it and breathed in and out through his nose as though to settle himself. With a clean flick of both wrists, he snapped the disc in two. Bits of iridescent plastic sprayed about the table.

Bunky started in his seat. "*Whatthefuck*," he yelped.

Eloise leaned back in her chair and eyed the door as though planning her escape. Malcolm wordlessly set about sweeping up the little plastic bits with his hands. Paul knew right then Stevie was batshit. Hell, you had to be batshit to manage bands. To place your well-being in the hands of people like him. Stevie held up the two jagged pieces of the disc like sacrament. He spoke as though issuing a verdict.

"This? This is good. If it wasn't, you'd already be gone. I'm not here to blow smoke up your culos." He pointed at each of them in turn. "Know what you're going to do tonight?"

Paul looked around at his bandmates. They were as stunned as he was.

Stevie looked at Malcolm. "Are they deaf?"

"Stevie would like to know if you know what you are going to do tonight," Malcolm said. "Related to the songs we just listened to of course."

"Um," Eloise ventured, "lock our doors and pray we don't wake up to you watching us sleep?"

"So nice of you to join the conversation," Stevie said brightly. Then his face fell. "No. Wrong. What you're going to do is you're going to set up a Spotify account for the band, okay? You are aware of its existence, yes?"

Paul squinted.

"Oh, don't give me that," Stevie said. "I know all about you record dorks."

"Yes," Bunky said. "We are aware of Spotify."

"Well, fan-fucking-tastic. Malcolm here will hook you up with an invite and you're going to upload two songs. And which two songs are you going to put up?" He locked his glare on Paul.

"Uh," Paul said.

Stevie's lips twitched and he seemed to delight in seeing him squirm.

"'Lights Go Out' and 'You'll Never Know?'"

Stevie shook his head. "Incorrect. Know why? I'll tell you why. 'Lights Go Out' is your best song. You never want to blow your load too quick." He waved a finger at Paul and Bunky. "You two know all about that, I'm sure." He raised a second finger. "And two, I can detect in 'You'll Never Know' a clearly identifiable sample. Which, does Gallo know about that?"

Paul could feel the burn of Bunky's glare and knew exactly what he was thinking, that he'd gone and fucked up again, put them in a jam. But Paul nodded. "He approved it. Gave us his blessing. Told you he and I went way back."

Stevie slapped the table again, but this time they were properly prepared. "You're not as dumb as you look, you know that? Any other samples hiding in there we should know about?"

Paul pulled at the wiry hairs on his chin and thought about the bits of music from Sara, Mika and Dante that he'd used.

"Fuck," Stevie said, "now you're making me nervous. I don't like being nervous. I prefer to make other people nervous."

"No," Paul said finally.

"No, what?"

"No other samples."

"You better not be shitting me, bucko. Because the goal here is to sell some records, is it not?"

Paul nodded.

"Hell, don't look too excited. Of course the goal is to sell some fucking records." Here he futzed with his rolled-up sleeves and calmed himself. "And speaking of records, five songs does not an album make. So. You're going to start a Spotify account and you're going to post 'King Kong' and the, uh, the other one, the instrumental." He squeezed the air as though the words might materialize from it.

"Friends," Malcolm said, expressionless.

Stevie snapped his fingers. "Yes. 'King Kong' and 'Friends.' And then you're going to go back to whatever little hole you came from and cook up some more tunes. But first, we're going to book you a show. We need to get some labels to start sniffing around."

Paul sat up a little straighter and felt his bandmates do the same.

"Labels?" Bunky said.

"Malcolm," Stevie said, "look into getting these guys out to L.A. end of this week. Hotel Café, The Mint. One of those joints."

Malcolm made little notes on a spiral pad.

"L.A.?" Paul said. "End of this week?"

Stevie glared at him, his stone eyes incongruous beneath that boyish haircut. "That a problem?"

Paul shook his head vigorously. "Absolutely not." But he felt a knot tightening in his stomach and could see the contours of Sara's face begin to take shape in the corner of his memory.

"Let me ask *you* something," Eloise cut in. "Why are you doing this?" She'd been mostly quiet throughout the meeting. Now she spoke with a suspicious edge.

Stevie maintained his stare. Paul caught Malcolm fire a glance from the corner of his eye, anticipating, no doubt, the eruption that was surely to come. "That's a hell of a question, isn't it," Stevie said. To Paul and Bunky, he said: "You two better keep her around. She's going to save your asses someday."

"She already has," Paul said, shaking free from drifting thoughts, "trust me."

"I'm doing this, Eloise," Stevie said, "because I see potential here. And in case you haven't noticed, things move very quickly nowadays with this whole internet superhighway, social media, hollow-brained attention span thing they got going. Therefore, I must move quickly."

"But isn't there such a thing as too quickly?"

"For you? Of course. But not for me. You want to talk frankly? We'll talk frankly. I bring you on and what's the worst that can happen? We press up a record, hook you up with a publicist, get you on tour and ..."

"No one gives a fuck," Bunky said.

"Right. I sink some time and money. Work hard to get you opportunities that you poop all over. You fade away into oblivion, back from whence you came. But guess what? I'm still here. I've got bands," he looked at Paul, "like your boy Gallo perhaps, to keep the lights on. But. And this is the thing: I pass on you and you connect? All the kiddies out there start arguing about who was a fan of yours first? I hear one of your songs in an ad for Fancy Feast or some shit? I'd look back on this meeting and want to cram my head into the corner of this fine maple table. See? I don't want to miss. And you?" He chuckled. "You won't miss with me. So, consider this a free consultation. And if I hear that you've been talking to anyone else?" He let the question linger as a threat. "Malcolm here will frown you to death. Ain't that right Malcolm?"

On cue, as though they'd rehearsed this routine a thousand times, Malcolm smiled.

14.

PAUL STARED BEYOND THE SCREEN OF HIS LAPTOP AT THE BLANK WALL where fine fissures had emerged in the plaster. He felt as if those same fissures had begun to web their way into his subconscious.

He found himself drifting into thoughts of Sara, trying to decide if he should reach out, to tell her about the L.A. show. He began to scroll his feed for photos of her. He had tried to avoid doing so since she'd left, to avoid the pain it might inflict. But seeing her, he felt, would help him decide what to do. He couldn't bring himself to search her name—a pointless boundary he had imposed on himself—so to get to her, he had to sift through the bloat of other people's lives. A flood of vacation photos from Spain. Hawaii. A place in Greece he couldn't pronounce.

Scroll.

Sunsets. Babies. Sandy feet. Always with the feet.

Scroll.

And there she was. The real reason he maintained an account to begin with. His pulse raced when he saw her face. His hands left a film of sweat on his phone. He scanned the context of the photo and realized with a wave of lightheadedness that he was holding his breath. She stood with a small group—tanned limbs, catalog teeth—beneath an arc of candied neon at the mouth of a pier. A watercolor sunset exploded beyond. The photo had been snapped before the group had settled into their camera-ready faces; mouths were caught open, gestures softened with faint blur: the self-conscious, anticipatory seconds before the crucial moment. Sara was the only one smiling in earnest. She wore a tank top and shorts, and her exposed skin was tanned and healthy. Next to her stood a guy who had been caught pointing, as though issuing instructions to the photographer. *A guy who takes control.* He was taller than Paul. And he wore cooler clothes: slim black jeans, white t-shirt with slick geometric designs. Was he good-looking? Well, sure, if you put a gun to Paul's head. But it didn't much matter, because he was holding Sara's hand—fingers interlaced and everything—and she looked happy. The cruel trick of social media was brought into sharper relief: the illusion of proximity. She was right *there.* If asked, he could say precisely what she'd been doing yesterday at approximately this time. He could see she'd cut her hair. That her legs looked fine as ever. A pair of legs you could climb. And yet, she couldn't have been more unclimbable.

He decided right then and there: he would text her. He would reach out, as a friend of course, and invite her to the show. All she could do was say no. But he had a feeling, deep in his gut, that she would accept the invitation and he would see her. He stopped short of indulging in the hope of some sort of fresh start; for now, the idea of seeing her in person was enough.

He was about to set down his phone when a post caught his eye, one in which Gallo had been tagged. Several hundred likes. A screed of comments. It was a photo from the *Chicago Tribune* that linked to a review of a show his band had played on their way across the country. "Feathers Take Flight," shouted the headline, "and they're bringing Americana to new heights."

The photo captured Gallo at the mic, mouth wide, the ropes of his neck taught as he belted one of their bouncy songs. Paul scanned the article: "infectious melodies ... front man Dee Gallo is having fun and it shows ... a breath of fresh air ..." *Mother-fucker was really doing it.*

Instinctually, he called up the page for the Spotify account he and Bunky and Eloise had set up after their meeting at Reese Management. As Stevie had instructed them, they'd uploaded the two tracks: "King Kong" and "Friends." An invite from Malcolm and two WAV files. That was it. That's all it took to take the songs from sacred, obscure, and private to sacred, obscure, and public. It had been oddly anticlimactic. When the songs went live, there were no streamers from the ceiling. No MacArthur Grants. Things were exactly the same as they had been, except perhaps worse: whereas before the songs rested safely in the security of Bunky's thumb drive, the possibilities for success and acclaim still endless, now they were out there in the ether of the internet where failure and insignificance were not only an option, but a mathematical likelihood. The little counter that marked the number of plays was static. Stevie's machine had yet to whir to life.

Next, he called up his bank account, entered his password and closed his eyes. He opened them, flinched at the number. Though his account was fuller than it had ever been, the sight of the figure made him feel empty as an abandoned well. The money wasn't his. His instinct was to figure out how to get rid of it, or at least spend it in a productive way. This, of course, meant spending it on the band, but he couldn't for the life of him understand how he would manage to do so without showing his hand. Bunky and Eloise knew he was living check to check. Acknowledging his funds meant having to come up with an alibi, and this reality was exhausting. He clicked out of the browser window and looked to the floor where Bunky's signed copy of *True Stories* sat atop a stack of records. He still had visions of the day he presented the record as a gift. A day when the band had broken through, and they could afford to laugh about it all. For now, he sat in his lonely studio with a fraudulent bank account and a tenuous dream. *Sink or swim.* Just like Bunky's knuckles proclaimed. Here he was, treading water, feeling the pull of the undercurrent, keenly aware of the murky depths that awaited his collapse.

***

He'd never been to L.A. Hell he'd never been west of the Mississippi. And for that matter, Eloise hardly had either, despite the fact that she'd grown up at its nexus. It was the two of them then, in the cab from LAX, who craned their necks to absorb the skinny, looming palm trees, the empty blue sky, the bungalows nestled in the hills. Bunky, of course, had traveled. He sat between them in the backseat unfazed, pecking at his phone, uploading photos to the Instagram page they'd set up for the band. He'd been quiet since they left New York, and Paul knew this meant he was anxious. Paul was anxious too, but he didn't want to show it, so he channeled his angst into gentle ribbing of his bandmate; he considered it his duty to get Bunky to lighten up. He tried to give Bunky shit for his new haircut; he'd let his haphazard buzz cut grow out and had it arranged into a clean fade with a whip-smart part. "Rivers Cuomo if he lost his glasses," Paul said to him as they boarded the plane, but Bunky's forced smile looked so pained that he resolved to leave his bandmate alone. Eloise, on the other hand, was wide-eyed.

"This is surreal," she said, almost to herself, and Paul found it hard to argue. The Hollywood sign drifted by in the distance as they cruised along the freeway. It looked cheap, almost fake, as though someone had placed the letters there on that arid hilltop as a blueprint for a grander statement, then got lazy and forgot all about it.

"You guys crack me up," Bunky said at last. "You'd think we just landed on Mars and not the 101."

"Let us have our moment, Mr. Jaded," Eloise said. "It's just hard to believe this is really happening."

Paul hadn't been entirely convinced it *was* happening until they'd checked into the hotel—a chicly slapdash boutique joint in West Hollywood—and he read the little *Welcome!* card on his pillow with his name on it. He just kept expecting a small disaster to bring it all crumbling down—a declined credit card, a lost reservation, a phone call from Stevie alerting them that it was all a big mistake—but no such thing happened. They'd managed, through a messy cocktail of luck, hard work, and borderline blackmail, to secure a label showcase, for real record labels in L.A.

They opted not to celebrate. To do much of anything the night before the show would have been premature, bad luck even; it would be an early night. Paul had the itch to do *something*, to enjoy the warm January air. After a few hours holed up in his room watching highlights for sports he didn't care about, he got dressed again and went up to Eloise's floor. He could see the light burning beneath her door. He knocked.

"Late night food run?"

"Ugh. You didn't have enough pizza? How can you eat?" Eloise palmed her stomach. She had on sweatpants and a white t-shirt rolled at the sleeves. For what felt like the first time, she wasn't wearing a bandana and her hair fell in disheveled waves to her shoulders.

"Metabolism?"

"Ugh," she winced.

"Besides, I'm not that tired. Too excited to sleep."

"Same," she shrugged. "I'll walk with you. Bunky coming?"

"Figure we let him crash. He seems stressed."

They walked along Sunset, quiet at this late hour. They could hear the clunk of changing street signs. Stores were closed. A few cars glided past like whales.

"Where's the farthest you've been?" he said.

"New York," she said, looking ahead, "now here."

He thought about how similar they were, their utter lack of worldliness compared to Bunky. That perhaps there was something to this fundamental difference that lent honesty and tension to their music.

"Bunky really wants to make it," he said then. "It's like it's do or die for that kid."

"He can be intense," she said. She put her hands in the pocket of her hoodie. "But you can't change someone, you know? I admire his drive. I do. I just don't want to see him devastated."

"There won't be anything for him to get devastated about. Trust me."

In the distance, a siren wailed.

"All I'm saying is there's more to life," Eloise said.

"For Bunky?" Paul exhaled. "I'm not so sure."

Eloise lowered her voice to imitate him. "*Let's make it so Stevie has no fuckin' choice*," she said. She smiled and Paul caught the glint of her silver tooth.

"Not bad," he said. "Throw a little more mumble in there. Avoid eye contact. But it's pretty much there."

Up ahead there was a diner. Angular and neon-drenched in the style of the 1950s. A sign in the window said *24 Hours*, a beacon for the restless.

"At least dinner number two will be healthy," Eloise said.

"Every place has low-cal options now. It's like a law or something."

"If you go to a late-night diner for low-cal options, you might be a serial killer."

Inside, the light was wickedly bright. The only other customer was a grizzled man in a heavy coat hunched over a cup of coffee at the counter. He leafed through shreds of old newspaper. They took a booth by the window. A young man approached their table. He wore the company-issued white shirt and a paper hat. Without speaking, he withdrew a pen and pad from the pocket at his waist and cocked his head.

"Um," Paul said, flipping through the thick menu, "I'll do a grilled cheese. And ..."

The young man looked out the window into the parking lot as he waited, tapped the butt of his pen on his pad.

Paul turned to Eloise.

"I'll hold out for breakfast," she said.

"Add some French fries," Paul said, "she's going to eat them all. Watch." The comment died in the air as the waiter collected their menus and set off to the kitchen without saying a word.

"Tough crowd," Paul shrugged. "Must have bombed an audition."

"Don't be mean," Eloise said. "That's more or less exactly what we're going to do tomorrow night."

"Bomb?"

"No, dummy." She rolled her eyes. "Audition. We're no better than that dude."

"I never said we were better. Takes a dreamer to know one."

They were quiet for a few minutes there in the booth until the waiter materialized once more and wordlessly slid the plate onto the table. Right away, Eloise reached over and snagged a few fries.

"Told you," Paul said to the waiter, but the young man's back was already turned.

"So," Eloise said as she chewed, "you invite her?"

"Who?"

"Don't play dumb. Your chick. I never got her name."

He dipped his sandwich in ketchup and took a bite.

"Sara," he said.

"Sara," Eloise said, nodding sagely.

"What?"

"Just sounds like a heartbreaker, that's all."

"Yes, I did invite her."

Eloise lunged back in the booth. "*Really?*"

"Yeah, is that bad? Fuck. Should I not have invited her?"

"No, you absolutely should have. I'm surprised you had the balls."

"Easy," Paul said, holding up his palms.

"I'm just saying. You never struck me as the ..."

"As the what?"

"You know, as the type who would extend an olive branch to the woman who ripped his heart out."

"I'm trying to grow up here."

"Admirable," Eloise said, nodding. "Also admirable that you acknowledge the need to grow up. Some say that's the first step."

"You want to hear about the day she left? I've never really talked about it with anyone."

"Are you kidding," Eloise said, leaning forward on her elbows, "hit me."

"Aright, so I had stayed at her place and—"

"Where'd she live?"

"Not far from Lincoln Center."

"Fancy. Was she rich?"

"No, it was more like Hell's Kitchen, but, can I—"

"Sorry."

"—finish."

"Please go."

"I remember I couldn't sleep that night. I was super restless, like I had a phantom limb or something. So I got out of bed—I still remember Sara was sleeping in one of my old Reds t-shirts, she still has it actually—and I went to the couch. I put the TV on and watched fucking like, *Law & Order* reruns on mute until I finally passed out. Early in the morning she shakes me awake and sits down next to me on the couch and I can tell right away by the look on her face. Like, I just *knew*. I even thought to myself right then, *I'm about to have my heart broken.* She pulled her knees to her chest, and we just sat there for a few minutes. I can still see the flecks of green nail polish on her toes. I felt like if I could just make her laugh everything would be okay, you know? So I reminded her about this time, this is back when I had a slot on a late-night radio show—we streamed it out of the Sweatshop actually—and she came by one night and I let her pick the whole setlist and we got drunk and laughed our asses off because she played 'You Sexy Thing' and we almost did it right there on the floor."

"You were going to fuck on the Sweatshop floor? That's disgusting."

"I know. But I'm telling you, it was probably one of the best nights of my life. We'd been together about a year. And of course she remembered, but that spark was just gone, you know?"

"I mean did you see any of this coming?"

"She'd been kinda distant for a couple weeks. Quiet. But she was really busy with rehearsals and work and stuff, so I chalked it up to that. Turns out she was trying to work up the nerve to leave me."

"Brutal," Eloise said, absently reaching for a few fries.

"You know what she told me? That I was a *good catch*. Like, what the fuck does that even mean?"

Eloise made a hook with her finger and tugged at her cheek and Paul almost laughed.

"Anyway," he said, "I guess what I regret most is that I never had the balls to tell her."

"The L word."

He nodded. "I just felt comfortable in my own skin with her. I don't even feel that way when I'm by my fucking self."

"And she's happy out here you think?"

He nodded again. "She's killing it with the Philharmonic and this smaller ensemble she put together."

"So, she drops the bomb on you with her green toenails, and then what?"

"Then I proceed to help her pack a few days later."

"No."

"Yeah. What was I supposed to do?"

"Uh, I don't know. *Not* help her pack? You got more balls than you give yourself credit for. Bigger balls than me."

"What would you have done?"

"Dropped two of these," Eloise held up her middle fingers, "and called it a day."

"Nah, it wasn't like that. Though I guess I'm leaving out the part where she deleted some songs we made together."

"Wait, wait, wait. Hold up. You two made *songs* together?"

"Good ones too."

"And she just deleted them?"

He sighed. "Yeah. I'm still not sure why."

"I gotta be honest with you. She sounds like a piece of work."

"All I can say is I loved her."

"So what all'd you say to her?"

"When?"

"When you invited her to the show."

"You really want to know?"

"Dude," Eloise said, snaking the last fries.

He withdrew his phone from his pocket, scrolled to the text. He passed over his phone for Eloise to read. She made a show of pushing nonexistent glasses up the bridge of her nose, clearing her throat. "Dearest Sara, I long for thee with the fire of a thousand suns—"

"You're hilarious," Paul cut in, "really."

"Okay, okay," she snickered. "Ahem. *Hey there. Know it's been a while. I wanted you to know my band is playing a showcase in L.A. Friday night. Love to see you there. Let me know if you're free.*" Eloise looked up from his phone. "That's it?"

"What do you mean, that's it? That text took a lot out of me."

"Damn," she said and slid the phone back across the table. "After that whole spiel you just gave me, I was hoping for some fireworks."

"Saving them for tomorrow night."

"Did she get back to you?"

Paul shook his head.

"It's been what, three days? You never know."

"I won't get my hopes up."

"Shit. I just want to see what this mysterious woman is like."

243

"Me too," he said. "I'm nervous."

"What if she's not what you remember?"

"Right."

Eloise shrugged, smiling warmly. "Then at least you'll know."

The waiter ambled over and began collecting their plates, laid down the tray with the hand-written bill on it. Paul paid with a twenty, left the balance for a tip, and as they walked out into the L.A. night, they looked back through the window to see the young man dutifully wiping down their table.

***

They hired a car from the hotel over to Silver Lake and arrived early for soundcheck. From the outside, the venue was a low-slung bungalow with a string of lights hanging from the eaves and a narrow marquee bearing four words: *They Is*, and *Ancient Futures*, the other band on the bill. The three of them couldn't help but linger at the curb and gawk up at it. Paul and Eloise took pictures with their phone. Bunky listed slightly on his feet and stared at the sign as though trying to decipher the letters. He was fucked up. And this made Paul very nervous. He and Eloise had shared an anxious glance when Bunky was the last to meet them in the hotel lobby, heavy-lidded and slow and wearing a beatific grin; his voice sounded as though it was stuck at the wrong RPM. He played dumb in the car, and it wasn't until they had lugged their gear down a set of stairs and onto the little stage of the venue that they got it out of him.

"Too much Xan," he shrugged as he plugged in his bass with a squelch for sound check. His words were doughy and opaque, and Paul knew right then they were in deep trouble.

There on the stage, before a shimmery curtain of silver and blue, Paul motioned Eloise over to the table where he'd begun to arrange his gear. She had her red Stratocaster slung over her shoulder and she was tuning as though to keep herself distracted. She too had been acting strange, quiet.

"What the fuck," Paul said in a low whisper. He had seen Bunky smoke plenty of weed, drink his share of booze, but pills were something different. Sure, he'd witnessed Bunky take anxiety meds once or twice, gulping down a pill or two with water when he was particularly jumpy, or depressed about his family, but then again, how well did you really know somebody?

"It's my fault," she said in a panicked whisper. Paul could see she was scared.

"What? What do you mean?"

"I gave it to him," she said through her teeth.

"You what?"

"Oh shit, Paul. What did I do?"

"What the fuck are you saying?"

"I'm saying I keep this little dropper bottle with me. After my brother—*shit*—I started having these really bad panic attacks. So I keep it as a security blanket."

"How much did he take?"

"I don't know. *I don't fucking know.*"

"Okay. Relax. We're going to be okay."

"I told him to take a drop or two. He must have overdone it."

"How do we pull him out of it?"

Before Eloise had a chance to answer, she caught something in her periphery and Paul followed her gaze to see Stevie emerge from the stairwell across the room. He was beaming and as he drew closer, he began a slow clap. At his arrival, the three of them stopped tuning and futzing and Paul could hear the squeak of Stevie's leather jacket as he moved.

"Well, well, well," he said, "if it isn't the fun bunch. And how are we feeling tonight? Ready to tear some faces off?"

The three of them set down their instruments and hopped down off the little platform to join Stevie at ground level. It was then that he took in Bunky's appearance. All at once, the energy and lightness drained from his face.

"The fuck happened to you?" he asked, eyeing Bunky head-to-toe. He turned to Paul and Eloise. "The fuck happened to *him?*"

Eloise averted her eyes. Paul scrambled for the right words, but they eluded him. "I, I—"

"Aye, aye, aye is fucking right." Stevie's face turned crimson, and he seemed capable of committing multiple homicide. "You know what? I don't even want to hear it."

"I didn't *do* anything," Bunky said in protest. But his eyes were moony and distant. He seemed to sway where he stood, as though balancing himself on the deck of a slow-moving boat.

Stevie stared at him for a moment, then let out a chortle, like he found the whole charade pathetically funny. Then he turned murderous again and pointed at each of them in turn. "If you fuck this up for me ..." He shook his head and didn't finish the sentence, but the implication was clear. He turned on his heels, headed for the stairs across the room and was out of sight.

Soundcheck went as expected. Bunky missed his cues, forgot words; they rehearsed in fits and starts. The venue's sound tech adjusted the levels and looked at them as though they were about to step into the ring with a heavyweight fighter. While Eloise took Bunky outside for some fresh air, Paul watched Ancient Futures run through their sound check. It didn't make him feel any better. They were a London band and riding a wave of buzz—they played a kinetic, infectious brand of Afrobeat-inspired jazz-funk—that carried them across the pond for a string of U.S. dates. He could tell by watching them warm up that they were seasoned. On stage, they were serious and efficient, yet still somehow effortlessly cool in that multi-cultural London sort of way. The drummer seemed to be the lead man; he was the one issuing instructions to both his band and the sound tech from behind his kit; all listened intently to him when he spoke. He wore all black, an easy smile, and a bandana tied around his high-top fade. Something about the way he doled out commands was both forceful and casual; he punctuated his wishes—a little more on the bass, some reverb on the trumpet—with jovial accents like *bruv* and *you with me?* to let everyone know they were a unified force. When he was happy with the levels, the band, rounded out by keys and sax, burned down one song all the way through. It was a steam-rolling groove of funky bass licks and spirited horn solos, Fela for the hip-hop generation, and Paul knew it would set fire to the dance floor.

When it was done, the drummer grinned, and the bandmates all nodded to each other. They put down their instruments and walked off stage. That was it. They had it down cold and wanted to preserve their firepower. All five of them acknowl-edged Paul warmly as they made their way outside. Paul told the drummer he couldn't wait to see their set. The drummer bowed and said, "Thank you, bruv, likewise," and Paul couldn't help but feel that he, Bunky and Eloise were very much out of their depth.

The room began to fill. Paul scanned the faces, didn't see the one he was after, and tried hard not to feel hurt. He and Eloise took Bunky to the bar that ran the length of the side of the room and made him slug glass after glass of water. Still,

Bunky looked out of it, and even seemed to find the whole bit amusing. Paul wanted to grab him by the shoulders and slap the shit out of him.

"I'm *fine*," Bunky said, heavy-lidded, stretching the vowel of the word like putty.

"You are *not* fine," Eloise snapped, for the first time truly losing her cool. "And you are scaring the shit out of me. Fuck. What did I do?"

"*Relax*," Bunky said. "Just like you always told me, right?" He shrugged, like, *Well?*

Paul took him by the collar of his camo button-down and tried to shake the cobwebs loose. He looked his bandmate right in the eye and what he saw behind the glaze was fear. He saw fear and loneliness, the look of someone hungry for connection, but so entrenched behind walls that he didn't know how to find it.

"Listen man," Paul said, "I have no problem calling Stevie and telling him the show is off. You tell me you need some help right now? I got you. No questions asked. Because I'll tell you this: we can't do this without you. You need to believe in yourself like *we* believe in you. You're the backbone of this shit, Bunky."

Bunky stared back, and for a moment seemed to verge on acquiescing, of setting down the front. But just as quickly, something clicked in those grey eyes of his and he slapped Paul's hand away and smoothed his shirt. He smirked. "Couldn't be readier."

They didn't have a choice. The room was full. Somewhere out there in the scrum were the label folks that would decide their fate. They made their way onstage to prepare for liftoff. Bunky made final adjustments to his bass and someone in the crowd went *whoop* and Bunky *whooped* right back into the microphone. He seemed to be enjoying the little game.

Eloise looked at him imploringly, as though willing him to be sober, then adjusted her bandana and stepped to her mic.

"We're They Is, and these are some songs. We hope you like them."

They very nearly didn't make it out of the gate. During the opening verse of "You'll Never Know," Bunky missed his prompt and dragged down the tempo and it was as though all the puzzle pieces had tumbled to the floor. Paul could feel it happening—the beginning of the end, a slow-motion train wreck in front of a room full of rubberneckers—and he could feel his t-shirt getting heavy with sweat. When the song lurched to a close, he could tell the crowd was unsure what to do. Perhaps that's how the music was supposed to be: angular, jaunty.

Paul caught Bunky's eye: *Get your shit together.*

Bunky glanced away, looked out at the sound tech manning the soundboard in the back corner. He pointed at his bass, then pointed to the sky. He thumbed his strings as the rumble grew louder. He kept pointing up, then he pointed at Paul and did the same.

There was no time to argue, so Paul tapped a steady beat, locking in with the pulse Bunky played until he could feel the pressure in his chest, a low, rumbling growl.

YEW, someone yelped over the murmur of the crowd.

This was how they were going to go out: in an earthquake of bass. The floor was going to split beneath them, and they would tumble into oblivion. As Bunky struck the notes that led them into "King Kong," something palpable shifted in the room, a touch of menace. The only way to prevent the bass from subsuming everything was to move, and not stop moving.

With "Lights Go Out," they were picking up speed, driven by Bunky's bass; it was as though by going faster, he sought to prevent the inevitable falling out. The intimacy of the vocal exchanges between Bunky and Eloise now carried with them a shade of danger: Eloise's movements, usually languid and sultry, now seemed poised for collapse. Bunky's croon was viscous, as though passed through molasses.

By the time they lit into "Crescent Line," they were moving much too fast, and Paul could feel the bolts starting to come loose. The crowd had stopped moving; faces craned to catch the moment when it would all hurtle off the edge and Paul prayed that Sara wasn't among them. He could hear Eloise's voice shake as she sang. They had practiced a flowing segue into "Love Will Tear Us Apart," Eloise's guitar casting out the frozen chords, but Bunky again played too fast, as though to compensate for his lethargy, and the transition was a mess. This was supposed to be Bunky's song. Where Ian Curtis's monotone had raised a screen between himself and the meaning of the words he sang— as though even he couldn't handle it—Bunky was to lay it bare. But there were holes in his verses, and again Eloise had to carry the slack. When they finished the song, the train had come off the rails, a steadily mounting wreck. Eloise, fed up, propped her guitar against the amp, sending waves of reverb tumbling out over the room, which by then had begun to thin out.

Stevie was nowhere to be found.

Outside they didn't speak to one another. They had blown it and it was difficult to look one another in the eye.

"I fucked up," was all Bunky could say. He looked dazed, trucked, and he said the words over and over again. Paul couldn't bring himself to console his bandmate.

"I'm going to take him back to the hotel," Eloise said, barely a whisper. Paul told them he wanted to be alone. The truth was that he was holding out hope. As they loaded their gear into a hired SUV and prepared to set off, Bunky looked at Paul from the backseat and seemed prepared to apologize. Instead, his face went rigid, and he said, "Don't fucking look at me like that."

"Like what?"

"Like you're disappointed in me." The sharpness had returned to his words; he must have finally resurfaced from his high. "Know how I can tell? Cause it's the same look I've been getting all my life." He pulled the door closed and the car drove off leaving Paul alone at the curb.

***

He flashed his wristband to the bouncer at the door to reenter the club. As he did so, he heard his name.

He knew instantly, but this didn't change the fact that he felt entirely unprepared to face her. She said his name again, as though he might not have heard the first time, so he spun on his heels and there she was.

She wore a jean jacket over a striped sailor shirt with a wide neck, slim black jeans and a pair of low-cut boots that showed off her ankles. Her legs looked fucking great. Her hair was short, clipped almost to her ears and he would have given anything to be able to kiss her neck. He said none of this of course. For a moment, he said nothing at all, until there was only one thing he could say that seemed to encapsulate the whirl of emotions winding their way around his brain stem: "Holy shit."

This made her laugh and she sort of lowered her eyes and looked away. Then she looked back up at him, curled a stray lock of hair around her ear and said: "Holy shit to you too."

"You came," he said dumbly, and it might have gone on like this, with him saying utterly stupid things to her right there at the entrance of the venue, had the bouncer not grown impatient with his obliviousness and ordered him to stop blocking the door. Paul apologized and he and Sara stepped aside and stood beneath the marquee that bore his band's name.

Sara gestured up to it and said, "Sorry you guys had a tough go of it in there. What happened?"

Paul shook his head. There were so many things he wanted to say, and it stung that not only had she witnessed such a colossal failure, but that he was also forced to explain it away. He stopped short of throwing his bandmate under the bus.

"We just didn't have it tonight," he said.

He could tell by the look on her face she knew there was more to it. But she didn't push.

"Well anyway, I really loved the songs you guys posted. Especially the one with the strings." This last word drew her lips into a smirk. "But I don't recall giving you permission."

"Oh that," Paul said and felt the blood drain from his face. "I saw it as a collaboration."

"Did you now?" She crossed her arms over her chest to make a show of giving him a hard time. "If I didn't think it was such a fantastic song, I might be inclined to ask you to kill it."

"Then I say we should make more together."

She studied him with those brown eyes of hers and it seemed as though she was considering not just the possibility of sharing more music, but the substance of their entire history together.

"Can I tell you something," he said.

"Please," she said.

He suddenly had the urge to tell her what he had been afraid to say while they were together. What he still felt. That he loved her. That he might never feel the same way about anyone again in his life. But he looked at her, how light she looked, and knew it wasn't fair. What was she supposed to do about it now? He changed course. "Well, I guess it's more of a question. Why did you delete our songs?"

"Paul," she said. The light in her eyes dimmed a bit and he knew he was in danger of pushing her away at the very moment he seemed to be erasing the distance.

"I'm sorry," he said, "forget it. I know you have your reasons. And I respect them. I really do. It's just—" *They were some of the best songs I've ever been a part of,* "how's the Philharmonic?"

At once, the spark returned and she grew animated, shifting the weight on her hips. "It's a dream," she said. "I can't believe it's what I wake up every day to go and do. It's strange, you know? To be doing what you set out to? And the smaller ensemble keeps it all fresh. We've got some more originals that we're going to record soon."

He looked at her, the way she beamed as she spoke, and tried, just for the moment at least, to let it go. "Look," he said, "I was thinking about going back in to catch the next set. But would you want to go somewhere? Get a coffee and catch up for real? As friends?"

"Oh, I don't know," she said, "rehearsal in the morning and everything."

She smiled at him with a touch of sadness; this was her way of telling him to let go, to leave the past behind. To enjoy this moment for what it was.

"Right," he said, "of course." And he felt grateful then. Grateful that she had shown up at all, had allowed him the chance to properly say goodbye.

"I really hope this all works out for you," Sara said. She reached out and squeezed his forearm. "I know how badly you want it. Lord knows you have the talent."

What he might have said a moment ago was that it didn't matter, that he'd give it all up for another night, another hour.

"There are bigger things," he said instead.

"Keep that attitude and you'll be just fine," she said.

She came in for a hug and as he felt her body pressed into his, he knew that he would never feel it again.

***

Inside, the crowd had redoubled, so he took a place against the rear wall. The room was dark, almost pitch black, the fuzzy static of anticipation before the main event. The only lights were the dim lamp above the soundboard in the back of the room, and the little red and green dots of the equipment onstage.

Without warning, the crowd exploded. He stood up on his toes to see five dark shadows emerging from backstage to take their instruments. At the very instant the first joyful chords burst from the speaker towers, a blinding strobe assaulted the crowd. Paul shielded his eyes. All around him, the throng danced with abandon, the strobe rendering them all an epileptic flip book. He squinted to see the drummer beaming, attacking his kit with gleeful chaos. By turns, the trumpet and sax players cast a cascade of emphatic sweetness into the air above. It was music as exorcism. Anxiety and tension couldn't grip what they couldn't hold. The only thing to do was to move and move and keep moving, until the mind at last submitted to the demands of the body.

15.

"Please," Bunky was saying, "please give us another chance." He had actually joined his tattooed hands together as a steeple at his chest. For once, Paul was not the one in a position to be begging for forgiveness, or apologizing, or generally feeling as though he was the scapegoat.

They were seated around Stevie's wooden conference table where Stevie sat at the head with a look of deranged contentment. He was leaning back in his chair with his arms folded across his chest. Next to him at the corner of the table was Malcolm, who struck a similar pose, as though boss and assistant were controlled by the same unseen force.

"Why?" Stevie shrugged. Malcolm performed a less exaggerated version of the same gesture. Both stared down at Bunky at the other end of the table. Paul and Eloise sat on either side of him.

Bunky hung his head, searching for an answer. Next to him, Eloise stared at her hands. Overhead, Feathers' second album was bouncing and noodling around the room. If the music was Stevie's idea of a joke, Paul had to give him credit. After news of their failure had begun to spread, and after Paul had landed back at his apartment in Red Hook, he received a fiery call from Gallo, during which his old friend proceeded to rip into him for making him look *like a fool*, for putting his reputation *on the line*, and *you know what else*, he steamed, Paul was *lucky* Stevie loved Feathers' new record and was reaping the benefits of a sold-out tour. Otherwise, it might have been *his ass*. And Paul had to sit there and take it. It didn't matter that Bunky had railroaded their set, it was Paul who had pushed Gallo to stick out his neck.

"Because," Bunky said then. He lifted his head and looked at Eloise, then Paul, and then square at Stevie. "Because these guys deserve better."

Stevie blinked, and if he felt any sympathy, he damn sure wasn't going to show it. "Well," he said, "maybe you should've thought about that before you went and swallowed the medicine cabinet. I mean, I knew you had some issues, kid, but I never thought towering idiocy was among them."

"I'm trying," Bunky said.

And, to his credit, he was.

A week after they had returned from L.A., Bunky invited Paul to his East Village studio for a meeting. Paul didn't know what to expect, and in fact, he would not have been surprised if They Is disbanded right then and there. But he climbed the four flights of stairs and Bunky opened his door and welcomed him in with a big embrace. Eloise was sitting cross-legged on his bed and her cheeks were puffy. Bunky was humbled and contrite and earnest, and it was hard, at first, for Paul not to think he was being put on. Bunky must have read his expression, because he lit into an apology, a sincere accounting of his profound gratitude for his two bandmates, an acknowledgement of just how goddamn lucky he was to have found the two of them. He thanked Paul for what he had said to him in the moments before the L.A. show, that it had meant a lot.

Paul was stunned Bunky had even been conscious enough to remember what he said, let alone that it had sunk in. But Paul told his bandmate he had meant every word of it. Then Bunky marched into the bathroom, opened his medicine cabinet, and proceeded to uncap several translucent orange canisters and empty them into the toilet. Eloise, for her part, retrieved a little bottle of brown glass, unscrewed the lid, and washed it down the drain drop by drop. Bunky was trying, he said, to work up the courage to extend an olive branch to his parents. He had even reached out to a therapist. Finally. And though he hadn't reached out to his parents yet, he would soon. Very soon. And all at once, though he projected a stance of firm support for his bandmate, Paul had felt a rush of fear.

Stevie stared down at the other end of the table and bit the inside of his cheek. Malcolm cast his boss a sidelong glance, and Paul could tell they were making some kind of progress.

"You guys really fucked me, you know that? I had several big swinging dicks at that show of yours. People that I love to hate, but that nonetheless bring me business and vice versa. You can imagine the explaining I had to do after you sent your performance careening off the road, over the guardrail and plummeting several hundred feet to a fiery ball of wreckage." Here Stevie uncrossed his arms and leaned forward on his elbows. Malcolm followed suit. "But somehow, a few of those very same individuals admitted that they could sniff a hint of potential behind that self-sabotage of yours." He pointed at Eloise. "Especially you. So, I'll tell you what I'm willing to do." Stevie raised a finger. "Actually, first, I'll tell you what I'm *not* going to do. And that's go out of my way to arrange any kind of performance or showcase or goddamn open mic night for you. But. If you can manage to pull together a show here in New York, and bring a crowd, and swear on your lives that you will not so much as drink a cup of fucking coffee before you step on stage, I'll see if I can whisper news of it to one or two people."

Paul glanced at Bunky, then Eloise, and watched as Bunky stood up at the table. "Thank you," he said. "You're not going to regret this." He was set to cross the room and shake Stevie's hand or invite him in for a hug, but Stevie raised his palm.

"Don't," Stevie said. "I don't do well with displays of emotion. Show your gratitude by playing the kind of music I know, and *you* know, you're all capable of playing." He nodded to Malcolm. Malcolm nodded back. "Malcolm, see them out, will you? And for the love of God, stop doing that."

Outside, Paul and Eloise followed Bunky up the steps to the Highline where they leaned against a rail and looked out over the Hudson, silver and slow on this January afternoon. Despite the cold, the park was still abuzz with foot traffic: people in big, shuffling groups, people with bulky cameras dangling from their chests, people wielding selfie sticks like weapons. At one point, a young French woman tapped Eloise on the shoulder and gestured with her camera for Eloise to take a photo of her and her friend. Eloise obliged, arranged the pair against the opposite rail to face the city streets below, counted off, and as the wind whipped up and sent hair and scarves flailing, snapped a photo. She showed the result on the back of the camera; the young women giggled and went on their way.

"I'm going to make this up to you guys," Bunky said. "We're going to bounce back from this. I promise."

"Guess we'll just dial up Greg, right?" Paul said. "See what kind of openings he's got in the next few days. If not? We might need to go the pay-to-play route somewhere else."

Bunky shook his head, looked off into the distance. "I know what we need to do," he said.

Paul and Eloise waited for him to say more. When he didn't, Eloise nudged him.

"When do we find out about it?" she said.

Their bandmate looked at each of them in turn, his grey eyes determined, zealous, even a little wild. "Just give me a few days and it will all make sense," Bunky said. He smiled. "Trust me."

***

They bumped along cobblestone in Bunky's old Pathfinder. In the rearview, Paul caught Eloise craning her neck to get her fill of the surroundings. Sometimes he forgot she was still new. Bunky drove in silence, eyes fixated, jaw set. As the plan had coalesced, Paul had begun to understand the ramifications, and he hoped, prayed really, for the first time since he was a boy. Even still, an urge had begun to burrow its way into his consciousness over the course of the last few days. He couldn't tell if it drew from exhaustion, a desire to stop running and hiding, or a sense of obligation. All he knew was that as he prepped his gear that evening, he found himself sliding the signed copy of *True Stories* into his record bag.

Bunky steered alongside a sidewalk splashed with light that poured out through the plate glass façade of an art gallery. It was an unseasonably warm night, the sky purple, indecisive. They unloaded gear, an archipelago of cases and bags at their feet. On the glass, in sleek sans serif was stenciled: *Carlo Bonucci— Your Playground is the World.* Paul let the words play around his brain and couldn't decide if it was brilliant or bullshit or both. At the reception desk, Bunky addressed the stubborn face of a gallery assistant, a young man with a long face divided in two by a thin mustache and adorned with green-framed glasses.

"We're here to play," Bunky said.

The face nodded, bored and interrupted. He shepherded them to a far corner. "So the patrons may maneuver," he whispered. He spoke gravely, with his hands clasped behind his back. "You must be heard, not felt. And the photographs? Always remember, *they* are the star this evening."

The photographs: stark, black-and-white images of swing sets. Each and every one of them. Swing sets rusting in backyards, engulfed in overgrown meadows, dwarfed in the shadow of project housing, cracked and bowed on vacant porches; they stood still and alone. The focus of the show hung behind them at the rear of the gallery, an enormous photo of a tire swing, hanging like a dead pendulum in the jigsaw shade of an oak. Despite his best efforts, Paul found himself thinking of Will. And despite his best efforts, he found himself succumbing to the art.

"Me and Robert hung one of those once," Eloise said. She stepped closer to the piece to get a better look and spent a few minutes quietly observing it.

From a backroom somewhere stepped two men. One young, one not.

"C," Bunky said through a smile.

The younger man, the artist, smiled back and they embraced, thumped each other on the back. He had wild but kind eyes, like he'd been up all night helping a friend through some difficulty, which was more or less what he had set about doing here.

Bunky nodded at his bandmates. "Gang," he said, "meet Carlo."

Carlo kissed Eloise on the cheek, then clasped Paul's palm. "Bunky gave me a sneak peek at the new tracks." His eyebrows jumped and he whistled.

Paul reddened. To establish an emotional connection with music was the goal. But to encounter someone he didn't know face-to-face, someone who had listened to and *liked* the songs, was something else entirely.

"So wait," Eloise said, "how do you two know each other again?"

Carlo and Bunky looked at each other. "Go for it," Bunky said.

"Man," Carlo said. He ran a hand through his blonde hair, folding his arms over his sport coat. "How *do* we—I mean, I guess my dad and your mom first met at RISD, right? Then kept in touch when they moved to the city?"

"*Kept in touch*," Bunky said with air quotes and a smirk.

"Exactly. But then I guess the universe had other plans and your pops and my mom entered the picture and—dude, I still have Polaroids of the six of us on the beach in Rockaway."

"And then in Newport—"

"Right, when things started happening. Anyway, my folks got out of the art game and into academics, but Bunky's parents blew up, and when I started doing my little photography thing, they hooked me up with—well, this fine gentleman standing next to me."

The gallerist forced his lips into a tight smile. He was a thin, bird-like man, with a navy blazer over a white shirt open too low, dark jeans, purple suede loafers and a wristwatch the size of a coaster. He looked like the kind of man who paid for expensive sex and expensive locations in which to have it. He clapped his hands together. "How fly is this going to be, guys?" he said.

Paul cringed.

Carlo introduced them. This was Mr. Fritz. One half of the $200 million-dollar Walker + Fritz enterprise. He wore the self-satisfied, yet somehow slightly pained, expression of the wealthy, as though Paul and his bandmates might threaten to scuff the floors or spill red wine on his dazzling white shirt.

"Carlo said he wanted a band for the opening," he said and laughed self-consciously. His teeth were so white they were almost blue. "Frankly, I thought he was insane. But he insisted. So I said, fuck it, who am I to stop this guy?" He exhaled and dropped his shoulders and drank in Eloise with a look that made Paul's stomach turn. "Just look at what he's done." Mr. Fritz raised a palm to the open room. "All we can do is watch him get brighter."

Star and star-maker left them to set up. Cords, mics, monitors, amps. Outside, a line had begun to wind. Hands cupped around faces to peek in through the window.

"This is it," Paul said.

"We're back in the Sweatshop," said Bunky like a coach. His eyes shifted around the room as though someone might sneak up on him at any moment and Paul couldn't help but do the same.

"If you'd told me there in the subway, when my only listeners were rats and commuters, that I'd be playing music in a fancy art gallery?" Eloise trailed off, smiled, wagging her head.

"All that's changed is the scenery," Bunky said.

"And the smell," Eloise said.

"From piss to bullshit," Paul said.

There was time to spare before the doors opened so Bunky and Eloise donned their coats and ducked outside for a smoke. Paul followed. The three of them leaned against Bunky's truck facing the street like a trio of high school toughs skipping class. Bunky and Eloise lit cigarettes, Paul lit his one-hitter, shaped and painted to resemble one. Instinctively, he held out the little pipe in Bunky's direction, then catching himself, he drew it back. "Sorry, I mean—"

Bunky waved him off. "All good." He pulled from his cigarette and exhaled. "I have a good feeling about this. Feels like it could be the start of something."

Eloise dropped her cigarette butt to the pavement. She ground it down with the toe of her black sneaker and crossed her arms. "Can we just enjoy the moment for once?"

Paul and Bunky waited for her to finish. Her cheeks, rosy from the chill, grew redder.

"It's just—I see all these kids, you know? Especially in this city. Running around, RPMs maxed out. And it's like, where are you going, buddy? And why? There's like this invisible plateau—and it changes for everybody—but it's like if they can *just* get over that plateau, *then* they'll be happy." She stuffed her hands in the pockets of her coat. "But what if they don't get there? What then? It's dangerous to be desperate, is all I'm saying." She looked at Bunky to her left, "I just don't want that to happen to you," then Paul on her right. "Us."

The word *desperate* had never occurred to Paul until that moment. He now had a name for what he'd been feeling since—well, since he could remember, really. He'd been so accustomed to spinning his wheels that he'd never taken time to consider where he'd end up if they ever gripped the road. It was this feeling, perhaps more than any other, that led him to make up his mind, to settle on the decision that would, in all likelihood, spell the end of it all.

"So, you're satisfied then?" Bunky said.

Eloise thought for a moment, looking at her feet. "Satisfied? Look, of course I want this to happen. How could I not? But like, if you'd knocked on my bedroom door back in Baton Rouge? And told me I'd be in New York City, in a band, with two lame-ass dudes—"

"Easy," Paul said.

She cracked a smile. "Two capital L, lames? And we'd be hanging out and making songs and about to play a show at a ... whatever the hell this is?" She thumbed over her shoulder. "Sometimes you just have to look around and say, *This is fucking hilarious.*"

She turned to make her way back toward the gallery, and as she did so, Paul gestured to Bunky.

"You got a sec?"

Bunky shrugged, pulled from his cigarette.

Paul turned to Eloise. "Keep the stage warm for us," he said.

She shouted over her shoulder. "Might just take it all for myself."

When she was out of range, Paul said, "Look, I got something for you. Open up your truck real quick." As soon as the words left his mouth, his pulse quickened with the realization of what he was about to do. He was lightheaded, anxious, and it was too late to change his mind.

"What is it?" Bunky said as he unclipped his keys.

"You'll see," Paul said, doing his best to keep his voice steady. He rounded the vehicle to the trunk, lifted open the hatch and withdrew his record bag. He slung it over his shoulder and returned to the side of the car where Bunky was stamping out his dead cigarette. Bunky nodded to the record bag, curious.

Paul started in. "So. You remember way back, one of the first shows we played? That basement dungeon off Lorimer?"

"Of course," Bunky said. "Might still be the best show I've ever played in my life."

"Right? And remember you drove me all the way back to Red Hook? We talked about what got us hooked on this whole music thing."

"*The Infamous.*"

"Exactly. And for you it was that Talking Heads show your mom took you to." Here Paul hesitated, for he knew he was wading into sensitive territory. Bunky narrowed his eyes to confirm it.

"Where's this going?"

"What I'm trying to say is we're lucky you went to that show. That you decided to make a go of it. Because nobody plays like you. You just gotta believe it as much as everybody else does."

Bunky squinted. "How strong is that herb you smoked?"

"Fuck it," Paul said, and as he did so, he lifted the flap of his bag and withdrew the signed record, handed it over.

For a few seconds, Bunky scrutinized the cover, turned the record over in his hands, and tilted it to catch the glow of the streetlamp above. Paul watched as the gears locked into place.

"What the—where in the fuck did you get this?" his bandmate said, almost giddy. It wasn't with anger that he said it, but confusion. Awe, really.

Paul could have made something up. He could have said something about how he found the record by chance on one of his digging adventures. That Bunky's parents must have sold off their collection, and that Paul's discovery of it was a sign, an aligning of the stars, a good omen. He could have kept the lie going just a *little* bit longer, improbable as it might have seemed.

Instead, he told the truth.

He told Bunky what he had done, step by step. He told him he had stolen records and CDs as a kid because he couldn't afford them. That it was the only way he could ever get the music that moved him. That stealing became second nature, indeed a way to eat. That this habit carried over to Dead Wax, that in fact stolen records had been the source of many of the samples they'd built their songs upon. That his compulsion had got him fired from the only job he truly loved. And he told him about the morning on Church and Chambers. That he'd stolen the records and sold them off to help his parents. That "Beat Bop" and its protean drums had inspired the foundation of "Crescent Line." That he'd had an encounter with Bunky's mother and that she told him she and Bunky's father were giving it another shot. That she wanted to see him.

As Paul spoke, Bunky looked him right in the eye and simply listened. The look on his face wasn't one of betrayal, or disappointment or rage, but disbelief.

"That it?" he said when Paul had finished spilling his guts. His face was blank now, a cipher, and Paul found this fact frightening.

"That's it, man." Paul let his hands fall heavily at his sides. He felt hollowed out. Numb. "That's all I got."

"Then I have two questions. One: how in the hell did you get in? And two: why, of all times, did you decide to spring this on me *now*?" Bunky wiped a hand down his face, lifted a palm. "Actually, don't bother answering that. It doesn't fucking matter."

Paul replied by digging in his pocket for his keys. He removed the apartment key from the loop and held it flat in his palm.

"Fuck me," Bunky said, stunned, "how in the world did you—" He shook his head and laughed in an abrupt way that seemed to surprise himself. And then, in a fluid sequence of efficient violence, he twisted up his face, drew back his elbow, and with the knuckles inked SWIM, delivered a punch that landed squarely on Paul's left cheekbone. Paul reeled back on his heels, clipped the nose of Bunky's truck with his hip, spun around in a sort of drunk pirouette and fell in a heap on the asphalt. What surprised him was not the punch itself—the word that dislodged in his brain as he stumbled to the ground was *finally*—but rather the ensuing sound. It was a resonant, high-pitched whine, as though someone was running their finger around the lip of a wine glass inside of his skull.

He lay on his stomach on the concrete and opened his eyes. From his vantage, he could see the worn tread on Bunky's front tire and beyond it, closer to the curb, the flattened, lipstick-stained cigarette Eloise had been smoking. The ringing in his ears fell a few octaves and settled into a deep, pressurized throb.

He groaned.

Bunky stood over him and said, "Get up. Before we make a scene."

Paul groaned again.

He rolled over onto his back to see Bunky scowling down at him and the black and blue sky beyond. He raised himself to a seated position and touched his cheek. He winced: it felt like someone was pressing a sharp piece of glass against his cheekbone.

"C'mon," Bunky said. He reached out a hand—the same one that had knocked Paul on his ass—and Paul clasped it and was pulled to his feet.

He was woozy. He blinked his eyes and worked his jaw until the world settled on its axis.

Bunky smoothed the front of his black hoodie and the motion made Paul flinch.

"You," his bandmate said, jabbing a finger into Paul's chest, "are a fucking *asshole*."

Yes. That's precisely what he was: an asshole. A fucking asshole. He had been one all his life, practicing to become the giant asshole who now stood wobbly on his feet with a blooming shiner outside a sniffy art gallery in Lower Manhattan.

"You're also lucky," Bunky went on, "because if it wasn't for this show we're about to play, I would absolutely wreck your shit."

Paul looked at his feet, though doing so made him dizzy, so he looked back at Bunky.

"I'm sorry," he said.

"Don't give me that bullshit."

"You don't have to believe me. But I am. About the records. About—"

"I don't give a fuck about the records, Paul. I don't give a fuck about which one *inspired* you, or that you're a fucking klepto. What I give a fuck about is that you went and meddled in my family. Just when things have started to turn a corner, you drop this on me?" He shook his head and sort of chuckled to himself. "Unbelievable. You are a royal fuck up."

At that moment, Eloise shouted from the entrance of the gallery: "Are you guys planning to join me? Or do I need to stall and tell some jokes?"

"*Give us a sec,*" Bunky shouted over his shoulder. Then he turned his attention back to Paul. "We're not done," he said. "You better play the show of your life tonight." His eyes flicked to Paul's cheek. "You're going to want to put some ice on that."

"What do I tell Eloise?"

"Whatever you want," Bunky shrugged. "That's your problem."

***

Back inside, Paul and Bunky made their way to the nook in the rear of the gallery to finish setting up. Eloise was tuning her guitar with a pick in her teeth, just like the first time Paul met her. She looked up, saw his face, took the pick from her mouth, and touched her cheek.

"What the fuck happened to *you*?" she winced. She shot a glance at Bunky, who ignored it and swung his bass over his shoulder.

"I'm fine," Paul said, "I'll explain later."

"Did *he* do that to you?" she said with an edge of anger.

"I said, I'll tell you later. For now? Forget it. We got a job to do."

"Fine," she said and shook her head. She turned her back to him and went on tuning her guitar.

It was definitely not fine. Paul felt guilty for shutting her out, guilty for all of it. And he felt, as he rounded the table that supported his gear, his eye beginning to swell shut.

The doors opened and the first patrons trickled in. They hardly seemed to notice the band, let alone that the guy behind the turntable had a welt growing on his face. Drinks were clutched. The room filled up. Carlo and Mr. Fritz welcomed guests, doled out hugs and kisses and handshakes. Lanky models accompanied short, keg-shaped men. More shades of black clothing than seemed possible.

But no Stevie Reese.

"Fuck him," Eloise said sharply as she adjusted the mic. "We don't need him."

"Nothing we can do about it now," Paul said. He steadied himself by leaning on the table that supported his drum machine and turntable. He was exhausted and the swelling had begun to blur the vision in his left eye. As best he could, he sought to fuel himself by the notion that he was no longer doing this to prove anything to anyone aside from his bandmates. "Let's just do this shit. Let's loosen these assholes up."

Bunky nodded, serious as ever, and Eloise nodded too. She turned and spoke aloud through the rising din of cocktail conversation.

"We're They Is," she said. "Get to know us."

Carlo hollered and a few people clapped, but it hardly mattered: they had already started in, launched right into "You'll Never Know." Paul could feel it right away: they were in lockstep. Bunky seemed to have channeled a deep well of focus: his lyrics were crisp, his basslines were tighter than perhaps they'd ever been. Eloise cloaked her voice in intrigue, improvised a wave of smoky tremolos. Paul fought through the fog of his thoughts and triggered the sample of Gallo's sped-up guitar. He looked out into the crowd as conversation slowed by degrees. Gradually, jaded looks grew curious. Pale faces, straight-lipped, arms locked in the self-conscious L of art appreciation, watched them guardedly. He knew this kind of crowd: finger on the pulse, but always waiting for someone else to tap the vein.

With "King Kong," a slower burn, they found it: chemistry. A fickle thing, visceral and unexplainable. Paul felt it begin to descend on them like a warm breeze and, for the moment, he forgot all about his transgressions. He forgot about Stevie and Gallo and Sara and Will and his parents. He didn't forget about his face, because the pulsing warmth blurred his vision, but he played through it, supported by the groove. Bunky and Eloise were in a union of spirit; theirs was a quiet confidence, a subtext. This was where they were meant to be.

But "King Kong" posed an altogether different problem. A sonic one. So deep was the rumble of Bunky's bass and Paul's punchy drums that the framed photographs rattled on their fasteners. The swing sets nearly swung. From the catering table in the rear, Mr. Fritz waved, manic. His hand cranked an invisible dial. *DOWN.* Bunky turned and, to Paul's surprise, slid him a mischievous grin. Paul nodded. They were nearing the end of the song, an outro in which Eloise's guitar and Bunky's thump fell away leaving only Paul's deep, screwed-down kick drum, a sonic ellipsis over which Eloise cast a few bewitching *Ooohs.* Paul bore down on his drum pads with a little extra pressure, as though trying to leave a watermark in the air. The rumble plunged lower, a sunken ship. Then silence. Someone in the crowd yelled, then a few others did too, and Paul caught Mr. Fritz bolting down a glass of wine and swimming through the thickening crowd in their direction. But before he could pull the plug, they were off, sprinters at the gun, into "Lights Go Out," Eloise's croon like WD40 on the stiffness of the room. It was then that Carlo materialized before them, holding the hand of a little girl—she couldn't have been older than three—in a frilly polka dot dress. They were dancing. Carlo bit his bottom lip and shimmied, cool, measured. The girl twirled in clumsy circles, bent her tiny, chubby knees, and bopped up and down. She smiled and Carlo smiled back, and Paul realized with a start she was his. It was as though he was saying to the room, "Cut the shit," and pockets of people did, allowing themselves to move.

But still, no Stevie Reese.

They charged on, and by "Friends," they'd swung the room. As they'd rehearsed, Paul took the wheel midway through, solo, knocking out a crisp breakbeat, working in a little extra flourish as his fingers flew around his machine. Eloise put her pick in her mouth and clapped. Clap. Clap. Clap. Reluctantly at first, but growing in number, led by Carlo and his little girl, the crowd clapped too, and a chill attacked Paul's back. Bunky's bass line slid in clean, like a partner in double Dutch, then Eloise did the same, smooth, magic.

As they tuned to lay into "Crescent Line," Paul noticed Bunky noticing something. He followed his line of sight to the back of the gallery and expected to see Stevie. Instead, he saw an older man with grey stubble and a baseball cap pulled low over deep-set eyes. Paul recognized him right away and, though he had been preparing for it, the sight of the man nearly knocked the wind out of him. His gaze shifted back to Bunky, who now seemed twenty years younger, a cowed child. Just as quickly, his resolve returned and he stood up a little straighter as he played, clutched his bass so tightly his knuckles turned pale against the dark ink that marked them.

To close, they segued into a cover of "Fade Into You," just as they'd planned. Eloise's voice floated through haze like it had that day on the subway platform. When she brought the song to a close and whispered *Thank you* as the last note rang around the room, there was silence. The crowd was struck dumb. Defense mechanisms razed to a smoldering pile of pretension. Then there was an eruption, a cascade of hollering and applause, and what Paul felt more than anything, more than the jubilation of a perfect show, more than the union he felt with his bandmates, more, even, than the pride at proving to himself that his journey was, at last, moving in the right direction, was dread. Because Bunky was aglow, and even the man with the baseball cap was clapping, and as Paul shared a look of beaming triumph with his bandmates, he feared it would never happen again.

After the set, he broke down his gear and went over to the catering table for a beer. For a moment, he held the cold bottle to his cheek and closed his eyes with relief. He stood there and drank the beer and watched as Bunky approached his father by one of the photographs on the far wall. Father and son observed each other for a moment, guardedly it seemed before the walls came down and they embraced warmly, rocking a bit as they thumped each other on the back. Bunky's father's eyes were shut tight over Bunky's shoulder, and Paul knew it was a physical manifestation of the private pain that families endure. He would never know what had led to the gulf that had opened between Bunky and his parents, but he knew he was witnessing the healing process begin.

Afterwards, to Bunky's credit, he didn't resume the confrontation with Paul there at the gallery. After all, they had just played the best set of their lives. They loaded their gear into his truck and set off for the East Village. Eloise, abuzz in the passenger seat, seemed to have forgotten about any tension as she provided a blow-by-blow of the show. Paul knew that she, far more than he or Bunky, deserved to bask in the glow. She had been swarmed post-show by well-wishers, people drawn to her magnetism—including a pretty woman with long braids Paul had noticed noticing her—and he knew then that she was going to be just fine, with or without them.

At East Seventh, he helped them unload their gear and carry it up to Bunky's apartment. There Bunky told Eloise that he was going to drop Paul in Red Hook; he'd be back soon. He was quiet the whole ride, and Paul was too: what was he supposed to say? It wasn't until they were idling out front of Paul's row house that Bunky at last broke the silence.

"You could've asked me for help," Bunky said. He studied his tattooed hands in his lap but couldn't bring himself to look Paul in the face. "I know you don't believe me, but if I had known you were really so desperate, we could have figured something out."

"You want to know something?" Paul said. "I didn't even know I was really going to do it until I was standing across the street from your apartment and watched your dad walk out of the building."

"How much did you even make on those records?"

"Ten grand," Paul said sheepishly. "And this might sound crazy but hear me out: what if I made it up to you by putting it into the band. Studio time. Equipment. Something."

"Hold up. You still have the money?"

Paul nodded. "I sent my dad a check and he straight up just ripped it in half."

"Why?"

Paul exhaled. "Because ... I don't know, man. I wish I understood."

"Ten grand," Bunky said. He shook his head. From his mouth, the sum sounded miniscule, almost pitiable. "I mean, what were you even *thinking?*" The tone of his voice climbed in volume and intensity, and it was as though the whole thing had snapped back into focus. "I'm your bandmate. Your friend. You fucking went into my apartment. My room. You stole a bunch of shit. And lied right to my mother's face."

"I know, Bunky. I know. I don't even know what to say."

"How can I trust you now?"

There in the dim cabin of Bunky's truck, Paul couldn't make out his bandmate's precise expression, but the message was clear. "I don't know," he said, "I wouldn't trust me either."

"Shit, you've seen my mother more in the past year than I have."

Paul thought carefully about what to say next, whether he should say anything at all, but decided at this point he had nothing to lose. "I know you think she's ashamed of you or whatever, but ... she's not. She told me as much. You should reach out."

Here Bunky laughed. A guffaw, really. "Classic," he said. "The kid who deceived me, lied, and stole from my family is now giving me advice. You're a special one, you know that?"

To this, Paul said nothing.

"Just tell me this," Bunky said. "Why did you do it? Is there even a real reason?"

He gave an answer that came naturally at last. "Because I wanted to prove to my family that I'm worthy of their love. Simple as that. And I still haven't gotten any closer to doing it. Matter fact, I feel farther away than ever."

The comment lingered in the air between them. Bunky looked out the window. "Shit," he said.

"So what now?" Paul said. He was referring to the band, but he might as well have been referring to the rest of his life.

Bunky turned from the window and looked at Paul. "First step? You figure out a way to explain this to Eloise. She deserves to know. After that, I'm not so sure."

"She might punch me in the other eye," Paul said.

"Like I told you," Bunky said, "that's your problem."

"I wonder why Stevie didn't show?"

Bunky shrugged but seemed unfazed. "Who knows? Maybe he gave up on us. And if so, that's my fault. But something good will come from that show. I know it. What I don't know is if you'll be a part of it."

Paul said nothing, unclipped his seat belt and held out his hand for Bunky to shake. Bunky considered it, then shook his head. Paul withdrew his hand, stepped from the vehicle then went around back to corral his gear. He made his way up the walk to the front door and heard the lingering idle of Bunky's truck, and for a moment, he half-expected his bandmate to roll down the window, say something more, something to help heal the wound. Anything. But as he unlocked the door and pushed it open, he heard Bunky press the gas and steer the truck from the curb.

***

The next day, Paul took the G to Fort Greene, found the little café on Dekalb where Eloise worked. He went in and saw her behind the counter with her back turned. She faced a hulking espresso machine and worked steamed milk into a little stainless-steel jug. She wore her trademark get up: all black everything, set off with her red bandana. She poured the milk into a steaming cup to make a squiggly design, turned to place the drink on the counter and nearly dropped it to the floor when she saw Paul standing there.

"*Oh Christ,*" she said, wagging droplets of coffee from her hands. "You scared the daylights out of me. And fuck, look at your *eye.*"

His eye was impressively gross. In the mirror that morning, he'd marveled at how many colors had begun to swirl together, a galaxy of purples, greens, and yellows right there beneath his eye. And the eyelid itself was swollen and puffy, as though he'd been stung.

"Yeah, well," he said, "I deserved it."

Eloise's face tightened with concern. "Are you okay?"

"I just need to fill you in on a couple things."

"Of course," she said. "Hang out for like, ten, and I'll take my break."

He did as he was told and took a little round table by the front window. He observed the six or seven other people in the café, a few of them solo, scrolling feeds or pecking at laptops, a few in pairs having hushed conversations as piano jazz tinkled overhead. The café was light-filled and elegant, minimal in a calming way that suggested one could achieve all sorts of creative breakthroughs just by being inside.

After a few minutes, Eloise came over and sat down. He could tell she was trying to mask her concern. "Can I get you something?" she asked.

He shook his head.

"So what is it then?"

He didn't hesitate. He went straight in and told Eloise the whole story. His parents. Bunky's parents' apartment. The records. The check. The fight. All of it. It flowed from him freely, and as he spoke, he watched Eloise's expression shift from confusion to anger and back around to confusion again. He told her about the conversation he'd had with Bunky that morning in which Bunky had devised a plan: as it turned out his father had been aiming to sell some of his collection. He and Bunky's mother were exploring, cautiously, the possibility of finding a new place together. But there were a dozen or so records that he wanted back, "Beat Bop" included. Paul would reach back out to the buyers on Discogs and do what it took to buy them back. If, by the end of it, he had any money left over—which he doubted since he'd now undoubtedly have to pay a premium—they'd buy some gear: a couple of mics and a new amp for Eloise. That was that.

When he finished, Eloise leaned back in her chair and looked at her hands. When she glanced up at him, he felt tiny. "So. Are you still in the group then?"

"I don't know," he said, and it was the truth. "I really don't know."

"Well," she said, "I'm not sure what to tell you to be honest. Seems like it's on you to figure it out."

And this was exactly what frightened him the most: that he didn't have what it took to become the man he hoped to be.

Eloise pushed back from the table. "I better get back." She stood and looked down at him. "Good luck, Paul. I care about you."

***

He didn't hear from either Bunky or Eloise for over a week, and as he came to terms with the future of the group and his absence from it, he began to assume he might never hear from them again. When at last he did, it was February. And it was his birthday. He was thirty years old. He was celebrating with a morning joint and a spin of Miles' *In A Silent Way* when his phone lit up with Eloise's number. He answered after the second ring.

"When's the last time you checked Spotify?" she asked straight away.

He had expected denouement, the last gasp of their relationship, so her excitability caught him off guard.

"I'm sorry?" he said.

"Check it," she said. "Check the account."

He did as he was told. He cradled his phone between chin and shoulder, pushed aside the clutter on his desk, opened his laptop and went to the page.

It took him a moment to notice what she was referring to.

"Oh my God," he said.

Eloise laughed.

Paul hesitated to say the number next to "Friends" out loud. To say it aloud threatened somehow to undo it all, to disrupt the miracle. "A hundred-and-fifteen?" he whispered.

"*Thousand*," Eloise said, a flutter of joy lilting the word.

"But how?"

It seemed impossible. He refreshed once more to ensure that it hadn't been some sort of glitch in the coding. But the number had climbed a few digits.

"NPR Music," Eloise said.

Paul shook his head. It was all so difficult to process.

"I don't get it," he said.

"Bunky's dad," Eloise said matter-of-factly. "He knows one of the producers and made a phone call. They put it on their Friday playlist. A lot of people follow that thing."

"Fuck," Paul said, and Eloise laughed again. "Why are you telling me this? I was starting to think I was done."

"Well," Eloise sighed, turning serious, "this wouldn't have happened without you. I thought it would be important for you to know that something you helped create is making people happy."

It was all very strange. To know that he had, in some measure, made a connection with a hundred thousand people that he would never meet. It was what he had set out to do when he first began making his own beats as a lonely kid, and now that it was a reality, he felt, not fulfilled exactly, but nostalgic—because the creation no longer belonged to him and the band—and a little sad too because of how impersonal, how oblique it all felt.

"Thank you," he wound up saying. "So does this mean—"

"Yes, asshole," he heard Bunky say, "we're not kicking you out. But it's not because I forgive you. It's because it would be a stupid business decision. You still need to get your shit together."

Paul wanted to tell him that even if he had been kicked out of the group, the pain it would have inflicted was nothing compared to the anxiety he had been living with for the last God-knows-how-long. Or the fact that he wasn't sure exactly how to free himself from it, or that it would ever really go away. Instead, all he said was, "Thank you."

"Don't thank me," Bunky said, "thank Eloise. She's the one who fought for you. And by the way: happy birthday, motherfucker."

***

The strangeness of the day did not end with the phone call from his bandmates, because he had hardly set about putting on another record when his phone buzzed once again. This time it was Will, who was excitable in his own dour way.

"Boy do I have news for you," he said. "Remember that client of mine who was looking for people to staff up a new advertising agency? Back when I found out you'd been unceremoniously dumped by Scrimshaw/Duff?"

"I wasn't dumped, Will. I quit, remember?"

"That's not important. What's important is that this client of mine—Meg Phipps is her name—seems to have heard of your little band. Turns out she listened to one of your songs on some playlist?"

"NPR."

"Right. Well, she liked the song and saw your name associated with it. In any event, she's looking for a song to soundtrack an ad her agency is working on for some big new wine app—"

"Get the fuck out of here."

"Some wine app called Grapeful, and she wants to use some of your music."

"Don't fuck with me, Will."

"I'm just as stunned as you are, trust me. She asked me if you had some sort of manager or agent to negotiate the clearance fee, which I'm guessing is a negative."

"Actually, there is someone," Paul said and relented to the grin that had taken shape on his lips. "His name is Stevie Reese."

16.

STEVIE NEGOTIATED A FEE OF $20,000, WHICH, FOR A GROUP WITHOUT
even a full-length album to its name, was generous, and Stevie
made a point of this fact. After his ten-percent cut, Paul, Bunky
and Eloise cleared six grand each, most of which would go into
recording. It was a start.

To top it all off, Stevie agreed to take on They Is as a full-time
client; he had, they learned, sent Malcolm to their gallery show
along with the A&R from a boutique label based in Greenpoint
that agreed to put their record out when it was finished. On the
phone, a conference call the three of them joined with Stevie
and Malcolm to hammer out the details, Stevie shared their
enthusiasm, but urged them, in his own way, to remain vigi-
lant.

"Whatever you shitheads do, do *not* take your foot off the
gas," he said. "Just because it's happy fun times with the first
two tracks, doesn't mean dick, okay? I wouldn't call this luck
exactly, but it's not far off. You know how many groups I've
seen who think they captured lightning in a bottle only for it
to turn out to be a giant turd ... in a bottle? More than I'd care
to count."

Paul bought a plane ticket home to help his parents move
into their new apartment. The day before he was to fly home,

he had several errands to run: a month's worth of dirty laundry, a visit to the bank, and a trip into the city where he went to the Farm, left a letter with the bartender addressed to Greg to thank him for everything. Then, against better judgment, he stopped by Dead Wax. His intention was, well, he wasn't sure exactly what his intention was, other than that he found himself walking along Bleecker Street and didn't know where he was headed until he got there.

He skipped down the treaded metal steps and opened the door and right away, Dante marked him from his perch behind the register. "Passin' Me By" grooved overhead and a handful of customers shuffled about or were transfixed in the bins.

"Well, well, well," Dante said, folding his arms, "had a feeling we'd see you back here. Smile, you're on camera."

"Look," Paul said, "I'm leaving town tomorrow for a bit. I just wanted to come in and—I don't know—say sorry I guess." He reached over the counter and offered his hand. Dante considered it for a moment, unfolded his arms and slapped Paul's hand with his own.

"This doesn't mean you're not still a dumbass."

"Tough, but fair."

"Where you going?"

"Home," Paul said. "For a little while."

"What's up with the group?"

"Been a wild few weeks, I'll put it that way." He ticked the events off on his fingers. "First, we bombed a showcase in L.A. Then we played the best show of our lives at an art gallery, and I almost got booted that same night."

Dante cocked his head.

"Then one of our tracks ended up on an NPR playlist. And *then* we got hit up to put a different song in a commercial for some wine app."

"Grapeful? I heard about that. White people love it."

"That's the one."

"And now you're going home."

"And now I'm going home. Need to be there for my family right now. But listen, can I play something for you?"

Dante shrugged. "Be my guest."

Paul handed over his phone, which Dante connected to an auxiliary cord that ran from the store's stereo. The Pharcyde faded out and the spare drums of "Crescent Line" faded up. Then came the groaning sample of Mika's mechanized ambience and shards of Dante's decaying vocals. Eloise began to sing:

Skip town on the back of an alligator
drag my blood in a paper sack ...

A grin took shape on Dante's face, and he began to nod his head. "Oh *shit*," he said, "you went and did it."

"You like it?" Paul asked.

But Dante's grin fell away as he listened more closely and studied the shapes and contours of the song. "You want to know the truth?"

"I mean, of course."

"I'll say this: the vocals?" He puffed out his cheeks. "Goddamn."

"That's Eloise. Unreal, right?"

"Crazy, bro."

"But ..."

"But yeah. I gotta be honest. The production just isn't hitting."

"Like what? The drums? Maybe they need more low end—"

"I'll tell you what. How about you let me control the boards on this one, and I'll let you use the sample. And, you know, I can talk Mika into letting us use her tune."

"Wait, you want to produce?"

"Hell yeah. And then you can let me know when to expect that royalty check."

Paul smiled. "Deal."

"But I gotta ask. That's not the tune that's gonna be in the commercial, right?"

"No, the one they want is an instrumental. Why?"

"Good. I mean I've played my tune for Mika before and she loves it, even if she'd never admit it to my face ... but if you said *her* stuff would be used to sell like, rosé?" Dante shook his head. "I don't know, bro. She'd probably cut you."

Paul couldn't help but laugh again.

"But check this," Dante said, "she's at a meeting right now. Turns out Black Diamond dug her stuff after all. They're going to put her record out."

"No shit," Paul said. He could picture Mika there in a label office playing hardball, and it warmed his heart. "Tell her congrats for me."

"I will. I'm proud of her, you know?" Dante's eyes became shifty, and his voice dropped to a conspiratorial tone. "Look, lemme ask you something: what do you think of Mika?"

"Uh. What do you mean?"

"Like, you know," Dante had begun to whisper, "what do you *think* of her? You think she's dope?"

Paul looked over his shoulder, as though he was being put on. "I don't get it."

"Just answer the question."

"Okay. Do I think Mika's dope ..."

As much as he loved Mika, *dope* might not have been in the top twenty adjectives he could think of to describe her. Maybe even the top fifty. *Cold. Mechanical. Ostrich-like.* Such words sprang to mind. "Of course," he found himself saying. He felt it was of critical import to Dante that he agreed. "She's really dope."

"Yeah?" The lightness returned all at once to Dante's voice and his face was awash with relief. "I think she's *so* dope. You're not messing with me?"

Paul stood up a little straighter. "No way," he said. "Would I lie to you?" He pictured Mika's big, blood-red framed glasses, a hipster Golden Girl. The pale skin. The lean physique. The straight lips. Shit. He had to admit: she *was* kinda hot in a kill-you-and-eat-you-after-sex, Praying Mantis-type of way. "She's smart. She's sexy. She makes music. She likes *Terminator 2*. What more could you want?"

"*Right?* That's exactly what I'm saying." Dante had let his voice begin to carry, caught himself, cleared his throat and lowered it once again. "Yo, don't tell anybody this, okay?"

"Uh. Okay."

"You gotta *swear*."

"Okay, okay. I fucking swear, Dante. Take it easy."

"Okay. Listen: I think I'm finally gonna ask her."

Paul stared at Dante and half-expected him to crack, to bust up and say *Gotcha*, or *What a sucker*, or any number of things he had said to Paul over the years to give him shit. But he said none of that. He just stared back, moon-eyed and earnest and the reality struck Paul over the head: He was dead serious.

Dante waved a hand in front of Paul's face. "Hello? You alive, bro?"

"I'm here, man."

"You hear what I said?"

"Yeah, I—I'm just—" An image came to mind of Dante and Mika holding hands in a theater, grinning in the bloody glow of a slasher flick. Of them collaborating on a limited run of Xeroxed zines, or a sludgy noise-rap mixtape, or both. Of them dressing an adorable little tyke in a Wu-Tang onesie. "You're going to ask her to marry you?"

At this, Dante recoiled and twisted up his face. "*What?* Marr— no, no, no." He broke into laughter. "*Marry?* Bro. I'm going to ask her to *record* something with me. No sampling or none of that. Like, finally together."

Paul began to laugh right along, but beneath the ridiculousness of it all, he had a feeling that Dante took this question as seriously as a proposal, and that for him it meant just as much.

"Well, good luck then," Paul said, "but when you do finally get married, let me know. I'm available to DJ."

"Fuck out of here," Dante said, "Mika wouldn't allow that if you were the last DJ on earth." Then he giggled. "But that *would* be hilarious."

***

As he settled into his seat on the plane, Paul considered the life he had led in New York for the last seven years. He was thirty now. Had he grown? Become a good person? He was afraid the answer was no. He held no illusions that his awareness of this fact made it any better or different. And the burgeoning success of the band, he now knew, was not a virtue in and of itself. What he hoped was that he was capable of charting a new course.

The plane began to taxi and as he retrieved his phone from his pocket to switch it off, it lit up with a pair of texts. The first was from Eloise. She sent him a link to an article on *Pitchfork*, which had, to his shock, posted a blurb about "Friends." The review was positive. It referred to a "New York trio" that had crafted "three minutes of wistful trip-hop perfect for that moment at the end of the party where you know you can't stay but you also don't want to leave."

The second text was from Cassie.

Hey. It began. *So it turns out Gallo wasn't the great guy I thought he was.*

Three little bubbles told him more was coming.

Reaching out to see if you'd be up for a coffee sometime soon? Just to catch up. Nothing serious. I hope the band is going well. Love to hear the new songs.

Paul began to type a response, to apologize, not about Gallo, but about himself. But the flight attendant came by his row and sternly instructed him to put his phone away. He deleted what he had written and obeyed the orders. He put away his phone, fastened his seat belt, leaned back, and closed his eyes. He would have plenty of time to explain to Cassie. Plenty of time to explain to his parents. Plenty of time to explain to everyone.

For now, all he could do was let his thoughts wash over him and dissipate into the recycled air as the plane hurtled headlong, then reached into the sky toward the Middle West.

ACKNOWLEDGEMENTS

This book is nearly ten years in the making and wouldn't be possible without the support of many kind and patient individuals to whom I am extremely grateful.

To Liz DeGaynor, Michael Haje, Jonathan Liebson, Carla Sacks and Aaron Taylor, whose thoughtful recommendation letters paved the path of my writing journey. To John Morris, whose early encouragement reignited my love of words.

To Michelle Valladares and the MFA students and staff at the City College of New York, especially Salar Abdoh and Nicole Dennis-Benn, whose care and attention made this book immeasurably better.

To Fern and James for your camaraderie and conversation. Those long subway rides would've felt a lot longer without you.

To Elizabeth Gaffney and my classmates at A Public Space for guiding this manuscript with such editorial empathy.

To Marshall Kuresman, Steve Li, Doug Midland, Ryan Parker and Eric Weiss for being early readers, confidants, and most importantly, friends.

To Ivan Ave, for the soul-enriching conversations about what it means to make art in a world that doesn't always make room for it.

To Evan Parter for being an incredibly generous ally and champion.

To the Boomshot crew for the unflagging support.

To Jessica and Amie at Vine Leaves Press, without whom this novel would simply not exist.

To Melanie Faith and Sue Bavey, for your patient and insightful edits.

To Danicah, for your love and for always listening.

To record stores everywhere.

VINE LEAVES PRESS

Enjoyed this book?
Go to *vineleavespress.com* to find more.
Subscribe to our newsletter: